The
Frontiersman

The
Frontiersman

William W. Johnstone
with J. A. Johnstone

PINNACLE BOOKS
Kensington Publishing Corp.
www.kensingtonbooks.com

PINNACLE BOOKS are published by

Kensington Publishing Corp.
119 West 40th Street
New York, NY 10018

PUBLISHER'S NOTE
Following the death of William W. Johnstone, the Johnstone family is working with a carefully selected writer to organize and complete Mr. Johnstone's outlines and many unfinished manuscripts to create additional novels in all of his series like The Last Gunfighter, Mountain Man, and Eagles, among others. This novel was inspired by Mr. Johnstone's superb storytelling.

All Kensington titles, imprints, and distributed lines are available at special quantity discounts for bulk purchases for sales promotions, premiums, fund-raising, educational, or institutional use. Special book excerpts or customized printings can also be created to fit specific needs. For details, write or phone the office of the Kensington sales manager: Kensington Publishing Corp., 119 West 40th Street, New York, NY 10018, attn: Sales Department; phone 1-800-221-2647.

PINNACLE BOOKS, the Pinnacle logo, and the WWJ steer head logo, are Reg. U.S. Pat. & TM Off.

ISBN-13: 978-0-7860-3945-6
ISBN-10: 0-7860-3945-0

First printing: April 2015

12 11 10 9 8 7 6 5 4

Printed in the United States of America

First electronic edition: March 2017

ISBN-13: 978-0-7860-3602-8
ISBN-10: 0-7860-3602-8

BOOK ONE

Chapter One

Death lurked in the forest.

It wore buckskins, carried a long-barreled flintlock rifle, and had long, shaggy hair as red as the flame of sunset. Death's name was Breckinridge Wallace.

Utterly silent and motionless, Breckinridge knelt and peered through a gap in the thick brush underneath the trees that covered these Tennessee hills. He waited, his cheek pressed against the ornately engraved maple of the rifle stock as he held the weapon rock-steady. He had the sight lined up on a tiny clearing on the other side of a swift-flowing creek. His brilliant blue eyes never blinked as he watched for his prey.

Those eyes narrowed slightly as Breckinridge heard a faint crackling of brush that gradually grew louder. The quarry he had been stalking all morning was nearby and coming closer. All he had to do was be patient.

He was good at that. He had been hunting ever since the rifle he carried was longer than he was tall. His father had said more than once Breckinridge should have been born with a flintlock in his hands. It wasn't a statement of approval, either.

Breckinridge looped his thumb over the hammer and pulled it back so slowly that it made almost no sound. He was ready now. He had worked on the trigger until it required only the slightest pressure to fire.

The buck stepped from the brush into the clearing, his antlered head held high as he searched for any sight or scent of danger. Breckinridge knew he couldn't be seen easily where he was concealed in the brush, and the wind had held steady, carrying his smell away from the creek. Satisfied that it was safe, the buck moved toward the stream and started to lower his head to drink. He was broadside to Breck, in perfect position.

For an instant, Breckinridge felt a surge of regret that he was about to kill such a beautiful, magnificent animal. But the buck would help feed Breck's family for quite a while, and that was how the world worked. He remembered the old Chickasaw medicine man Snapping Turtle telling him he ought to pray to the animals he hunted and give thanks to them for the sustenance their lives provided. Breck did so, and his finger brushed the flintlock's trigger.

The crescent-shaped butt kicked back against his shoulder as the rifle cracked. Gray smoke gushed from the barrel. The buck's muzzle had just touched the water when the .50-caliber lead ball smashed into his side and penetrated his heart. The animal threw his head up and then crashed onto his side, dead when he hit the ground.

Breckinridge rose to his full height, towering well over six feet, and stepped out of the brush. His brawny shoulders stretched the fringed buckskin shirt he wore. His ma complained that he outgrew clothes faster than anybody she had ever seen.

That was true. Anybody just looking at Breckinridge who didn't know him would take him for a full-grown man. It was difficult to believe this was only his eighteenth summer.

Before he did anything else, he reloaded the rifle with a ball from his shot pouch, a greased patch from the brass-doored patchbox built into the right side of the rifle's stock, and a charge of powder from the horn he carried on a strap around his neck. He primed the rifle and carefully lowered the hammer.

Then he moved a few yards to his right where the trunk of a fallen tree spanned the creek. Breckinridge himself had felled that tree a couple of years earlier, dropping it so that it formed a natural bridge. He had done that a number of places in these foothills of the Smoky Mountains east of his family's farm to make his hunting expeditions easier. He'd been roaming the hills for years and knew every foot of them.

Pa was going to be mad at him for abandoning his chores to go hunting, but that wrath would be reduced to a certain extent when Breckinridge came in with that fine buck's carcass draped over his shoulders. Breck knew that, and he was smiling as he stepped onto the log and started to cross the creek.

He was only about halfway to the other side when an arrow flew out of the woods and nicked his left ear as it whipped past his head.

"Flamehair," Tall Tree breathed as he gazed across the little valley at the big white man moving along the ridge on the far side.

This was a half hour earlier. Tall Tree and the three men with him were hunting for game, but Flamehair was more interesting than fresh meat. The lean Chickasaw warrior didn't know anything about the red-haired man except he had seen Flamehair on a few occasions in the past when their paths had almost crossed in these woods. It was hard to mistake that bright hair, especially because the white man seldom wore a hat.

"We should go on," Big Head urged. "The buck will get away."

"I don't care about the buck," Tall Tree said without taking his eyes off Flamehair.

"I do," Bear Tongue put in. "We haven't had fresh meat in days, Tall Tree. Come. Let us hunt."

Reluctantly, Tall Tree agreed. Anyway, Flamehair had vanished into a thick clump of vegetation. Tall Tree moved on with the other two and the fourth warrior, Water Snake.

Bear Tongue was right, Tall Tree thought. They and the dozen other warriors back at their camp needed fresh meat.

Empty bellies made killing white men more difficult, and that was the work to which Tall Tree and his men were devoted.

Three years earlier, after many years of sporadic war with the whites, the leaders of the Chickasaw people had made a treaty with the United States government. It was possible they hadn't understood completely what the results of that agreement would be. The Chickasaw and the other members of the so-called Five Civilized Tribes had been forced to leave their ancestral lands and trek west to a new home in a place called Indian Territory.

Tall Tree and the men with him had no use for that. As far as they were concerned, the Smoky Mountains were their home and anyplace they roamed should be Indian Territory.

They had fled from their homes before the white man's army had a chance to round them up and force them to leave. While most of the Chickasaw and the other tribes were headed west on what some were calling the Trail of Tears, Tall Tree's band of warriors and others like them hid out in the mountains, dodging army patrols, raiding isolated farms, and slaughtering as many of the white invaders as they could find.

Tall Tree knew that someday he and his companions would be caught and killed, but when that happened they would die as free men, as warriors, not as slaves.

As long as he was able to spill plenty of the enemy's blood before that day arrived, he would die happily.

Now as he and the other three warriors trotted along a narrow game trail in pursuit of the buck they were stalking, Tall Tree's mind kept going back to the man he thought of as Flamehair. The man nearly always hunted alone, as if supremely confident in his ability to take care of himself. That arrogance infuriated Tall Tree. He wanted to teach the white man a lesson, and what better way to do that than by killing him?

He could think of one way, Tall Tree suddenly realized.

It would be even better to kill Flamehair slowly, to torture him for hours or even days, until the part of him left alive barely resembled anything human and he was screaming in agony for the sweet relief of death.

That thought put a smile on Tall Tree's face.

Water Snake, who hardly ever spoke, was in the lead because he was the group's best scout. He signaled a halt, then turned and motioned to Tall Tree, who joined him. Water Snake pointed to what he had seen.

Several hundred yards away, a buckskin-clad figure moved across a small open area. Tall Tree caught only a glimpse of him, but that was enough for him to again recognize Flamehair.

Tall Tree understood now what was going on. After Water Snake had pointed out the white man to Big Head and Bear Tongue, Tall Tree said, "Flamehair is after the same buck we are. Should we allow him to kill it and take it back to whatever squalid little farm he came from?"

"No!" Big Head exclaimed. "We should kill him."

Bear Tongue said, "I thought you wanted to hunt."

"I do, but Flamehair is only one man. We can kill him and then kill the buck."

"Even better," Tall Tree said, "we can let *him* kill the buck, then we will kill him and take it for ourselves and our friends back at camp."

The other three nodded eagerly, and he knew he had won them over.

Now they were stalking two different kinds of prey, one human, one animal. Tall Tree knew that eventually they would all come together. He sensed the spirits manipulating earthly events to create that intersection. His medicine was good. He had killed many white men. Today he would kill another.

Tall Tree knew the trail they were following led to a small clearing along a creek that wildlife in this area used as a watering hole. Before his people had been so brutally torn away from their homes, so had they.

It was possible Flamehair knew of the spot as well. He came to these hills frequently, and it was likely that he was well acquainted with them. Tall Tree decided that was where he and his men would set their trap. The buck would be the bait.

They circled to reach the creek ahead of the buck and concealed themselves in the thick brush a short distance downstream from the clearing. A fallen tree lay across the creek. Tall Tree had looked at that log before and suspected Flamehair had been the one who cut it down.

As they waited, Tall Tree began to worry that the buck wasn't really headed here after all and would lead Flamehair somewhere else. In that case Tall Tree would just have to be patient and kill the white man some other day.

But he was looking forward to seeing if the man's blood was as red as his hair, and he hoped it was today.

A few minutes later he heard the buck moving through the brush and felt a surge of satisfaction and anticipation. He had guessed correctly, and soon the white man would be here, too. He leaned closer to his companions and whispered, "Try not to kill him. I want to take him alive and make his death long and painful."

Big Head and Bear Tongue frowned a little at that. They had killed plenty of whites, too, but not by torture. Water Snake just nodded, though.

A few more minutes passed, then the buck appeared. Almost immediately a shot rang out, and the buck went down hard, killed instantly. It was a good shot. Tall Tree spotted the powder smoke on the far side of the creek and knew that if all they wanted to do was kill Flamehair, they ought to riddle that spot with arrows.

Instead he motioned for the others to wait. He was convinced he knew what the white man was going to do next.

He was right, too. Flamehair appeared, looking even bigger than Tall Tree expected, and stood on the creek bank reloading his rifle, apparently unconcerned that he might be in danger. Reloading after firing a shot was just a simple precaution that any man took in the woods. Any man who was not a fool.

The other three warriors looked at Tall Tree, ready and anxious to fire their arrows at Flamehair. Again Tall Tree motioned for them to wait. A cruel smile curved his lips slightly as he watched Flamehair step onto the log bridge and start across the creek. He raised his bow and pulled it taut as he took aim.

This was the first time he had gotten such a close look at Flamehair, and a shock went through him as he realized the white man was barely a man at all. For all his great size, he was a stripling youth.

That surprise made Tall Tree hesitate instead of loosing his arrow as he had planned. He wanted to shoot Flamehair in the leg and dump him in the creek, which would make his long rifle useless and ruin the rest of his powder.

Instead, as Tall Tree failed to shoot, Big Head's fingers slipped on his bowstring and it twanged as it launched its arrow. Big Head's aim was off. The arrow flew at Flamehair's red-thatched head, missing as narrowly as possible.

But somehow it accomplished Tall Tree's goal anyway, because as Flamehair twisted on the log, possibly to make himself a smaller target in case more arrows were coming his way, the soles of his high-topped moccasins slipped. He wavered there for a second and fought desperately to keep his balance, but it deserted him and he toppled into the stream with a huge splash.

Tall Tree forgot about his plan to capture Flame-hair and torture him to death. All that mattered to him now was that this white intruder on Chickasaw land should die. He leaped up and plunged out of the brush as he shouted in his native tongue, "Kill him!"

Chapter Two

Breckinridge had good instincts. They told him where there was one Indian there might be two—or more. He knew he was an easy target out here on this log, so he tried to turn and race back to the cover of the brush on the creek's other side.

Despite his size, he had always been a pretty graceful young man. That grace deserted him now, however, when he needed it most. He felt himself falling, tried to stop himself, but his momentum was too much. He slipped off the log and fell the five feet to the creek.

He knew how to swim, of course. Like shooting a gun, swimming was something he had learned how to do almost before he could walk.

So he wasn't worried about drowning, even though he had gone completely under the water. His main concern was the charge of powder in his rifle, as well as the one in the flintlock pistol he carried. They were wet and useless now. The powder in his horn was probably all right, but he figured his attackers wouldn't give him a chance to dry his weapons and reload.

Sure enough, as he came up and his head broke the surface, he saw four Chickasaw burst out of the brush. Three of them already had arrows nocked, and the fourth was reaching for a shaft in his quiver.

Breckinridge dragged in as deep a breath as he could and went under again.

He still had hold of his rifle—it was a fine gun and he was damned if he was going to let go of it—and its weight helped hold him down as he kicked strongly to propel himself along with the current. The creek was eight or ten feet deep at this point and twenty feet wide. Like most mountain streams, though, it was fairly clear, so the Indians could probably still see him.

Something hissed past Breckinridge in the water. He knew it was an arrow. They were still trying to kill him. He hadn't expected any different.

When he was a boy, he had befriended and played with some of the Chickasaw youngsters in the area. The medicine man Snapping Turtle had sort of taken Breckinridge under his wing for a while, teaching him Indian lore and wisdom. Breck liked the Chickasaw and had nothing against them. He didn't really understand why the army had come and made them all leave, but he'd been sorry to see them go.

Not all the Chickasaw had departed for Indian Territory, however. Some of them—stubborn holdouts, Breckinridge's pa called them—had managed to elude the army and were still hidden in the rugged mountains, venturing out now and then for bloody raids on the white settlers. Breck figured he had run into just such a bunch, eager to kill any white man they came across.

He had known when he started into the hills that he was risking an encounter like this, but he had never let the possibility of danger keep him from doing something he wanted. If that made him reckless, like his pa said, then so be it.

Now it looked like that impulsiveness might be the death of him.

His lungs were good, strengthened by hours and hours of running for the sheer pleasure of it. He had filled them with air, so he knew he could stay under the water for a couple of minutes, anyway, probably longer. He had to put that time to good use. Because of the thick brush, the Indians couldn't run along the bank as quickly as he could swim underwater. All he needed to do was avoid the arrows they fired at him, and he had to trust to luck for that since he couldn't see them coming while he was submerged.

Breckinridge continued kicking his feet and stroking with his left arm. Fish darted past him in the stream, disturbed by this human interloper. It was beautiful down here. Breck might have enjoyed the experience if he hadn't known that death might be waiting for him at the surface.

He didn't know how long he stayed under, but finally he had to come up for air. He let his legs drop so he could push off the rocky bottom with his feet. As he broke the surface he threw his head from side to side to sling the long red hair out of his eyes. When his vision had cleared he looked around for the Indians.

He didn't see them, but he heard shouting back upstream a short distance. He had gotten ahead of his pursuers, just as he'd hoped, and once he had grabbed a couple more deep breaths he intended to go under again and keep swimming downstream.

That plan was ruined when strong fingers suddenly clamped around his ankle and jerked him under the surface again.

Taken by surprise, Breckinridge was in the middle of taking a breath, so he got a mouthful of water that went down the wrong way and threatened to choke him. Not only that, but he had a dangerous opponent on his hands, too.

He could see well enough to know that the man struggling with him was one of the Chickasaw warriors. He must have jumped off the log bridge into the creek and taken off after Breckinridge as fast as he could swim. The warrior was long and lean, built like a swimmer. He slashed at Breck with the knife clutched in his right hand while keeping his left clenched around Breck's ankle.

Breckinridge twisted away from the blade. It scraped across the side of his buckskin shirt but didn't do any damage. His movements seemed maddeningly slow to him as he lifted his other leg and rammed his heel into the Indian's chest. The kick was strong enough to knock the man's grip loose.

The Chickasaw warrior shot backward in the water. Breckinridge knew he couldn't outswim the man, so he went after him instead. If he could kill the Indian in a hurry, he might still be able to give the slip to the others.

Breckinridge had never killed a man before, although he had been in plenty of brawls with fellows his own age and some considerably older. This time he was fighting for his life, though, so he wasn't going to have a problem doing whatever he had to in order to survive. Before the man he had kicked had a chance to recover, Breck got behind him and thrust the barrel of his rifle across the warrior's neck. He grabbed the barrel with his other hand and pulled it back, pressing it as hard as he could into the man's throat.

The Chickasaw flailed and thrashed, but Breckinridge's strength was incredible. He managed to plant his knee in the small of the Indian's back, giving him the leverage he needed to exert even more force.

The warrior slashed backward with his knife. Breckinridge felt the blade bite into his thigh. The wound wasn't deep because the Indian couldn't get much strength behind the thrust at this awkward angle, but it hurt enough to make red rage explode inside Breck. The muscles of his arms, shoulders, and back bunched under the tight buckskin shirt as he heaved up and back with the rifle lodged under the warrior's chin.

Even underwater, Breckinridge heard the sharp crack as the man's neck snapped.

The Chickasaw's body went limp. Breckinridge let go of it and kicked for the surface. As soon as his enemy was dead, Breck had realized that he was just about out of air. The stuff tasted mighty sweet as he shot up out of the water and gulped down a big breath.

An arrow slapped through that sweet air right beside his head.

Breckinridge twisted around to determine its direction. He saw right away that the other three Chickasaw had caught up while he was battling with the one in the creek. Two of them were on the bank even with him, while the third man had run on downstream, where he waited with a bow drawn back to put an arrow through him if he tried to swim past.

They thought they had him trapped, and that was probably true. But the realization just made Breckinridge angry. He had never been one to flee from trouble. He shouldn't have tried to today, he thought. He should have stood his ground. He should have taken the fight to the enemy.

That was what he did now. He dived underwater as the two Indians closest to him fired, but he didn't try to swim downstream. Instead he kicked toward the shore, found his footing on the creek bottom, and charged up out of the water bellowing like a maddened bull as the warriors reached for fresh arrows.

The rifle wouldn't fire until it had been dried out, cleaned, and reloaded, but in the hands of Breckinridge Wallace it was still a dangerous weapon. Breck proved that by smashing the curved brass butt plate against the forehead of the closest Indian. With Breck's already considerable strength fueled by anger, the blow had enough power behind it that the ends of the crescent-shaped butt shattered the warrior's skull and caved in the front of his head. He went over backward to land in a limp heap.

The other Indian loosed his arrow, and at this range Breckinridge was too big a target to miss. Luck was with him, though, and the flint arrowhead struck his shot pouch. The point penetrated the leather but bounced off the lead balls within.

Breckinridge switched his grip on the rifle, grabbing the barrel with both hands instead, and swung it like a club. He was proud of the fancy engraving and patchbox on the stock and didn't want to break it, but pride wasn't worth his life.

The Chickasaw dropped his bow and ducked under the sweeping blow. He charged forward and rammed his head and right shoulder into Breckinridge's midsection. Breck was considerably taller and heavier than the Indian was and normally would have shrugged off that attempted tackle, but his wet moccasins slipped on the muddy bank and he lost his balance. He went over backward.

The Chickasaw landed on top of him and grabbed the tomahawk that hung at his waist. He raised the weapon and was about to bring it crashing down into Breckinridge's face when Breck's big right fist shot straight up and landed on the warrior's jaw. The powerful blow lifted the Indian away from Breck and made him slump to the side, momentarily stunned.

Breckinridge rolled the other way to put a little distance between himself and the enemy. As he did an arrow buried its head in the ground where he had been a split second earlier. The fourth and final Chickasaw had fired that missile, and when he saw that it had missed, he screeched in fury and dropped his bow. He jerked out a knife and charged at Breck.

As he rolled to his feet, Breckinridge snatched up the tomahawk dropped by the Indian he had just walloped. He dodged the thrust of the fourth man's knife and brought the tomahawk up and over and down in a blindingly swift strike that caught the warrior on the left cheekbone. Breck intended to plant the tomahawk in the middle of the man's skull and cleave his head open, but the Indian had darted aside just enough to prevent that fatal blow.

Instead the tomahawk laid the warrior's cheek open to the bone and traveled on down his neck to lodge in his shoulder. Blood spouted from the wounds as he stumbled and fell.

Breckinridge would have wrenched the tomahawk loose and finished off the injured Chickasaw, but at that moment the man he had punched rammed him again. This time the impact drove Breck off the bank and back into the creek. He floundered in the water for a moment, and by the time he was able to stand up again the two surviving warriors were disappearing into the woods. The one who had just knocked him in the stream was helping the wounded man escape.

Breckinridge felt confident that they didn't have any fight left in them. He might not have admitted it to anyone but himself, but he was glad they felt that way. He knew how lucky he was to have lived through a fight with four-against-one odds . . . especially when the one was an eighteen-year-old youngster and the four were seasoned Chickasaw warriors.

There was no telling if other renegades might be in the vicinity, so he figured he'd better get out of the hills and head for home pretty quick-like.

He wasn't going back without his quarry, though, so without delay he gathered up his rifle and started for the clearing where the buck had fallen. It would take time to put his rifle and pistol back in working order, and he didn't think it would be smart to linger that long.

When he reached the clearing the buck was still lying there, undisturbed as yet by scavengers. Breckinridge stooped, took hold of the carcass, and heaved it onto his shoulders. Even his great strength was taxed by the animal's weight as he began loping through the woods toward home.

He thought about the four warriors he had battled. Two of them were dead, he was sure of that, and the one he'd wounded with the tomahawk probably would die, too, as fast as he had been losing blood.

What would the fourth man do? Would he go back to the rest of the renegades—assuming there were any—and tell them that he and his companions had been nearly wiped out by a large force of well-armed white men?

Or would he admit that all the damage had been done by one young fella who hadn't even had a working firearm?

Breckinridge grinned. Lucky or not, he had done some pretty good fighting back there. He knew now that in a battle for his life he would do whatever it took to survive. He wondered if he ought to tell anybody the truth about what had happened. Chances were, they wouldn't believe him.

But he knew, and he would carry that knowledge with him from now on.

It was all Tall Tree could do not to cry out in pain as he leaned on Bear Tongue while they hurried through the forest. He was weak and dizzy and knew that was from losing all the blood that had poured out from the wounds in his face, neck, and shoulder.

"We must get you back to camp," Bear Tongue babbled. His voice was thick because his jaw was swollen from the powerful blow Flamehair had delivered to him. "If you don't get help, you will bleed to death."

"No," Tall Tree gasped, even though it caused fresh explosions of terrible agony in his face every time he moved his lips. The pain was nothing compared to the hatred that filled him. "I will not die. The spirits have told me . . . I cannot die . . . until I kill the white devil Flamehair!"

Chapter Three

Robert Wallace had come to Tennessee as a young man in 1810. His father Ebenezer had immigrated from Scotland to what was then the British Colony of North Carolina and had later fought in the revolution, taking part in the Battle of King's Mountain. Awarded land for his service, Ebenezer had trekked over the Great Smoky Mountains into Tennessee, taking his family with him. That included his son Robert.

Growing into manhood on the family farm not far from the newly settled town of Knoxville, in due time Robert had taken himself a wife, the redheaded beauty Samantha Burke. He had claimed land of his own, built a fine cabin there with his own two hands near a spring that bubbled crisp and cold from the ground, and settled down to farm and raise a family.

Four sons had come along in reasonably short order: Edward, Thomas, Jeremiah, and Henry. Samantha made no secret of the fact that she wanted a daughter to go with all those strapping sons, and when she found herself with child again she hoped and prayed this would be the one.

Those prayers were answered, but only to a certain extent. The child was a girl, all right, but she was stillborn. Embittered, Samantha had declared that she would tempt fate no more by bringing additional children into the world.

Such things being beyond frail mortal control in most cases, Samantha conceived again several years later and brought forth another healthy son. Robert named him Breckinridge.

The boy was more than healthy. Robert sometimes said that Breckinridge entered the world squalling and never stopped. He grew like the proverbial weed and was just as hardy. Childhood illnesses barely touched him. As the years passed he shot up and his shoulders broadened. He was tireless and could do more work on the farm than any of his older brothers. Not only that, he was also handsome and usually had a devil-may-care grin on his face. He was known to burst into song out of sheer exuberance. Any parent would have adored him.

Any parent except for his mother, Samantha, who looked at him and saw the daughter Fate had cheated her out of. She loved her youngest son, no doubt about that, but she always harbored an unjustified resentment toward Breckinridge that led her to be sharp and critical with him.

Robert came to feel much the same way, although for different reasons. Breckinridge's great size, boundless enthusiasm, and reckless nature led him into trouble on a regular basis. Also, Breck's numerous appetites did not include a hunger for work. Although he could accomplish more around the farm than anyone else when he put his mind to it, getting him to buckle down and do chores instead of skylarking off on some "adventure" was an endless battle, one that Robert usually lost.

In Breckinridge's uncomplicated mind, he knew these things. He was aware that he was a vexation and a disappointment to his parents and his older brothers, who he regarded as dour and humorless. He would have done something about it if he could, but to his way of thinking, the Good Lord had made him the way he was for a good reason, although he might not know what it was just yet, and it would be blasphemous for him to interfere with the Lord's handiwork.

Because of that knowledge, when Breckinridge got back to the farm he wasn't surprised to find his father waiting for him with an angry scowl on his weatherbeaten face.

Robert's frown eased a little as he looked at the carcass draped over his youngest son's shoulders.

"Where'd ye get that?" he asked.

"Up in the hills," Breckinridge replied.

"While ye were supposed to be plowin'."

It was an accusation, not a question.

Breckinridge lowered the buck to the ground in front of the cabin and said, "I swear, Pa, it was like I heard him callin' to me. I knew he was there, and I knew I could get him."

"Ye nearly always hear something callin' to you when there's work to be done, don't ye?" Robert waved a hand. "Never mind. I grow weary of scoldin' ye." He frowned again and pointed. "There's blood on yer ear."

Breckinridge touched the lobe where the arrow had clipped it and said, "I caught it on a sharp branch.

Wasn't watchin' where I was goin' close enough, I reckon."

Robert grunted and said, "I would'na be surprised."

He didn't seem to have noticed the rip in Breckinridge's buckskin leggings where the Chickasaw's knife had struck during the battle in the creek. The wound was just a shallow scratch, and the water had washed it out. Breck barely felt its sting anymore.

Robert nodded toward the buck and went on, "Ye brought it in, ye can dress it out. Best get to work before the meat spoils."

"Yes, sir," Breckinridge replied. He picked up the carcass again and carried it to the area near the smokehouse where the men did their butchering.

While he set about the bloody task, he wondered why he hadn't told his father about the encounter with the Chickasaw. Somehow, he knew instinctively that that wouldn't be a good idea. It would give his pa one more good reason to insist that Breckinridge stay close to home—and staying close to home was boring.

Did he have a duty to let folks know that there were renegade Chickasaw in the hills? Well, they already knew that, didn't they? Half a dozen farms had been raided in the past year. Several cabins had been burned. A number of settlers had been killed. Men went about their daily chores with a rifle or a musket or a fowling piece close at hand.

The government had promised help in rounding up the renegades and forcing them to go to Indian Territory with the rest of their tribe, but Breckinridge knew better than that. He might be young, but he wasn't naïve enough to believe the government's promise about anything. Government wasn't good for much except a bunch of hot air and empty words.

A footstep behind him made him look around. His mother stood there, and Breckinridge felt embarrassed somehow for her to see him with deer blood smeared up to his elbows.

"Your father was stomping around here earlier, saying that you'd run off for good this time," Samantha Wallace said. "I figured you'd just gone hunting and would be back sooner or later."

"I'm sorry about neglectin' my chores, Ma. I know that when I do that, one of the other boys has to make up the work for me. I'll pay them back, I swear."

"Don't waste your breath making promises you won't keep, Breckinridge," she told him with a sigh. She folded her arms across her chest and cocked her head a little to the side as she regarded the carcass. "That's a good buck you brought home. With your appetite, you'll probably want a whole haunch for yourself tonight."

"The way you cook it up, I reckon I do," he said, grinning at her.

Much of Samantha's beauty had faded with time, as had the red of her hair she had passed on to her youngest son. Every so often, echoes of the way she must have been were visible to Breckinridge, but he had never really seen that in his life. The tragedy that had altered her had occurred before he was born.

She smiled now at the compliment to her cooking, but only for a second. Then she said, "The next time you run off from your chores, I'm taking a strap to you."

"Yes, ma'am. Whatever you think is best."

Breckinridge meant it, too. He would take a hiding

from her without complaint. He had done so in the past and had no doubt that he would again.

Samantha went back into the cabin, and Breckinridge hung up the meat he had carved out of the buck. He went to the spring, drew a bucket of water, washed his hands and arms in it, then drew another and dumped it over his head. As he shook the water from his hair, he thought about how he planned to spend the evening.

He was going to call on Maureen Grantham, and even though he hadn't told his father about the encounter with the Indians, he figured he would tell Maureen. He would tell her how bloodthirsty the renegades had been and how close they had come to skewering him with arrows or braining him with a tomahawk, and she would shudder and say how perfectly dreadful and terrifying that was, and then he would take her in his arms and comfort her and tell her not to worry about him, that no Chickasaw was ever going to get the best of him.

He might even kiss her if she let him. She had allowed it on a couple of occasions in the past, and he'd spent many a night since with a fever burning in his blood as he remembered the warm, soft sweetness of her lips.

Breckinridge was no innocent. The older girls on neighboring farms had started to notice him several years earlier when he grew larger than the boys their own age. One of them, Charity McFee by name, had lived up to that moniker and freely given him quite an education in the hayloft of her father's barn. Since then Breck had engaged in a bit of slap and tickle with a few other girls in the area, none of whom were any better than they had to be.

Ah, Maureen, though, Maureen was different. Breckinridge had no desire whatsoever to settle down just yet, but he had made up his mind what the future held for him.

She didn't know it yet, but one of these days, Maureen Grantham was going to be his wife.

Supper that evening was rather tense. Breckinridge's brother Henry had taken over the plowing after Breck vanished, and he was angry and resentful about it. Breck put up with the scowls and the snide comments from his next-oldest brother as long as he could before saying sharply, "Just because I don't want to be tied to a piece of ground for the rest of my life is no reason for you to lambaste me, Henry."

Robert said, "A piece o' ground like the one that's given ye a home all these years, lad, is that what ye mean?"

Breckinridge flushed and looked down at the greasy bone with a few shreds of meat still clinging to it. He'd been gnawing the last bits off when he'd finally lost patience with Henry's complaining.

"I know you and Ma have been happy with this life here," he said quietly, which was unusual since his voice usually boomed no matter what he was saying. "But that don't mean that being a farmer is the right thing for me."

"What do you want to do, Breck?" his brother Edward asked. Edward was the most scholarly of the bunch, having attended the school in Knoxville for a good five years. "Run off to the woods and be a hunter and adventurer like Daniel Boone, Davy Crockett, and Natty Bumppo?"

Breckinridge's pulse sped up a little as he nodded and said, "That sounds good to me. Who's Natty Bumppo?"

"The hero of some books by Fenimore Cooper. I just read the latest one, *The Pathfinder*, if you'd like to borrow it."

"I'm, uh, not much of one for readin'," Breckinridge said. "But if he's like Boone and Crockett, this Bumppo sounds like my sort of fella."

"Crockett went off adventuring to Texas and died there, slaughtered by Santa Anna's army at the Alamo. And Boone died an old man, sitting in a rocking chair on the porch of his son's house."

"Only after he had plenty of excitement in his life," Breckinridge countered. "And as for Crockett . . . well, dyin' while you're fightin' for what's right don't sound like such a bad way to go."

Samantha said, "Hush up all this bloodthirsty talk at the dinner table. Land's sake, the way you men go on, you'd think you were in a tavern or something!"

"Yes, ma'am," all five of the Wallace sons murmured automatically.

After supper, Breckinridge went up into the loft where he slept with his brothers and put on a clean homespun shirt. His brother Thomas caught him at it, reaching the top of the ladder leading to the loft just as Breck was pulling the shirt over his head, and said, "You're going courting, aren't you?"

"That's none of your business," Breckinridge said.

"Going to see Maureen Grantham?"

"What if I am?"

"Better not let Richard Aylesworth catch you there if you do."

Anger boiled up inside Breckinridge. He clenched

both hands into big, ham-like fists and declared, "I'm not afraid of Richard Aylesworth."

"You should be, Breck. You should at least be worried about him. He has his eye on the Grantham girl, too."

What Thomas said was true, although Breckinridge didn't like to think about it. Richard Aylesworth was interested in Maureen, all right, and as the son of a well-to-do merchant in Knoxville, he had advantages that Breck didn't, such as money and schooling. He was also several years older, in his early twenties, which might make him more impressive to a girl. His father had sent him to an academy all the way up in Philadelphia for a year, and it was rumored that he had fought a duel while he was there, giving him an air of mystery and danger.

Breckinridge was willing to wager, though, that Aylesworth had never battled four bloody-handed Chickasaw renegades to the death.

Thomas followed his brother outside and said, "Just be careful, Breck. I've known Dick Aylesworth all my life. I don't like him, and I don't trust him. Whenever he sets his sights on something, he feels like it ought to be his by natural right, and he gets mad when anybody interferes with that. I once saw him hand a beating to a man who'd bought a horse that he wanted."

"All I'm going to do is sit with Maureen on the porch of her father's house," Breckinridge said. "I don't see how anybody could get angry about that, even Richard Aylesworth."

His declaration wasn't strictly true. He planned to regale Maureen with his blood-and-thunder tale of battling the Chickasaw, then steal a kiss . . . but

Thomas didn't need to know about that. None of his family did.

"All right," Thomas replied gloomily. "Just don't say I didn't warn you."

Breckinridge went to the barn and saddled Hector, the only one of the plow horses that was a halfway decent mount to ride. A faint fan of reddish-gold from the sunset lingered in the western sky as he headed for Knoxville, five miles away.

What did the sunset look like from the vast plains and the towering mountains he had heard about, the ones that lay hundreds of miles farther west across the continent? Such distances were almost beyond Breckinridge's imagining. He had never been more than ten miles from the cabin in which he'd been born.

He felt a stirring inside whenever he thought about such things. Just like that buck had seemed to call to him from the hills earlier today, something was pulling on him from the other direction, from the sprawling wilderness that now made up so much of the American nation.

He remembered Edward talking about another story he'd read, a tale about one of those ancient Greeks or some such who had gone off to fight in a war and then taken the long way home, having all sorts of adventures along the way. One of those adventures involved a bunch of beautiful women on an island who sang songs so pretty that they were irresistible to any sailors who happened to pass by. That was sort of the way Breckinridge felt about the frontier, like it was calling to him so powerfully that sooner or later he would have to answer.

Of course, those sailors who listened to the song

the women were singing usually came to a bad end, Breckinridge recollected. But anything in life that was worth doing had some risks that came along with it, he supposed.

With those thoughts occupying his mind, the ride to Knoxville passed quickly. Almost before he knew it, he was entering the outskirts of the settlement, and he soon came to the house of Alonzo Grantham, who owned a successful livery stable and wagon yard. Breckinridge reined in sharply when he spotted the lantern hanging from a hook and lighting up the porch of the Grantham house.

Maureen was already out there, but she wasn't waiting for him to come calling. She was sitting there with someone else, and Breckinridge knew instantly who it was.

Richard Aylesworth!

Chapter Four

Breckinridge sat there stiffly on Hector for a long moment, just outside the reach of the light, and pondered what he should do next. He wasn't the sort who was given to a lot of heavy thinking, but he sensed that his next actions might turn out to be important.

Unfortunately, the decision was taken out of his hands. Maureen leaned forward on the bench where she was sitting with Aylesworth and called, "Is someone there? Who is it, please?"

Blast it, the girl had good eyes, Breckinridge thought. He would have sworn it was too dark where he sat for her to spot him, but obviously that wasn't true. He nudged his heels against Hector's side, and the big, docile horse plodded forward into the light.

"Breckinridge Wallace!" Maureen exclaimed. "When I saw how big the visitor was, I thought it might be you. What errand are you about tonight?"

Breckinridge muttered a curse under his breath. After the kisses they'd shared, she knew good and well why he was here. She ought to, anyway.

Aylesworth stood up and swaggered over to the

porch railing. He rested one hand on the rail and struck a pose that was anything but casual, showing off his expensive clothes and the fine figure he cut. He was big and well built, although not as large and powerful as Breckinridge, and undeniably handsome with a shock of dark hair and clean-cut features. He smiled and asked, "Yes, Wallace, why were you lurking out there in the shadows like a red-skinned savage?"

Breckinridge could have told Aylesworth something about that, but he didn't want to share his story with the man. Instead he said, "I wasn't lurkin'. Just on my way past and thought I'd stop and pay my respects to Miss Maureen."

"On your way past to where?" Aylesworth prodded.

"I, uh, thought I'd pick up a few things at Porter's store. I need some black powder, and my ma needs some salt."

The lie was the first thing Breckinridge could think of. Aylesworth looked even more smug as he responded, "I hope the poor woman doesn't mix up the two. That would make for an interesting dish, wouldn't it?"

Maureen laughed, normally a sound that Breckinridge loved to hear. The fact that she was laughing at something Richard Aylesworth had said, though, grated at his nerves like a rasp.

Breckinridge felt himself flushing. He said, "My ma would never do that. She's the best cook in these parts."

"Of course she wouldn't," Maureen said. "Richard was just joking, Breckinridge."

"Yes, merely a jest," Aylesworth said. Breckinridge longed to smash that self-assured grin right down his throat.

Instead he lifted Hector's reins and got ready to turn the horse around as he said, "Reckon I'll be goin' now—"

"Oh, no," Maureen said. "You just got here. Come up and sit on the porch with us for a bit."

Now it was Aylesworth's turn to look less than happy. He said, "I'm sure Wallace has other things to do—"

"He can't go to Mr. Porter's store," Maureen broke in. "It's too late. The store will be closed for the night already. I don't want Breckinridge to have ridden all the way into town for nothing. We can all visit for a spell."

"Of course," Aylesworth said, although the glance he shot toward Breckinridge was a surly one. Maureen couldn't see that, however, from where she was sitting.

Breckinridge thought about telling Maureen he couldn't stay, but he knew it would annoy Aylesworth if he accepted Maureen's invitation. That was enough to make up his mind for him. He said, "I'm obliged for the hospitality," and swung down from the saddle.

"I'm going to fetch a pitcher of buttermilk from the cellar," Maureen announced as she stood up. She was a little bit of a thing, short but well-rounded in the right places, with glossy, dark brown hair and a lovely heart-shaped face. "The two of you sit there on the bench and talk."

She waited expectantly until Breckinridge and Aylesworth had taken their seats as far from each other as they possibly could, then she went into the house. An awkward, unfriendly silence descended on the porch.

Finally, Aylesworth broke that silence by saying, "I know why you're really here, Wallace, and I can tell you that you're wasting your time. More important, you're wasting Miss Grantham's time—and mine."

Stiffly, Breckinridge replied, "I reckon Miss Grantham can make up her own mind how she wants to spend her time—and I don't rightly care about yours."

Both young men leaned forward as they eyed each other. Breckinridge's hands rested on the thighs of his buckskin trousers. His impulse was to go ahead and clench them into fists, but he resisted the urge. He didn't want Maureen to come back out onto the porch and find him getting ready to fight . . . unless Aylesworth made it come to that.

Instead Aylesworth tried a different tack. He said, "Surely you can see that it's entirely inappropriate for you to be courting Maureen. She's a sweet, gentle girl. She lives in town. She's been pampered and protected her entire life. She's not the sort of earthy backwoods lass you're accustomed to, Wallace."

"I always act like a gentleman," Breckinridge insisted.

Aylesworth laughed, and the sound made Breckinridge's hands tighten. He couldn't help it.

"You have no concept of what it is to be a gentleman, Wallace. You're an uncouth, unlearned barbarian." Aylesworth straightened his jacket. "I, on the other hand, attended the Schofield Academy in Philadelphia and received a classical education."

"I heard they kicked you out after a year for causin' trouble. Somethin' about a duel fought over a gamblin' debt? Or was it because of some other fella's wife? Maybe I'll ask Maureen if she's ever heard the truth about what happened up there."

Aylesworth shot to his feet as his face flushed darkly with rage. Breckinridge was up, too, turning to meet any charge or block any punch Aylesworth threw at him.

"Keep your tongue off my affairs, you damned ridge runner," Aylesworth grated. "And if you say anything to Maureen, I'll—"

He stopped short as the door opened. Maureen came out carrying a tray that held a pitcher of buttermilk and three cups.

"What was that, Richard?" she asked with an interested smile. "What are you and Breckinridge discussing?"

"Nothing," Aylesworth replied. His voice was tight with anger. Breckinridge could hear it, even if Maureen seemed unable to. "I was just telling Wallace that I have to be going."

"Really? But you haven't had your buttermilk yet."

Aylesworth put a forced smile on his face and told her, "Another time, perhaps?"

"Of course. You're always welcome here, Richard, you know that."

Aylesworth nodded and reached for his beaver hat, which was perched on the railing. He put it on, set it at a jaunty angle, and said, "Good night, Maureen." He gave Breckinridge a curt nod and added, "Wallace."

As Aylesworth went down the steps and strode away from the house into the darkness, Maureen set the tray on a small table next to the bench and said, "My, that was odd. I never expected Richard to leave so abruptly. Did the two of you have harsh words, Breckinridge?"

"Not so's you'd notice," Breckinridge said. "He was tellin' me about the time he spent at that fancy academy in Philadelphia."

"Oh, I see. What did he tell you?"

Breckinridge hesitated. It would serve Aylesworth right if Breck told her about some of the rumors he'd heard . . . but that would make him a gossip, and Breck didn't want anybody ever accusing him of that. So instead he said, "He was just talkin' about, uh, learnin' Latin and philosophy and readin' books and things like that."

"I'd love to do that, wouldn't you?" Before Breckinridge could reply, Maureen went on, "But proper young ladies aren't encouraged to study such things, of course." She smiled. "Sit down, and I'll pour the buttermilk."

Breckinridge's anger disappeared and he forgot about Richard Aylesworth as he sat there on the bench with Maureen, talking and drinking buttermilk. He kept his head turned so she could see his wounded ear, and sure enough after a while she said, "Oh, you've been hurt! What happened there?"

With a casual shrug, Breckinridge said, "A bunch of Indians jumped me in the woods today, and one of their arrows nicked me."

Maureen's eyes widened appropriately. She gasped. "You were attacked by Indians?"

"Chickasaw renegades," Breckinridge replied, still acting nonchalant about the incident. "I was over in the hills huntin', and I'd just brought down a fine buck. I reckon they wanted to take it away from me, or else they just wanted to kill me 'cause I'm white. Those renegades have been causin' trouble for quite a while now."

"That's terrible! How many of them were there?"

"Four, I think. Yeah, four."

"Were your brothers with you?"

Breckinridge shook his head and said, "Nope, just me."

"There were four savages trying to kill you . . . and you survived?" Maureen seemed astounded by the idea. "How on earth did you get away?"

"Well, I fought back, of course," Breckinridge said.

"You drove them away?"

"Two of 'em ran off after they tangled with me."

"What about the other two?"

"Why, I killed 'em, of course." Caught up in his own heroic glories, Breckinridge went on, "Snapped the neck of one of 'em clean in two and stove in the other one's head with my rifle butt."

He didn't notice until it was too late the horrified expression that had stolen over Maureen's face as he answered her question. She said, "You . . . you murdered them, just like that?"

"No, you couldn't call it murder," Breckinridge said hastily. "You see, they were tryin' their dam—tryin' their best to kill *me*, so I figured I had to defend myself. Otherwise it'd be me layin' out there in the woods now, gettin' gnawed on by scavengers."

A shudder ran through Maureen, and Breckinridge realized that he'd let his mouth run away with itself again. He had assumed she would be impressed by the grisly details of his tale of derring-do, maybe even so moved by the thrilling yarn that she would want to kiss him.

He could see now that he'd been wrong about that. He had forgotten that Maureen was a city gal. The renegades stayed far away from town. She had probably never even seen a hostile Indian.

"I don't see how anyone can live like that," she said.

"To be in so much danger that you have to respond with such terrible brutality . . ."

She shuddered again.

"Maybe we should, uh, talk about somethin' else," Breckinridge suggested.

Maureen shook her head and got to her feet. Breckinridge quickly stood up, too.

"No, I think it'll take me some time to get those dreadful images out of my mind," she said. "I'm sorry, I don't want to be inhospitable, Breckinridge, but perhaps it would be best if you didn't come calling for a while."

Breckinridge felt crushed. He wasn't quite sure how the situation had fallen apart so quickly. He had believed everything was going along just fine. Aylesworth was gone, Maureen was smiling and laughing, and he'd been so sure she would be impressed by his story . . .

Instead she was telling him to leave and not come back, at least for a while. Some instinct told him that arguing would just make things worse, so he swallowed and said, "All right, Maureen, if that's what you want, I'll go. But I sure never intended to upset you."

She gave him a weak smile and said, "That's all right, Breckinridge. Sometimes I just forget how . . . how very different you and I really are. But I still consider you my friend, I assure you of that."

Well, it was something, anyway, Breckinridge thought. Although the idea of being just a friend to Maureen Grantham didn't appeal to him at all. He had figured that sooner or later they would be much, much more than that.

But this was just a minor setback, he told himself. Sooner or later she would get over the revulsion she felt toward him at this moment, and he would work his way back into her good graces. It wasn't like this changed anything permanently.

"I reckon I'll say good night, then."

He thought maybe she would touch his arm or something, but she made no move to do so. She just said, "Good night, Breckinridge," and turned to go into the house.

Breckinridge waited until the door closed behind her, then sighed and shook his head. He blew out the lantern to save Mr. Grantham the trouble of having to come out and extinguish it, then untied Hector's reins from the picket fence where he had fastened them, swung up into the saddle, and headed home.

Chapter Five

Richard Aylesworth scowled down into the mug of beer in front of him. He was seated at a table in a Knoxville tavern, one of his favorite haunts. He seemed to see images swirling in the brew's amber depths.

Those images formed a picture of Maureen and that lout Wallace sitting together on the bench on her father's front porch. Aylesworth's fingers tightened on the mug as that mental portrait shifted and Wallace took Maureen in his arms to kiss her.

He wanted Maureen to pull away and slap the big lout's face, but she didn't. Instead she responded eagerly, passionately, to Wallace's caresses, and the pictures playing in Aylesworth's head became more and more obscene until his teeth ground together so hard it seemed they might snap.

Aylesworth was so caught up in the bitter fantasy he didn't notice his friend Jasper Carlson approaching until Jasper slapped him on the back and greeted him, "Hello, Dick!"

Startled, Aylesworth jumped a little. The lurid images

in his head disappeared. Breathing a little hard, he looked around and said, "Ah, Jasper, it's you."

"Of course it's me," Jasper said as he pulled out an empty chair and sat down. He was about the same age as Aylesworth, but the marks of dissolution were already starting to appear on his lean face under a shock of curly blond hair.

The two of them had spent many nights drinking, gambling, and paying discreet visits to houses of ill repute. Both young men had to be careful because their fathers were respectable citizens, pillars of the community, influential businessmen. They couldn't risk bringing too much shame on their families because then they might be cut off from their generous allowances.

"You look like you're brooding about something," Jasper went on. "What's wrong?"

Aylesworth didn't really want to talk about it, but he knew Jasper would hound him until he replied. So he said, "I called on Maureen Grantham tonight."

A grin creased Jasper's face. He said, "Ah, the beautiful and nubile Maureen. Did you convince her to take a step closer to coming to your bed?"

Aylesworth clenched his right hand into a fist and thumped it on the table.

"Damn it, Jasper, I don't just want to bed that girl. I intend to marry her in a couple of years, when she's old enough."

"Marriage?" Jasper cocked an eyebrow so pale it was almost white. "I thought you didn't intend to settle down for quite a while yet. There are still plenty of whores in Knoxville we haven't slept with."

Aylesworth let out a disdainful snort.

"Since when does getting married mean that a man can no longer sleep with whores?" he wanted to know.

"Well, there is that to consider," Jasper replied with a chuckle. "Some people believe in the sanctity of holy wedlock . . . but we've never been much for sanctity and propriety, you and I, have we?"

Aylesworth drank some of his beer and didn't reply. He looked around the dim, smoky tavern and saw several other young men he knew. A vague idea began to form in the back of his mind.

"So what happened at the Grantham house to upset you?" Jasper persisted.

"Who said anything upset me?"

"Ah, we've been friends too long for that, Dick. I know your moods too well."

Aylesworth shrugged and said, "Breckinridge Wallace showed up. He had courting on his mind, too."

"Wallace . . . That big, redheaded oaf? The farm boy?"

"That's right. He's interested in Maureen, too. I've heard that this isn't the first time he's called on her. She treated him in quite the friendly fashion, as if he'd been there many times before."

Jasper signaled to a serving girl, who brought him a mug of beer. As she set it on the table he rested a hand on her backside, digging his fingers into the soft flesh. She smiled at him.

"I'll see *you* later, my dear," he told her as he tossed a coin to her, then watched with a smile as she walked away with a sensuous sway to her gait. He downed some of the beer and turned back to Aylesworth. "Surely you can't regard that bumpkin Wallace as serious competition for the fair Maureen's affections."

"He's big and handsome, and she's female. Other

than how much money is in a man's purse, that's all they really care about."

"True, but Maureen is a smart girl. She couldn't be interested in an uneducated lout like Wallace." A look of understanding appeared on Jasper's face. "But that might not stop her from playing him against you. Women are devils for such games."

"I know. And before you know it, she might actually start to have feelings for him." Aylesworth's fingers tightened on the mug again. "I won't allow that to happen. I can't allow that. And there's something else."

Jasper leaned forward and asked, "What?"

"While Maureen was in the house and Wallace and I were alone, he threatened to gossip to her about what happened in Philadelphia."

"No! He can't do that. He doesn't know what really went on up there. Only a few people do."

"The whispering has just died down," Aylesworth said grimly. "I don't want it to start again. There's been more than enough speculation, and I won't have Breckinridge Wallace fueling the whole thing again."

With a shrewd smile, Jasper said, "It sounds to me as if someone needs to teach young Master Wallace a stern lesson about interfering in the affairs of his elders and betters."

"I was just thinking the same thing," Aylesworth admitted. "Do you think you could gather up some of the boys . . . ?"

"There are enough right here in this room who would be happy to help you, Dick. Do you know where we can find Wallace?"

"It hasn't been that long since I left him at the Grantham house. If we were to wait on the road east of town, he'll have to come along there when he starts back to his family's pathetic little farm."

"An excellent idea." Jasper shoved his chair back and stood up. In the tavern's smoky light, the grin on his face made him look like a blond devil. "Before this night is over, Breckinridge Wallace will regret intruding where he doesn't belong."

Breckinridge was still upset as he followed the road that twisted through the wooded, gently rolling hills east of Knoxville. Because he knew this route well, he didn't really have to think about where he was going as he guided Hector along the trail. Instead he was able to cast his thoughts back over everything that had happened this evening.

Now he was able to see the mistakes he had made, and if he got a chance to see Maureen again in the future, he knew he could repair the damage he had done. She thought he was as brutal and bloodthirsty as those Chickasaw renegades. All he had to do was show her that she was wrong.

He was so deep in thought he never noticed the slight rustling in the branches of the tree limb that hung over the road ahead of him. The night was fairly dark, with only the light of the stars and a quarter-moon washing over the landscape, so even if he had been more alert he might not have noticed anything out of the ordinary in time.

He was still thinking about Maureen as he rode underneath the limb. He didn't know he was in danger until a heavy weight smashed against his back and drove him out of the saddle.

Breckinridge's reflexes were swift. As he felt himself falling he kicked his feet out of the stirrups so Hector wouldn't drag him if the horse decided to bolt. An instant later he hit the ground hard enough it knocked the breath out of him. The weight remained on his back, pinning him to the hard-packed dirt of the trail as he gasped for air.

He heard the crackle of leaves and the sound of running footsteps as several people rushed out of the brush alongside the road where they apparently had been hiding. His first thought was that he had been ambushed by highwaymen. Like the renegade Indians, normally they didn't venture this close to town to rob unwary travelers, but anything was possible.

All he felt certain of was that these strangers meant him harm, and if he just lay there in the road there was no telling what they might do to him. They might even kill him.

So for the second time today, Breckinridge figured he was fighting for his life.

That thought sent anger surging through him. He bucked up from the ground like a wild horse. That gave him room to get his hands and knees under him and thrust himself to his feet, spilling the man who had tackled him from above.

A faintly heard swishing sound in the air warned him. He twisted away from it. A club of some sort struck him on the shoulder and sent pain shooting down his arm, but that was better than letting the weapon brain him.

"Grab his legs!" a man yelled. "We've got to get him down!"

"He's built like a damned bear!" another man complained.

Breckinridge didn't recognize either voice. He didn't expect to, because he still thought the men were cutthroats and thieves. Seeing half a dozen shadowy shapes moving around him, he clenched his fists and turned with his attackers, watching for one of them to get close enough for him to land a punch.

"You've made a bad mistake, you brigands!" he roared at them. "I don't have anything worth stealing!"

That brought a laugh from one of the men, who said, "He's right about that."

That was a voice Breckinridge knew. He had heard it earlier tonight. He couldn't hold back a surprised exclamation.

"Aylesworth!"

"We're going to teach you a lesson, you oaf," Richard Aylesworth said. "You'll stay away from Maureen Grantham in the future, and you won't say a word about me to her or anyone else."

"Go to hell!" Breckinridge shouted. He had run out of patience waiting for the men to come to him. He had never liked letting someone else make the first move, anyway.

So he charged at the nearest man, lashing out with rock-hard fists.

That took Aylesworth and his friends by surprise. Breckinridge got close enough for one of his powerful punches to land solidly on a jaw and send that jaw's owner flying backward. Two of the men closed in and tried to grab hold of his arms, but his hands shot out with blinding speed and locked around their necks instead. With a heave he banged their heads together, and both men dropped like rag dolls.

Just like that, Breckinridge had reduced the odds to three to one in a matter of seconds. One of the men still on his feet had that club, though, and he slammed it into Breck's lower back across his kidneys. The agonizing pain from that blow sent Breck stumbling forward and threatened to drop him to his knees.

Aylesworth straightened him up by stepping in and smashing a right and a left to his face. Breckinridge hated Aylesworth, but the man was big and he could fight, Breck had to give him that. Aylesworth tried to throw another punch, but Breck caught his balance, forced himself to ignore the pain in his back, and blocked the blow. He countered with a jab to Aylesworth's face.

The man with the club darted closer and struck again, this time whipping the weapon against Breckinridge's upper right arm. The whole arm went numb from the impact. Breck wheeled around and swung his left arm in a sweeping backhand, but the man with the club leaped out of the way. He was lean and fast and nimble on his feet.

The third man grabbed Breckinridge from behind and yelled, "I've got him, Dick!"

"Hang on to him!" Aylesworth said. He closed in and started slugging Breckinridge in the stomach. With one arm still dead, Breck couldn't break free of the grip by the man behind him. Aylesworth sank his fists into Breck's belly again and again. A burning pain filled the younger man's gut.

"You've softened him up, Dick," the man with the club said gleefully. "Now I'll finish him off!"

Breckinridge believed the man intended to do just that. This may have started out as an attempt to give him a thrashing, but Breck sensed that it was more serious now. They would kill him if they could, and if he allowed that man to start bashing him with the bludgeon, that was what would happen.

He let his knees buckle, using his weight to throw himself forward. The man behind him couldn't hold him up. They both spilled onto the ground. That loosened the man's grip, and Breckinridge kicked free. He rolled over and came back up, and as he surged to his feet he realized that the feeling had returned to his right arm.

The man with the club slashed the weapon at Breckinridge's head. Breck was out of breath and hurting, but he managed to avoid the blow, if only barely. The other man was off balance for a second because of the miss, and in that instant Breck caught hold of the front of his jacket and slung him toward the trees beside the road.

He was turning to try to locate Aylesworth when he heard an ugly thud and a crunching sound behind him. He looked around to see the man drop the club and pitch forward on his face. Breckinridge realized that the back of his head had struck hard against one of the tree trunks.

"Jasper!" That frightened exclamation came from Aylesworth. Breckinridge stood there numbly as his enemy rushed past him and dropped to his knees beside the fallen man. Aylesworth rolled his friend over onto his back, lifted him by the shoulders, and shook him. Breck felt a sick horror in his stomach as he saw the way the man's head lolled loosely on his shoulders. Aylesworth cried again, "Jasper, can you hear me?"

There was no response.

Aylesworth clutched the dead man, looked up at Breckinridge, and howled in a ragged, broken voice, "You bastard! You've killed him! You've killed Jasper!"

Chapter Six

For a terrible moment all Breckinridge could do was stand there, stunned by what had happened. He hadn't really meant to kill any of the men, even though he was convinced that his own life was in danger.

At the same time he felt no guilt. They had jumped him, outnumbered him six to one, and planned to thrash him within an inch of his life, if not worse. Whatever happened, Aylesworth and his friends had brought it upon themselves.

Aylesworth had the dead man clasped in his arms as he screamed curses at Breckinridge. Three of the other men were still unconscious, and the one fellow still on his feet seemed even more stunned by this turn of events than Breck was.

"You'll hang for this!" Aylesworth ranted at Breckinridge. "You're a murderer, Wallace! I'll have the law on you!"

"I was defending myself—" Breckinridge began.

That argument didn't work any better with Aylesworth than it had with Maureen. The wealthy young man shouted, "You'll hang, I tell you! You attacked us! You struck down poor Jasper from behind like the killer you are!"

"That's a damned lie! It was you and your friends—"

This time Breckinridge stopped short on his own without being interrupted. A chill raced through him. Sick fear clawed at his stomach.

If Aylesworth and his surviving friends blamed this encounter on Breckinridge, there was no doubt who the law would believe. Breck could insist from now until doomsday that he wasn't to blame for what had happened, that Aylesworth and the others had started the fight and he was only trying to protect himself, but it wouldn't do him any good. The authorities wouldn't accept that story.

This wasn't like his battle with the Chickasaw, either. Nobody was going to be upset about him killing a couple of renegades. If anything, he would be cheered for it.

But killing a white man was different. Especially when the dead man was the son of Knoxville's most prominent banker. Aylesworth had called him Jasper, and Breckinridge recalled now that one of Aylesworth's friends was Jasper Carlson, whose father wielded a great deal of wealth and influence in this end of the state.

He was doomed, Breckinridge thought. He could see himself being marched up the thirteen steps to the top of the gallows, where a noose awaited him . . .

Those thoughts raced through his brain in a matter of seconds as he came to their inescapable conclusion.

"No!" he cried involuntarily. "No, I won't hang for something that's not my fault!"

"You'll hang," Aylesworth said with utter certainty. The faint moonlight glittered on tears that ran down his cheeks as he held his dead friend. "And when they haul down your corpse I'll spit on it before they dump it in a pauper's grave."

Breckinridge looked around, jerking his head from side to side as wild desperation filled him. He spotted Hector standing about fifty yards away, cropping peacefully at the grass along the side of the road. The horse had run that far after Breck was knocked off his back and then had stopped to graze.

Breckinridge suddenly broke into a run. He headed for the horse as Aylesworth howled behind him, "Stop him! For God's sake, stop him!"

The other man didn't budge, never made a move to try to prevent Breckinridge from getting away.

Hector shied a little as Breckinridge ran toward him, but he didn't go far. Breck caught the trailing reins, stuck his left foot in the stirrup on that side, and hurriedly swung up into the saddle. He banged his heels against the horse's flanks. Hector blew air through his nose in an offended manner at this rough treatment, but he broke into a run.

Breckinridge's heart pounded so hard it felt like it might burst out of his chest. He had never been in real trouble with the law. He had gotten some stern warnings from the constable about fighting but had never spent a night in jail, much less faced the threat of being tried for murder, convicted, and hanged.

Yet he was convinced that was exactly what would happen if he was arrested. He would never be free again. His parents would probably plead for mercy because of his youth, but such pleas were likely to go ignored because of his great size. People would look at him and see a grown man, whether he really was or not.

As far as Breckinridge could figure, he had only one choice, one hope of saving his life.

He had to flee. No matter how much it went against the grain for him to run away from trouble, he had to do it.

Unless his pa or maybe Edward could come up with some other idea. Pa had a lot of hardheaded Scots common sense, and Edward was smart as a whip. Breckinridge felt a faint glimmering of hope inside him. He would go home and ask his father and oldest brother for help.

Besides, he couldn't run away, maybe forever, and not say good-bye to his ma first.

A bitter taste filled his mouth as another thought occurred to him. Richard Aylesworth had gotten what he wanted, after all.

Breckinridge would probably never lay eyes on Maureen Grantham again.

By the time he got back to the farm, his pulse wasn't racing as fast and his head was clearer. He had put aside the stirrings of horror he felt at the knowledge that he had killed yet again. This morning when he woke up he had never taken another human being's life. Now there were three men who would never take another breath because of him.

Breckinridge didn't let himself think about that as he dismounted. He had ridden in pretty quickly, and Hector's pounding hoofbeats had roused the dogs, young Sammy and the ancient, silver-muzzled cur called Max. Both of them came out of the barn to bark loudly at him.

Robert Wallace appeared at the doorway wearing a nightshirt and holding a shotgun. He demanded, "Who's out there? Who— Oh, it's you, Breckinridge." Robert snorted. "I might have known. Who else would come barging up in the middle of the night, causing a ruckus? Boy, have ye no sense?"

Breckinridge ignored the irritated question and said, "Pa, I'm in trouble."

"Over what? Brawlin' again? If the constable be after you, son, ye'll just have to take yer medicine—"

"I killed a man."

Robert's mouth drooped open. He stepped forward on the porch and stared at his youngest son. He tried to speak, but it took him a moment to force the words out.

"Ye . . . ye killed a man? Who . . . how . . . Good Lord, boy, what were ye thinkin'?"

Breckinridge dismounted and looped Hector's reins around a porch rail. He stepped up next to his father and said, "It wasn't my fault, Pa—"

"Aye, 'tis never yer fault when ye get in trouble, is it?" Robert bellowed. "Saints preserve us, lad, this is serious!"

"I know. But I swear I was just defending myself. It was an accident."

"Who did ye kill?" Robert asked in a flat, hard tone.

"I'm pretty sure it was Jasper Carlson."

Robert gasped and staggered as if he'd been struck. His voice was hollow with fear now, rather than angry, as he repeated, "Jasper Carlson. The banker's son?"

"Yeah. He was with Richard Aylesworth and some more of that bunch. They jumped me on the road outside of town and tried to give me a beatin'. I fought back and . . . well, Jasper hit his head on a tree. I reckon it, uh, stove in his skull, from the sound of it when he hit."

Edward stepped out of the door onto the porch. Clearly he had gotten there in time to hear Breckinridge's explanation, because he clutched Breck's arm and asked, "You said Aylesworth and more of his friends were there?"

"Yeah. And Aylesworth said they'd tell the law it was all my fault, that I attacked them and hit Jasper from behind. That's not the way it happened, though."

Edward reached up and put both hands on Breckinridge's shoulders now.

"Oh, Breck," he said despairingly, "the authorities will never believe that."

"I know." Breckinridge swallowed hard. "They'll believe whatever Aylesworth tells them . . . and he told me that I was gonna hang for what happened."

Robert squinted at him and asked, "Do ye swear that yer tellin' the truth about it, lad?"

Breckinridge nodded and said, "I swear, Pa."

"Then ye'll not hang! We'll put a stop to this. We'll talk to the law and tell them the truth—"

"And they'll put Breck in jail, have a sham of a trial, and string him up," Edward broke in. "You know that, Pa. People like us . . . we've got no chance against the likes of Richard Aylesworth. And Jasper Carlson's father will want blood, too. Breck's blood." Edward looked at his youngest brother and went on, "You've got to get out of here."

Breckinridge sighed.

"That's what I was thinkin', too," he said. "But I

sure hoped you could come up with some other idea, Edward. I don't want to leave home."

"It's your only chance," Edward urged. "You need to head west into Missouri. Maybe even beyond Missouri. If you go far enough the law won't be able to find you. They may not even try if you vanish into the frontier. You have to take Hector, too. You'll need a good horse."

"But you use him for the plowing. I thought I'd go on foot—"

"They'll catch you in a matter of days if you do," Edward said. "Maybe hours."

"Wait a minute, wait a minute," Robert said. "Yer sayin' Breckinridge has to go away? To never come back?"

"Not any time soon. It's too dangerous for him."

"My God." Robert leaned the shotgun against the wall and stepped over to Breckinridge. He said again, "My God," then put his arms around his youngest son, who was almost twice as big as the old man. "My baby boy. I . . . I . . ."

Emotion choked his voice so that he couldn't go on.

Breckinridge's eyes burned, and his throat felt like it had something huge caught inside it. He used a big hand to pat his father on the back and forced himself to say, "It'll be all right, Pa. I . . . I'll come back one of these days. You'll see."

Robert hugged him fiercely, then said to Edward, "Fetch yer mother and yer brothers. If Breckinridge has to leave, he won't do it without everybody sayin' good-bye to him."

Edward nodded and ducked into the house. Robert put an arm around Breckinridge's shoulders, reaching up quite a bit to do so, and steered him toward the door.

"Come inside, son. Ye've got to say yer farewells."

"It needs to be fast, Pa," Breckinridge said. "Aylesworth's probably already gone to the law by now."

The next few minutes were hectic indeed. Breckinridge's mother wailed with grief when she learned that her youngest son was leaving, most likely for good. Despite the resentment she sometimes felt toward him, he was still one of her boys.

Breck's brothers were all upset, too. Jeremiah and Henry, the most hotheaded of the clan other than Breck himself, declared that he should stay and fight the law with them at his side.

"They'll only take you out of here over our dead bodies!" Jeremiah vowed. That made Samantha sob even more.

"Nobody else is gettin' killed, and sure as blazes not on account of me," Breckinridge said. "That's why I'm leavin', and nobody can stop me."

In the light from the candle on the table, Edward rubbed his chin and said, "The law is bound to ask questions. We'll tell them you said you were going to Texas." He smiled sadly. "Like Davy Crockett."

"Anybody who knows Breckinridge will believe that," Thomas said.

"You'll need supplies," Samantha said. "I'll gather up some food."

"And your rifle and pistol and plenty of powder and shot," Edward said. "We'll get all we have on hand. We'd better get busy. There can't be much time."

That was true. Breckinridge could imagine a posse of lawmen galloping toward the farm at that very moment, aiming to arrest him and start him on the road that led inevitably to the gallows.

When all the supplies had been gathered and hung on the saddle in canvas bags, Breckinridge stood on the porch and hugged each of his brothers in turn, slapping them on the back. He might have gotten a little carried away by emotion, judging by the way they staggered a bit, but they returned the hugs and exhorted him to take care of himself.

He hugged his father next, and Robert gruffly advised him, "Ye've got to learn to control that reckless nature o' yers, boy. 'Twill land ye in trouble every time."

Breckinridge wanted to point out that he hadn't done anything reckless in this instance other than calling on a pretty girl, but he didn't want to waste any of what might be his last few precious moments with his family in arguing. Instead he promised, "I'll try, Pa. I'll do my best not to let you down again."

He hugged his mother then, and through her tears Samantha said, "I've never been fair to you."

"Now, Ma, that's not—"

"It's true," she insisted. "I've always been harder on you than any of the others, and yet all the time I knew you might turn out to be the best of us."

"The best? I'm runnin' away from the law because I killed a man—"

"This is just the start of your life, Breckinridge. What happens from now on is up to you, not anyone else. You'll be all right, especially if you stop to think every now and then. You don't *always* have to do the first thing that comes to your mind, no matter what the circumstances." She dabbed at her eyes with the sleeve of her nightdress. "And there I go again, fussing at you. Just remember that we all love you, Breckinridge."

"And I love you," he said. "I'll never forget you, any of you. And if I can come back someday, I will."

With those painful farewells out of the way, Breckinridge mounted up. He sat there on Hector for a moment, looking at his home and family that he might never see again. Then he lifted a hand to wave good-bye, turned the horse's head, and nudged Hector into motion.

"Ride south a good long way before you turn west," Edward called after him. "Stay as far away from Knoxville as you can."

That was good advice. Breckinridge waved again to signal his acknowledgment.

He struck out across country, following the valley as it angled southwest. The dark bulk of the Smokies rose to his left. He had spent so much time in those mountains that they were like his second home, and he regretted leaving them, too.

But he had heard that the Rocky Mountains were even taller and more majestic. Despite being upset about everything that had happened, he felt the first flush of excitement. Maybe he would actually see the Rockies for himself someday. He had dreamed about such things without really thinking they might come true.

Now there was nothing holding him back. He could go wherever he pleased and do whatever he wanted.

Assuming, of course, that the law didn't catch him and hang him for killing Jasper Carlson.

Breckinridge forced those thoughts out of his mind. He knew the danger existed and he would do everything in his power to avoid it, but he wasn't going to dwell on it. Instead he was going to think about the endless possibilities before him.

He leaned forward, patted Hector on the shoulder, and said, "I know you've carried me quite a ways already tonight, old fella, but I have to depend on you for a while longer. If you can keep it up, we'll have a rest later."

Hector tossed his head and didn't slow from the ground-eating trot he had established. He and Breckinridge moved on, skirting trouble—at least Breck hoped so—moving steadily toward the frontier . . . and the future.

BOOK TWO

Chapter Seven

Many times over the next few weeks, Breckinridge dreamed of being chased. He heard the thundering hoofbeats of a posse pursuing him. The baying of bloodhounds haunted his dreams, along with the angry voices of men shouting "String him up!" and "Hang the murderer!"

From time to time he even dreamed about that night on the road east of Knoxville, and it seemed that he could change what had happened. All he had to do was wake up while Jasper Carlson was still alive . . .

But when he woke, Jasper was still dead, and there wasn't a blessed thing Breckinridge could do about it. He was still a wanted fugitive, and he always would be.

For all practical purposes, though, every mile he put between him and Knoxville increased his chances that so-called justice would never catch up to him. Rich man's justice, he thought bitterly sometimes as he rode through the night, along narrow trails and through unfamiliar woods, guided only by the stars as he listened to the lonely hooting of owls and fought against the empty feeling inside him.

Fortunately, it wasn't like that all the time. At first he traveled only at night, hiding out in gullies or thickets during the day when he might be seen, but as he began to curve more to the west, farther from Knoxville, he grew bolder. He hadn't spotted any signs of pursuit and thought it might be safe to ride during the day as long as he avoided the main roads.

That allowed him to take a good look at the new country through which he passed. It really wasn't that much different from the landscape around home—rugged, wooded hills slashed with gullies and divided by valleys where farmers earned their living from the land—but it was new territory to Breckinridge and he savored everything about it.

He avoided settlements and people as much as he could. Now and then he would meet somebody on the road, usually a farmer driving a mule-drawn wagon, but they were as taciturn as he was and had little or nothing to say.

That went against Breckinridge's nature, because he'd always been the sort to talk to anybody and everybody, and his pa had said sometimes that Breck could talk the ears off a brass monkey. Breck had never actually *seen* a brass monkey, but he'd heard plenty about them from Pa.

He shot game when he could, filled his water skin at every passing creek. He began to long for company. He enjoyed exploring like this, but he wasn't really cut out for a solitary life.

Both Breckinridge and Hector began to grow lean, almost gaunt. Breck's supplies were low. He didn't want to venture into a town. Folks would be liable to remember somebody as big as he was, and if the law came around looking for him and asking questions, they might pick up his trail.

He figured he might could risk stopping at some isolated farm, though. Maybe if whoever lived there had enough supplies on hand, he could trade some work for a few staples. He had never really liked chores, but he could do them. He was a regular wizard, in fact, at things like splitting firewood.

When he spotted a farmhouse and a small barn sitting by themselves in a valley, he sat for a long time on the ridge overlooking the scene. After a good while, he decided to ride down there and see how things went.

A heavyset old man limped out of the barn as Breckinridge rode in. The farmer wore overalls and had a floppy-brimmed hat pushed back on a mostly bald head. Tufts of white hair stuck out above each ear. When Breck came closer he saw that the old-timer had a face like a bulldog. The old man grinned and said, "How do. Lord have mercy, you're a big 'un, ain't you?"

Breckinridge returned the grin and said, "Yeah, and I'm not sure I've got my full growth yet."

"I hope for the sake o' that there hoss that you have, otherwise you're liable to break the poor animal's back. Light and stay a spell, if you're of a mind to. Name's Yancy Humboldt."

"B-Bill," Breckinridge said. He'd almost given the old man his real name out of habit. He had to break that habit, and the sooner the better.

"Well, Buh-Bill, are you gettin' down or not? If you ain't, I'll get back to my work."

"What are you doin'? Maybe I could lend a hand."

"In return for some supper?" Yancy Humboldt asked shrewdly.

"And maybe a few supplies?"

Humboldt frowned in apparent thought for a second or two, then waved Breckinridge forward.

"Mule kicked some slats outta his stall. Sound like somethin' you could fix?"

"Sure," Breckinridge answered. He had done some carpentry work around the farm, although Edward was always better at that sort of thing.

"Do a good job and we'll see. Might be able to spare a few things." Humboldt pointed. "You can water your hoss at that trough over there. I can find some grain for him, too. Poor critter probably needs some rest if he's been carryin' you for very long."

"He's pretty strong," Breckinridge said as he dismounted.

"He'd have to be."

As they went into the barn, Breckinridge could tell that Humboldt limped because of a twisted right leg. He nodded toward it and asked, "What happened to your leg? If you don't mind talkin' about it, that is."

"And if I do mind?"

"Well, it ain't none of my business, so I wouldn't ask again. I'm just curious, that's all."

"Bear got hold of it when I was a young man and durned near pulled it off. Ripped the hell out of it with his claws, too. Reckon I'd have been a goner if my friend Dan'l hadn't shot the bear, patched me up as best he could, and then packed me outta the woods back to where I could get some real help."

"Dan'l, eh?" Breckinridge chuckled. "Wouldn't be talkin' about Dan'l Boone, would you?"

"As a matter o' fact, I am," Humboldt replied. "This was up in Kentucky, not far from Boonesborough."

Breckinridge stared at him and said, "You're serious."

"I should hope to smile I'm serious!"

"You really knew Daniel Boone?"

"Broke many a trail with him in the old days, at least until I tangled with that dang bear." Humboldt pointed into a stall with several broken planks on one side. "There she be. I'll leave you to it. You ought to be able to finish by suppertime. If you don't, you won't eat. Do a poor job, and you won't eat, neither. Understand?"

Breckinridge barely heard the question. He said, "Can you tell me about Daniel Boone?"

"Best man I ever knowed at times, and a damned fool at others. Just like most men. I thought you was gonna fix that stall. Boards and a hammer and nails are out back."

Breckinridge had a hunch that Humboldt could be talkative, but only when he wanted to be. It might be better to go ahead and repair the stall and save the conversation for later.

One thing he had to know first, though.

"Has anybody, uh, come around here lookin' for somebody like me?" He added hastily, "I mean, there might be some friends of mine in these parts."

"You mean has anybody been lookin' for a galoot as tall as a tree, with bright red hair? Naw, I reckon I'd remember somethin' like that . . . Buh-Bill."

Breckinridge could tell from the old farmer's voice that Humboldt suspected he was running from something. The old-timer didn't seem worried by that possibility, though. He repeated the warning about

getting done with the task by suppertime and then left
Breckinridge in the barn.

Breckinridge pried out the broken boards and
nailed new ones in their place. It was a pretty simple
job, really. The mule that had caused the damage
stood inside the stall, stolidly ignoring him. Breck
worked from outside the stall, not wanting to venture
in there with a mule that was known to kick. That was
a good way for a fella to get his head bashed in.

When he was finished, he took hold of the new
boards and gave them a good shake. They seemed
plenty solid, so he nodded in satisfaction and put the
hammer and the rest of the nails back where he'd
found them. He walked out of the barn and went
toward the house.

Yancy Humboldt must have seen him coming. The
old-timer stepped out onto the porch, and this time
he had a shotgun tucked under his arm.

"Got done out there, did ya?" he called.

"That's right," Breckinridge said. "You want to
come have a look at what I did?"

Humboldt shifted the shotgun's twin barrels so
they pointed more in Breckinridge's direction and
said, "Maybe later. Right now you can just stop right
there where you are."

Breckinridge stopped thirty or forty feet short of
the house as the old-timer said, but he frowned in
confusion.

"What's wrong, Mr. Humboldt?" he asked. "I thought
we were makin' a trade. The work I done in exchange
for supper and some supplies."

"That's right, but there weren't nothin' said about

you comin' in the house to eat that meal or pick up them supplies. You can do that just as good out here."

Breckinridge was puzzled by the farmer's attitude, but then he saw the crude homespun curtain over one of the windows twitch a little, and when he looked closer he caught a glimpse of a face peering out at him.

It was a girl's face, and from what Breckinridge could see of it, a pretty one, too. But then the curtain dropped back and he couldn't see her anymore.

Breckinridge understood now. Humboldt didn't want him setting foot in the house because he had a daughter or a granddaughter or, shoot, maybe even a wife in there, and he didn't trust Breck to be around her.

That was a mite insulting, Breckinridge thought. His ma had raised him to always be polite to females. He could be a little rough around the edges sometimes, that was true, but he liked to think he was a gentleman when he needed to be, too.

He supposed he could see how come Humboldt felt the way he did, though, living out here a good long ways from civilization. It was natural for him to be protective of the girl, whoever she was.

"That's fine, Mr. Humboldt," Breckinridge said. "Out here or in there, it don't really matter to me. I appreciate your hospitality either way."

Humboldt looked a little flustered by Breckinridge's politeness. He let the shotgun's barrels sag toward the ground.

"I reckon you can come up here and sit on the porch," he said gruffly. "But that's all."

"Thank you kindly, sir."

Breckinridge climbed the three steps to the porch while Humboldt went back inside. A few minutes later the old-timer brought him a bowl of stew with chunks of roast beef and wild onions and carrots floating in it. Humboldt handed him a piece of bread torn off a larger loaf, as well, and asked, "You got anything to carry those supplies in?"

"There's an empty burlap sack on my saddle."

Humboldt fetched the sack and limped back inside. When he came back out the sack was bulging with provisions.

"You set right there and eat while I go take a look at that work you done," Humboldt said. "You budge off this porch and you'll be sorry."

"I'll be right here," Breckinridge promised. Since all the trouble back home, he was more determined than ever not to get mixed up in any more ruckuses. Knowing himself as he did, he wasn't sure that resolve would last, but he was going to try to stay out of hot water, anyway.

The stew was good. He figured the girl he'd seen at the window had made it, although he couldn't be sure. He wondered idly if Humboldt was keeping her here against her will. He didn't seem like the sort of fella who would do such an ungodly thing, but you couldn't ever tell. Just because the farmer had been friends with Daniel Boone didn't mean the old man could do no wrong.

Humboldt came back from the barn and said, "You done a fine job, young fella. I'd say we made a fair trade. Now you can finish up that stew and be movin' along."

"It'll be night soon," Breckinridge pointed out. "I'll be lookin' for a place to stay."

"It won't be here." Humboldt's voice was flat, brooking no argument.

"Sure," Breckinridge said with a shrug of his broad shoulders. "Whatever you say, Mr. Humboldt."

"Dang right."

Breckinridge used the bread to sop up the last of the juices from the stew, then handed the empty bowl to the farmer. Breck picked up the sack of supplies and said, "I'm much obliged to you. I'd say that I'll stop by and say howdy if I'm ever in this part of the country again, but I don't expect to be."

"No, I reckon you better keep on to wherever it is you're headed, Buh-Bill. But tell you what . . . if those so-called friends you mentioned come around lookin' for you, I'll tell 'em I ain't seen you."

"That'd be best," Breckinridge agreed solemnly. He tied the supplies to the saddle, then mounted up and rode out without looking back.

He had ridden about half a mile before he said out loud, "Dang it, I never did get him to tell me about bein' on the scout with Daniel Boone!"

Breckinridge traveled another couple of miles before he found a place to camp for the night in a thicket of trees. Since he'd already had his supper, he didn't even have to build a fire. At this time of year the weather was pleasant enough that he didn't need one for warmth, either, although it could still be a mite chilly early in the mornings.

Instead he picketed Hector where the horse had some graze, spread his blankets in a reasonably comfortable spot, and rolled up in them to go to sleep.

His rifle, pistol, and knife were close beside him, and when something roused him from slumber an unknown amount of time later, his hand reached out unerringly in the darkness and closed around the pistol butt. He lifted the weapon from the ground in complete silence and curled his thumb over the hammer, ready to cock and fire.

Renegade Indians could be anywhere, and so could thieves. If somebody wanted to rob him, either of his hair or his belongings, they were in for an unpleasant surprise.

Instead he was the one who got the surprise as a female voice called softly, "Hey! Hey, mister, are you in there? Don't shoot, I'm comin' in."

Chapter Eight

Breckinridge had never heard the girl at Humboldt's place speak, so he couldn't recognize her voice. Despite that, every instinct in his body told him she was his late-night visitor.

He didn't trust that this wasn't some sort of trick or trap, but there was only one way to find out. He raised the pistol and eared back the hammer, just in case, and said, "Here I am, gal. I'm warnin' you, though . . . You best not try anything funny."

The undergrowth crackled a little as the girl made her way toward him. She stepped out of the brush and into the little clearing where he had camped. Even though there was almost no light from the moon and stars under the trees, his keen eyes spotted her. She was only an indistinct shape in the gloom.

"That's far enough," Breckinridge told her. "Who are you, and what are you doin' here?"

"My name's Sadie Humboldt," she answered without hesitation. "I followed you from my grandpap's farm, mister. I saw which direction you went and hoped I could find you."

"Why?"

"Because wherever you're headed, I want you to take me with you. Otherwise I'm gonna be stuck there takin' care of Grandpap until he dies, and then I'll just have to marry some ol' farmer who'll be more of the same. I want to get out and have me some fun before that happens."

To a certain extent, Breckinridge could sympathize with her. Back home, he had spent many pleasant hours daydreaming about running away from his family's farm and having adventures instead of spending all his time either working like a dog or sleeping an exhausted sleep.

Now he had left home, but it wasn't anything like what he had envisioned. Parts of his current existence weren't really that bad—he liked being out in nature and seeing new places and things—but he could never forget that he was a wanted fugitive, on the run from the law forevermore.

Breckinridge climbed to his feet and asked, "How old are you, anyway, girl?"

"I'm sixteen," Sadie said. "But don't let that worry you, mister. I don't care how much older than me you are."

She had mistaken him for being older than he really was, which was a pretty common occurrence. Rather than correct her, he said, "You ain't old enough to be runnin' away from home, especially with a strange man. Your grandpap would be comin' after me with a posse. I don't need the extra trouble."

"Yeah, Grandpap said you were likely on the run from the law. He liked you anyway. I don't think he'd be too upset if he knew I was with you. That's why I left him a note tellin' him I'd gone after you and planned to travel with you. I can't write that good, but I was able to manage that much."

Breckinridge bit back a groan of dismay. All his good intentions of staying out of trouble, and Sadie had gone and landed him right in the middle of it anyway. He bet that if the law showed up on the Humboldt farm now, the old man wouldn't be so generous about not mentioning that he'd seen Breck.

"All right, you've got to turn around and head home right now," Breckinridge said. "When you get there, you be sure and tell your grandfather that I never laid a finger on you, you hear?"

His eyes had adjusted to the darkness well enough that he saw her give a defiant toss of her head as she said, "Oh, shoot, is *that* all you're worried about? I ain't what anybody would call a good girl, mister, and I ain't been for a long time. Most of six months. Plenty of gals in these parts, by the time they're my age they're married and swole up with child. Not always in that order, neither."

Breckinridge still held the pistol, although he had lowered the hammer and pointed the weapon at the ground beside him. He used his free hand to scrub at his face in frustration for a moment, then he said, "I don't care about any of that other stuff, but you can't go with me. Where I'm goin', I can't be saddled with no girl-child."

"I just told you, I ain't no child. Where *are* you goin'?"

"The Rocky Mountains," Breckinridge answered without thinking about it. "I'm gonna be a fur trapper."

He knew when he heard those words how right they sounded. When he'd left home he hadn't had any clear idea of his goals except not to get hanged, but now he knew what he wanted to do.

"That sounds mighty excitin'," Sadie declared. "I'll come with you. I'll be a fur trapper, too."

"Ain't you listenin'? I just told you you can't!" Breckinridge paused. "Anyway, there ain't no gal fur trappers. None I've ever heard of, leastways."

"Then I'll be the first."

Breckinridge felt like a man who couldn't swim, being drawn into deeper and deeper water by an irresistible current. If Sadie wasn't going to cooperate, he didn't see how he could make her go back to her grandfather's farm short of picking her up and carrying her there. And if he did that she'd probably fight him every step of the way. He couldn't afford to lose that much time, either, when the law might be on his trail.

Somehow, he had to talk her into going back on her own, and he could tell he wasn't going to be able to do that tonight. She was just too blasted determined to get her own way. Maybe he could risk letting her travel with him for a day or two. Once she had seen how hard it was to live on the trail like he'd been doing, she would turn around and head home on her own.

With that hope in his head, Breckinridge said, "All right, since you're so damn stubborn I reckon you can come along. You got to promise, though, that if your grandpap comes after us or sets the law on us, you'll tell them the truth of the matter, that this was all your idea and that I never took advantage of you."

She came closer to him and said, "It ain't takin' advantage if it's what I want, too, is it, mister?"

"Blast it, girl, stop that! Did you bring anything with you?"

"A blanket and a little food."

Breckinridge pointed and said, "You take your blanket and curl up on the other side of the clearin'. I got my side of camp, and you got your side."

"All right," she said with a saucy lilt to her voice. "Just remember it don't have to be that way."

Breckinridge went back to his bedroll and listened to Sadie getting settled on the other side of the clearing. He said, "You don't even know my name, do you?"

"You told my grandpap it was Bill, but he said he could tell that was a lie."

"Your grandpap's too damned smart," Breckinridge muttered. "For now we'll just say it's Bill, all right?"

"Sure." A moment later, Sadie added brightly, "Good night, Bill."

Breckinridge's sleep was restless that night.

When he woke in the morning it was to the smell of coffee brewing, a pleasant sensation he hadn't experienced since leaving home. And he shouldn't be experiencing it now, he thought as he sat up sharply and looked around.

Sadie had a small fire going, just big enough to boil a pot of coffee and fry some strips of salt pork in a little pan. She must have brought all that with her, Breckinridge thought. At the moment, his stomach was glad she had come after him whether his head was or not.

The sun wasn't up yet, but there was enough light in the sky for him to get his first good look at her as she hunkered next to the fire in what Maureen would surely think was an undignified, unladylike position. Thick ropes of honey-colored hair hung around Sadie's face. It was a nice face, too, even if it was a little dirty.

She wore a plain gray homespun dress that looked like it was a little small for her. Either that or she was just pretty womanly for her age. In Breckinridge's experience, hill girls tended to mature early. Sadie had been right about one thing: most places she'd be considered marriageable enough.

However, the last thing in the world Breckinridge was looking for was a wife.

She had noticed that he was awake. Hard not to, when he'd sat up the way he had with a gun in his hand. She smiled across the fire at him and said, "Good mornin', Bill."

Breckinridge wasn't a liar by nature. It bothered him that he had given her a name not really his own. But under the circumstances, it was the best thing for him to do, he thought as he grunted, "Mornin'."

"Hope it's all right I started a fire and put some coffee on to boil. I figured if you're gonna make me sleep *way* over there on the other side of the camp I ought to make myself useful to you in other ways."

"Yeah, it's fine." Breckinridge couldn't help licking his lips at the smells filling his nostrils. "I got to admit, that coffee smells mighty nice. It's been a while since I had any."

"You're welcome," she told him, even though he hadn't thanked her.

Breckinridge stood up, stretched, and went to tend to his morning business. While he was doing that, he got to thinking that maybe the fire hadn't been such a good idea after all. If anyone was close behind him on his trail, they might be able to follow those smells right to the camp.

It was too late to worry about that now, he told himself. In the meantime he was going to enjoy the coffee and salt pork. He might even wind up enjoying Sadie Humboldt's company, although he vowed he wouldn't let her share his bedroll. That would be an unwanted complication and an invitation to even more trouble that he didn't need.

The breakfast was a good one, he discovered when he rejoined her. He wasn't sure, but when he complimented her on her cooking he thought she blushed a little. He didn't expect that from somebody as brazen as she apparently was.

By the time they had eaten and cleaned up, the sun was scarcely above the horizon. It was time they were moving on, Breckinridge thought. He fastened the two bedrolls behind Hector's saddle, hung the supplies Sadie had brought with his own, and then told her, "Come here."

She stood in front of him, the top of her head barely up to the bottom of his chest.

"What do you want?" she asked.

"Hold still," he told her. Then he grasped her under the arms and hoisted her into the air. She exclaimed in surprise and started kicking her feet, which were shod in well-worn work shoes.

"Put me down, you big ox!" she cried.

Breckinridge set her on her feet again.

"What was that about?"

"I was just seein' how much you weigh," he told her. "Hector's a strong horse. I reckon he can carry both of us without too much trouble. But if I see that he's gettin' tired, you may have to get down and walk for a spell."

She raked her hair back from her face and said, "You could always walk, you know."

"Yeah, but he's my horse," Breckinridge said. "And I don't recollect invitin' you to come along on this trip."

"All right, fine," she snapped. "If I have to, I'll walk."

Breckinridge nodded and swung up into the saddle. He extended a hand to her. She hesitated, then took it and climbed up in front of him. Breck heeled Hector into an easy walk.

As they rode, Breckinridge asked, "Your grandfather, did he mistreat you?"

"Grandpap?" Sadie said. "Shoot, no. He's one of the nicest fellas you'd ever want to meet. He was good friends with Dan'l Boone, you know."

"Yeah, he mentioned that."

"He never treated me bad at all," Sadie went on. "He just never saw that I was pinin' away for somethin' different. Somethin' better. I don't want to spend my life as no farmer's wife, workin' from before dawn to past dark and raisin' a bunch of squallin' brats. That's no way to live."

The way she talked about it, Breckinridge couldn't help agreeing. It sounded like a life of misery and drudgery, all right.

Then he reminded himself that his mother had lived that way, and it never seemed to bother her that much, although she had her times of melancholy, sure enough. He supposed that whether a person's life was good or bad depended more on what was inside them than anything else.

Breckinridge's route still angled southwest. For one

thing, the lay of the land made that the easiest route for traveling, because he and Sadie could follow the valleys between the numerous ridges that ran in that direction.

For several days they drifted along in that fashion. At night Sadie still made a comment now and then about how she was willing to warm his blankets, but Breckinridge was steadfast in his refusal. Morality didn't come easy to him, so he knew he had to be stubborn and not give an inch, or else there was no telling what he might do.

Eventually they came to a crossroads where a little whitewashed church sat. Nobody was around at the moment, but a signpost stood at the intersection and on it were written the words CHATTANOOGA 10 MILES, with an arrow pointing to the southwest, the way they had been going.

"I never heard of a town called Chattanooga," Breckinridge said. "It must be new. But if it's big enough to have a sign pointin' toward it and sayin' how far away it is, I don't reckon I want to go there."

"You try to stay away from towns, don't you?" Sadie said. "What's the matter, ain't you the sociable sort?"

"Of course I am. I love bein' around people. But it ain't a wise idea right now."

Sadie nodded solemnly and said, "Because you're on the run from the law."

"Because I got a wild, runaway gal with me," Breckinridge said, not admitting that he was a fugitive. He turned Hector onto the trail that led almost due west. "Come on, we'll see what's this way."

Sadie sighed. She said, "I thought I was runnin' away to a more excitin' life. Instead all I ever see is you, Bill. You ain't hard on the eyes, but a gal gets a little tired of lookin' at the same thing all the time, especially when it's a fella who won't even spark her."

"It was your choice to come along."

"You're gonna keep throwin' that in my face, ain't you?"

"As long as it's true, which is gonna be from now on."

Sadie snorted and then fell silent.

A few hours later, Breckinridge reined in at the top of a hill and looked down at the biggest stream he had ever seen. There were lots of creeks and a few rivers around home, but nothing like this. The blue water stretched for a hundred yards from shore to shore. He figured it had to be the Tennessee River, which started up at Knoxville where the Holston and the French Broad rivers flowed together.

"Son of a gun," Breckinridge said. "How are we gonna get across that?"

"Look!" Sadie said excitedly, pointing at the near shore. "There's a ferry."

So there was, Breckinridge saw as he looked down the hill. The ferry landing had a cluster of buildings around it, too, a village that had no doubt grown up because this was a place where folks could cross the river.

Breckinridge felt worry stir inside him. So far he had avoided being around people very much on this journey, and it had worked out well for him.

Now, though, he didn't seem to have much choice. He wanted to continue heading west, and he couldn't do that without crossing the river.

"You're nervous about goin' down there, aren't you?" Sadie asked.

"Yeah, a little."

"I'll behave myself, I promise. And that ferry looks like the only way we're gonna get across."

"I know." Breckinridge heaved a sigh and nudged Hector into motion again. "Let's go."

He felt like he was riding into trouble, but there wasn't a damned thing he could do about it.

Chapter Nine

A board with jagged ends mounted on a post at the edge of the tiny settlement had the words COOTERS LANDIN burned into it in shaky letters. Breckinridge hadn't heard of Cooter's Landing any more than he had Chattanooga. This part of Tennessee was all unexplored territory to him.

The ferry landing, which consisted of a dock and a shack built of rough-hewn planks, was at the far end of the broad, muddy expanse that passed for a street. Four buildings stood on the right: a combined blacksmith shop and stable, a general store, a lawyer's office, and a tavern. The opposite side of the street occupied another tavern and a doctor's office. Half a dozen log cabins were scattered around haphazardly behind the business buildings.

"Well, this don't look like much of a place," Sadie commented as they rode along the street toward the landing.

"It probably hasn't been here very long," Breckinridge said. He wasn't really interested in Cooter's

Landing. He just wanted to board that ferry, get to the other side of the river, and keep going.

As they passed the store, Sadie said, "Oooh, can we go in there and buy some things, Bill?"

"With what?" Breckinridge asked. He had a few coins in his pockets that he had brought from home, but he had managed not to spend any so far. He considered the coins to be for emergencies only, and he didn't want Sadie or anybody else to know that he had them.

"I've got some money," she said. "I, uh, brought it with me from Grandpap's place."

Breckinridge felt his eyes widening. He said, "You mean you stole it!"

"I got a right to it," Sadie replied in sullen tones. "I been cookin' and cleanin' for him ever since my ma died, and that was almost three years ago!"

"Maybe so, but you shouldn't have just took it like that."

"What else could I do? I couldn't very well tell him I was leavin' and ask for it, now could I? If I'd done that, he never would've let me off the place. He's a good man, but he's set in his ways." She twisted on Sadie's back to gaze longingly at the store as they rode past it. "Please, Bill?"

"You can do whatever you want," he told her, "but I ain't stoppin'. I'm boardin' that ferry and headin' across the river as soon as the ferryman will take me."

Sadie pouted and made angry noises, which Breckinridge ignored like he had all the sultry looks she had given him and the seductive noises she had made over the past few days.

As they approached the landing he realized he was going to have to part with some of his carefully hoarded coins after all. A sign was nailed up on the side of the shack announcing that riding the ferry cost ten cents per person and five cents per horse. Breckinridge recognized the writing as being the same that was on the sign at the edge of the settlement. The prices seemed awfully high to Breck, but he didn't really know anything about the ferry business.

A man in overalls and a floppy-brimmed hat stood next to a capstan with a thick rope looped around it. He had his hands on his hips and looked disgusted. Off to one side was a pole corral holding a couple of mules. Normally those mules would be hooked to the capstan, which was attached to the pulley that provided a means of locomotion for the ferry. As the mules plodded around and around, the rope dragged the ferry first one direction and then the other, depending on which side of the river it was on.

Now, however, the big ferry made of logs floated on the river next to the landing, its only movements in response to the gentle current.

Breckinridge reined in and called to the man, "Hey, mister, how long before the ferry goes across the river again?"

The man turned to glare at him. His face was angular and unfriendly.

"As soon as I get this damn capstan to workin'," he replied, "and I don't know when that's gonna be. Blasted thing's seized up. I can't get the ferry across the river and back without it."

Worry crawled along the back of Breckinridge's neck. He felt like trouble was closing in on him from behind, and the last thing he wanted was to be delayed.

"An hour or two, maybe?" he asked.

The ferryman snorted and shook his head.

"More than likely it'll be tomorrow mornin' at the earliest," he said. "If you're in a hurry you'll have to go on downstream to Chattanooga."

"We're in no hurry," Breckinridge lied. His instincts told him to avoid the bigger towns, and he was going to stick with that as long as he could.

"You and your missus can get a room for the night at Rollins's tavern, I 'spect," the ferryman said. "He's got a couple o' rooms he rents to travelers. I'll try to get you across the river by the end o' the day tomorrow."

He pointed to the closest of the two taverns.

Breckinridge didn't correct the man's assumption that he and Sadie were married. It was simpler not to, plus a married couple traveling together wouldn't attract nearly as much attention as a man and woman who weren't hitched doing the same. Breck nodded, said, "Thank you kindly," and turned Hector around.

"That man thought we'd jumped the broomstick," Sadie said as they rode toward the tavern.

"I know."

"I don't mind pretendin' we're married if you don't," she purred.

Breckinridge tried not to sigh. Sadie was doing an almighty good job of testing his resolve, and these circumstances sure weren't making it any easier.

They dismounted at the tavern. Breckinridge tied Hector's reins to the hitch rack out front, and they went inside.

Breckinridge had been in taverns before, although some people—mostly his pa and brothers—figured he was too young to be drinking. Once he'd gotten his full growth, though, nobody tried to keep him out. He liked to have a bucket of beer now and then, but he didn't care for the taste of hard liquor or the way it burned going down his throat.

He enjoyed the way some of the serving girls fawned over him, too, if he was being truthful about it. They liked to sit on his lap and run their fingers through his long red hair, and they didn't seem to mind if he got a little frisky with them.

But that was the old Breckinridge, he told himself. The new one behaved himself and tried to stay out of trouble.

Problem was, he was getting damned sick and tired of behaving himself.

The air inside the place was thick with pipe smoke and whiskey and beer fumes, as well as the smoke from candles that burned on wagon-wheel fixtures hanging from the low ceiling. The floor was hard-packed dirt. Tables made from empty barrels were scattered around. Men used kegs as seats. A rough bar filled up one wall. On the far side of the room a blanket hung over a doorway. It was pushed back part of the way to reveal a dim hallway beyond.

Three men stood at the bar drinking, two together and one down at the far end. Half a dozen more were split between two tables. A skinny, white-haired man with a face ravaged by time and alcohol stood behind the bar wearing a gray canvas apron. He nodded to Breckinridge and Sadie.

"Something I can do for you folks?"

"Fella at the landing said you might be able to rent us a room for the night," Breckinridge explained.

The bartender nodded and said, "Waitin' for the ferry to be fixed, are you?"

"That's right."

One of the men at the bar said, "That capstan's busted more'n it works. Cooter has to work on it almost ever' day just to keep it goin'."

"He's the one the settlement's named after, is he?"

"I wanted to call it Rollinsville," the bartender said. "That's my name. But Cooter claimed he was here first and had the right to name the place. I couldn't argue with that."

"What about that room?" Breckinridge asked.

"Oh, yeah. Sure, I got a couple of rooms in the back that ain't bein' used right now. You can sleep in one of 'em. Cost you a dime apiece."

"That's what it costs to ride the ferry."

Rollins shrugged and said, "It's the goin' rate." His watery eyes narrowed as he gazed at Sadie. "Unless you'd care to make a business arrangement. The gal can use the room, split whatever she makes with me, and you and her can sleep there for free once she's done with her customers."

Sadie wasn't so brazen now. She shrunk against Breckinridge's side. Breck felt himself getting angry and said, "You just watch your tongue, mister. I never said that this here girl is . . . is a trollop!"

The man rubbed his chin and said, "Well, if she ain't, she could be. She's comely enough. If you ain't ever considered hirin' her out, you ought to. She could make you a pretty penny."

"Bill," Sadie said in a voice that quavered a little with nervousness, "I ain't sure I want to stay here after all."

"Ain't no other place in Cooter's Landin' to stay," the bartender said reasonably.

One of the men at the bar edged closer. He was

stocky and had a thick sandy mustache that drooped over his mouth. He said to Breckinridge, "Mister, I'll give you two bits for half an hour with the girl. Now, you got to admit that there's a fair price. Maybe more than fair."

"Forget it," Breckinridge snapped. He took hold of Sadie's arm and started to turn her toward the door. "We'll just find us a place to camp—"

He stopped as he saw that three men who had been sitting at one of the tables had stood up and moved to place themselves between him and the entrance.

"It's just that there ain't been a gal that nice lookin' in Cooter's Landin' for quite a spell," Rollins said from behind the bar. "When one like her comes along, we sure do hate to let her go before we all get to know her better."

"Bill . . ." Sadie said, and she really sounded scared now.

"Don't be afraid," Breckinridge told her. "None of these fellas are big enough to scare me."

"You're a big one, all right," Sandy Mustache said, "but put us all together and we're a heap bigger 'n you."

The three men from the other table had joined the first trio in blocking the way out of here. They spread out some and started to close in on Breckinridge and Sadie. Breck backed against the bar, taking her with him. Sandy Mustache had a friend, and the bartender had declared himself in with the others.

That meant Breckinridge was outnumbered nine to one. The man down at the far end of the bar was the only one not making a move to join in. He concentrated on the mug of beer in front of him.

So things could have been worse, Breckinridge supposed. The odds could have been ten to one.

Another thought flashed through his mind. Despite all his vows to avoid trouble, it had found him anyway. Maybe that was just the natural order of things where Breckinridge Wallace was concerned.

"You can see things ain't gonna go your way, mister," Rollins said. "Might as well be reasonable. The offer to go in halves on what the girl earns still stands." The man's voice hardened. "Make us take her away from you and you won't get a thing out of the deal except a busted head."

They weren't leaving him any choice. Breckinridge said quietly, "Sadie, you stay close behind me."

"What—"

Before she could finish the question, he grabbed the nearest table and hoisted it in the air. The barrel out of which it was made was heavy, and two normal men would be needed to move it.

Breckinridge Wallace was no normal man, however. He let out a roar, because he knew that would give him strength, and lifted the table even higher. For a second the men blocking the tavern's front door forgot about threatening him and stood there open-mouthed, gaping at this incredible feat of strength.

Then they realized what was about to happen and tried to get out of the way, but they were too late. Breckinridge heaved the table in their direction. It crashed into two of the men and drove them off their feet. They went down hard with the table on top of them.

That created a gap on the group trying to keep Breckinridge and Sadie from leaving the tavern.

Breck grabbed Sadie's hand and charged toward that opening.

The sheer surprise of the devastating attack should have been enough to let Breck and Sadie get clear, but one of the men recovered quicker than Breckinridge expected. The man lunged at them and left his feet in a diving tackle. His arms went around Breck's knees.

At the same time, another man made a grab for Sadie. He managed to snag the collar of her dress. The material gave with a loud ripping sound and the garment came half off of her. Sadie screamed.

Breckinridge tried to kick free of the man who had hold of his legs, but while he was doing that another of the varmints hit him high and knocked him off balance. He lost his grip on Sadie as he felt himself falling.

Men piled on as he hit the dirt floor. Punching, kicking, gouging, they swarmed over him. The man who had torn Sadie's dress had his arms around her now. Still screaming, she writhed and struggled against him, but she was no match for his strength.

Breckinridge could take a pounding better than most men, but this rain of violence was too much punishment for even him to absorb and shrug off. His head spun crazily after a couple of kicks. He bellowed and swept his arms around in an attempt to get some breathing room. It worked, but only for a second. Then the brawlers closed in again, driven on by Rollins exhorting them from behind the bar, "Kill him! Kill the big son of a bitch!"

It looked like that stood a mighty good chance of happening.

Chapter Ten

The gunshot was deafening in the low-ceilinged tavern, pounding against the ears like a physical blow.

The sound made everything stop. Breckinridge almost groaned in relief as fists and feet stopped crashing into him. As the shot's echoes died away, a man's voice said into the resulting hushed silence, "Let go of that girl, my friend, or I'll put a pistol ball through your brain."

"You . . . you just got one shot," another man said. "You can't get all of us."

"That's absolutely right," the first man replied with a note of amusement. "Confer among yourselves and decide which one of you would like to die."

A voice Breckinridge recognized as belonging to Rollins, the proprietor of the place, said worriedly, "Better do what he says, boys. That's Jack MacKenzie. He's a crack shot. They say he's killed three men in duels down in Chattanooga."

"That's right," the man identified as MacKenzie drawled. "And those are just the ones that people know about." His tone became more brisk as he went on, "The rest of you, back away from that man."

"He jumped us!" somebody protested.

"Only after you threatened to rape his lovely companion. Now move!"

A couple of men were still on top of Breckinridge, holding him down. It felt good as their weight went away. He pushed himself up to a sitting position. His head still spun a little as he looked around, but he was getting his wits back.

The man who had been standing at the far end of the bar, enjoying a solitary drink, now had a pistol in each hand. The one in his left hand was down at his side, a tiny tendril of smoke still curling from its muzzle. The one in his right hand was leveled at the brawlers, and he held the weapon rock-steady.

The man reminded Breckinridge of Richard Aylesworth. He was well dressed and sleekly handsome, with dark hair under a beaver hat. He didn't have Aylesworth's air of smug arrogance about him, though. His demeanor was more one of quiet confidence.

Freed from the grip of the man who had half torn her dress off, Sadie hurried over to kneel next to Breckinridge. She had to hold the ruined garment around her with both hands as best she could, and even her best effort didn't prevent a considerable amount of creamy flesh from showing. She risked further exposure by putting a hand on Breck's shoulder and asking, "Are you all right, Bill?"

Breckinridge knew he would be bruised and sore by the next morning, but all his muscles seemed to be working and his head was settling down. Lucky for him his skull was too thick to be damaged easily. He said, "Yeah, I'll be fine."

"You want me to help you up?"

"No, I can manage. You just, ah, keep that dress on if you can."

Grimly, she stood up and tightened her grip on the torn dress. Breckinridge put a hand on the floor and levered himself up. He was shaky once he got on his feet, but that passed quickly.

MacKenzie motioned with the cocked pistol in his right hand and ordered, "All of you clear out, right now. This place is closed for the time being."

"You can't do that," Rollins protested with a yelp. "I make my livin' from this tavern."

MacKenzie set the empty pistol on the bar, reached into one of his waistcoat pockets, and took out a gold coin. Without really looking to see what he was doing, he tossed it unerringly to the bartender, who plucked it out of the air with avaricious deftness.

"There," he said. "I've just rented the entire establishment for the night for me and my new friends here."

Rollins bit the gold piece and nodded in satisfaction. He said, "You got yourself a deal, Mr. MacKenzie."

"That's more consideration than you deserve. You helped start this trouble. But I tend to choose the simplest solution to a problem, and it's easier to pay you off than to kill you."

Rollins swallowed hard and said, "I appreciate that, sir." He waved a hand at his sullen customers. "Shoo, the lot of you. You can come back and drink again tomorrow."

"Maybe we will and maybe we won't," one of the men said in a surly voice. "We won't forget the way you just turned on us. This ain't the only tavern in Cooter's Landing, you know."

"It's the only one that serves anything besides hog swill," Rollins said. "Now go on, git."

The men left, muttering resentful curses under their breath. When they were gone, MacKenzie finally lowered the loaded pistol and said to Rollins, "We'll be wanting some supper, and we'll take both rooms, of course. What I paid you ought to cover everything."

"Yes, sir. I'll see to it. Food won't be anything fancy, but it'll be good."

"I hope so."

"Listen, mister," Breckinridge said to the well-dressed man, "I'm obliged to you for your help, sure enough, but I can pay for our own food and lodgin'—"

"Nonsense," MacKenzie cut in. "I've taken you under my wing for the moment, and that's that. I never like to see anyone being ganged up on, and the way you leaped into the fray without hesitation to defend your lady tells me all I need to know about your character." He shifted the loaded gun to his left hand and extended the right. "We haven't been formally introduced. I'm Jack MacKenzie."

Breckinridge shook hands and said, "I'm Bill Walters." That was close enough to his real name he hoped he could remember it. "And, uh, this is Sadie."

He didn't claim that she was his wife, but he didn't say that she wasn't, either.

"It's my pleasure," MacKenzie said to her with a smile. "I trust you have another dress to replace the one that lout ruined."

"That's just it," Sadie said with a little quaver in her voice. "I don't. This dress I have on my back is my one and only."

"Well, that won't do. Stay here. I'll go over to the store and pick one up for you."

Breckinridge said, "We couldn't ask you to do that—"

"You didn't," MacKenzie pointed out. "I offered. Don't worry about the money. I sat in on a poker game in Chattanooga a couple of nights ago and had a run of exceptionally good luck."

"You're a gambler?"

"Among other things. I do a little bit of whatever strikes my fancy."

That would be a wonderful way to live, thought Breckinridge. MacKenzie looked like he enjoyed it, too.

"Go on back to one of the rooms," MacKenzie went on. "I'll return shortly." He glanced at Rollins before he left. "Don't try to double-cross me, friend, or you'll live to regret it. Not much longer than that, though."

"No, sir, Mr. MacKenzie," Rollins said hastily. "We done made a deal, and I'll stick to it, you can count on that."

Taking both pistols with him, MacKenzie strode out of the tavern. Breckinridge glanced at Rollins and couldn't stop his hands from clenching into fists. Less than a quarter of an hour earlier, the white-haired bartender had been urging those ruffians to kill him. Breck hadn't forgotten about that.

For the time being, though, he supposed it was best to put his anger aside. He growled, "Show us them rooms."

"Yes, sir, right back here." Rollins waved them toward the blanket-draped doorway.

The rooms were as squalid as Breckinridge expected, airless cubicles furnished with rope bunks that had straw ticking mattresses on them. The only other items of furniture in each room were a crude chair and a tiny table that held one lonely candle. Pegs had been driven into chinks in the log walls for patrons to hang their clothes. Blankets hung over the door to each room. At the moment the only light came through cracks in the walls and roof.

Breckinridge took a look around and his mind rebelled at the thought of spending the night in one of these pestholes. But Jack MacKenzie had paid for the accommodations and Breck figured it would be rude to turn them down.

Besides, Sadie seemed more impressed with the place than he was. As she held the torn dress around her, she said, "My, it's nice. And it'll be better than sleepin' on the ground again tonight, won't it, Bill?"

When she'd decided to run away with him, she hadn't known what she was letting herself in for, he thought. Life on the trail had been harder than she'd expected.

Maybe once she slept in a real bed again, even a mighty poor one, she might decide it would be better to go on home to her grandpap.

"All right," Breckinridge said to Rollins. "One room's as good as the other, I reckon. We'll stay here. Sadie, you wait here for Mr. MacKenzie. I'll go tend to Hector. Figure I can get a stall for him in that livery stable I saw down the street, next to the blacksmith shop."

"Ernie Muller runs it," Rollins volunteered. "He'll take good care of your horse, Mr. Walters."

Breckinridge fixed the man with a cold stare and

added, "Better not anybody bother this gal while I'm gone."

"No, sir. Nobody'll come back here but Mr. MacKenzie. I give you my word on it."

Breckinridge wasn't sure why he should be so quick to take the word of a man who'd urged his murder only a short time earlier, but that seemed to be the way things had developed. He waited until Rollins left, then turned toward Sadie to tell her to holler if anybody bothered her.

He didn't get the words out because Sadie chose that moment to give up the fight with the torn dress. She let go of it, and the ruined garment slid over her body and dropped to the floor around her feet. She wasn't wearing anything under it, so she stood there naked and unashamed in front of Breckinridge.

There was an awful lot of pink and white and gold for him to look at, and he didn't figure he should be looking at any of it. So he averted his eyes—although not without a struggle—and grabbed the threadbare blanket from the mattress.

"Here," he said as he thrust the blanket at her. "Wrap this around you."

"I'm not worried about you seein' me, Bill. It don't bother me at all. We're supposed to be hitched, ain't we?"

"Supposed to be ain't the same as the real thing. Now cover up, blast it."

She sighed and took the blanket from him. When he dared to risk a glance, he saw that she had wrapped it around her, covering herself completely.

"I don't like this," she said. "It's hot and itchy."

Breckinridge felt hot and itchy sensations of a

whole other sort, but he didn't say that to her. Instead he told her, "I won't be gone long," and stalked out of the room.

Ernie Muller was a fat, stolid Dutchman who knew horses. He looked at Hector and said, "This is a good horse. Not for show and not fast, but he will never let you down, Herr Walters."

"You're right about that," Breckinridge agreed. He handed one of his precious coins to the liveryman in return for a stall and care for the night.

Some of the men he'd clashed with at Rollins's place were hanging around in front of the other tavern. They stared at him from across the street with hostile expressions as he went back to Rollins's.

When he got there, Sadie was waiting for him in the main room. She wore a blue dress now, nothing too fancy or expensive but a lot nicer than the gray wool dress that had gotten torn. She sat at one of the tables with Jack MacKenzie, who lounged back in his chair with a drink in front of him. The bottle stood next to his glass.

Smiling brightly, Sadie said, "Look at this beautiful dress Mr. MacKenzie brought me, Bill. Ain't it just the loveliest thing you ever saw?"

"It's made much lovelier by the woman wearing it," MacKenzie said. "And I told you, you can call me Jack."

Breckinridge started to scoff and say that Sadie was a girl, not a woman, but as he looked at her, the words died on his tongue. It was true she looked older in the dress. Girls were full grown sooner than fellas, he reminded himself.

MacKenzie looked up at Breckinridge and said, "As for you, my large young friend, sit down. Have a drink. Rollins promises that our dinner will be ready soon."

Breckinridge lowered himself on one of the chairs made from an empty keg. He said, "I never cared much for the taste of whiskey."

"That just tells me that you've been drinking the wrong whiskey," MacKenzie said with a smile. He signaled to Rollins for another glass, and when the bartender brought it, MacKenzie splashed a couple of inches of amber liquid in the bottom of it. He urged Breckinridge, "Give that a try."

Breckinridge did. He made a face at the way the stuff burned his gullet, but even so, he had to admit it was smoother than the whiskey he'd tried in the past.

"What do you think?" MacKenzie asked.

"Not too bad, I reckon."

"It gets better," MacKenzie said with a smile as he poured more liquor in Breckinridge's glass.

Rollins brought them roast beef, potatoes, and bread. Simple fare, as he had said it would be, but the beef wasn't too tough and the bread was actually good. Once Breckinridge started eating, he realized how hungry he really was. He put away more food than his two companions combined, washing it down with shots from MacKenzie's bottle.

The gambler was right. The whiskey got to tasting better and better as the evening wore on.

Something was nagging at Breckinridge, though, a thought that he couldn't quite put out of his mind. He wondered what had happened when MacKenzie got back to the tavern from the store. Had Sadie still been wrapped up in that blanket when he gave her the blue dress? Or had she acted as brazen with him as she had with Breck? Had MacKenzie left the room while she got dressed, or had she allowed him to watch the whole thing?

Breckinridge told himself it was none of his business. He had no claim on Sadie. She had tried to give herself to him more than once, and he had refused. She could do anything she wanted with anybody she wanted, and he wouldn't have the right to say a blessed thing.

Breckinridge knew that, but the things he *didn't* know bothered him anyway.

Luckily the whiskey sort of dulled any worries that he had. Between the liquor and the big meal, he found himself getting sleepy. He tried to shake off the lassitude but couldn't.

He put his hands on the table and rumbled, "Reckon I'm gonna have ta . . . turn in. Don't know how come . . . I got so sleepy . . . all of a sudden."

"The evening's young yet," MacKenzie said. He reached for the bottle, which somehow never seemed to empty. "Have another drink."

Breckinridge shook his head with what seemed to him like agonizing slowness.

"No, I don't reckon . . . that'd be a good idea . . ."

He tried to push himself to his feet, but it suddenly seemed like he weighed as much as a mountain. He couldn't budge his enormous bulk. He grunted and strained and finally rose from the chair, but he couldn't take a step. He just stood there swaying.

His vision swam in and out. He looked at Sadie and she was just a blue and gold and pink blur. Then those shaky images came together for a moment and he saw her gazing up at him with a look of both worry and anticipation.

"Sadie," he said thickly, "you really are pretty . . ."

"Oh, Bill," she said.

Then everything went blurry again and the room started to spin faster and faster. Alarm bells clamored in the small part of Breckinridge's brain that was still working. Jack MacKenzie's face whipped past him, and the sight of it caused rage to well up inside Breck.

"You . . . you son of a bitch!" he gasped. "You—"

Whatever accusation he was going to make went unsaid. The world fell out from under him. He caught a glimpse of the dirt floor rushing up to meet him.

He didn't feel it hit him. He was out cold by then.

BOOK THREE

Chapter Eleven

Breckinridge was sick when he woke up . . . sick both physically and spiritually. At first he had only a vague memory of what had occurred in the tavern, but as comprehension returned to him more and more, he realized the truth. It had been written on Sadie's face.

She had been waiting for him to pass out. Whatever Jack MacKenzie had done to him, she had known it was going to happen.

That understanding was like a knife in his heart.

After everything he had done for her—after he had treated her like a gentleman when he had every reason not to—she had thrown him over for MacKenzie. Betrayed him. Sat there with a sweet smile on her face while the gambler plotted against Breckinridge.

His stomach lurched violently. Everything he had eaten and drank earlier began to come up, and there was nothing he could do about it except lie there and let the spasms wrack him. Before it was over, he wished he could just go ahead and die. Anything would be better than this.

After what seemed like an eternity, he was empty. He shuddered a couple of times and then lay there in the reeking darkness that surrounded him.

"I'm glad I dragged you outside," a man's voice said somewhere nearby. "Figured if I didn't I might have a big mess to clean up inside."

Breckinridge struggled to raise his head and look around. He still couldn't see anything, and for a terrible second he believed that he had been struck blind.

Then somebody struck a lucifer with a rasping sound. Even though the flame didn't provide much light, it was enough to make Breckinridge wince. He turned his head and saw Rollins sitting on a log step at the rear of a building, probably the tavern. The white-haired man held the match to the bowl of the pipe he had clenched between his teeth. He puffed until the tobacco was burning. That created an orange glow that rose over his face and made him look like one of the demons Breck's ma had read about in the Bible, when she read aloud from the Good Book sometimes after supper by the light of the fireplace.

"Where . . . how . . . ?" Breckinridge gasped.

"The where's easy," Rollins said. "You're out back of my place. Like I told you, I dragged you out here because I had a hunch you'd be sick when you woke up. Let me tell you, it wasn't easy, either. You must weigh damn near a ton, young fella."

Breckinridge couldn't hold his head up any longer. He let it sag back to the ground, being careful to keep his face away from what he had thrown up, and let out a groan that came from deep inside him. He had a headache the likes of which he had never experienced before. Maybe his skull wasn't as thick as he'd thought it was.

When he could speak again, he asked miserably, "What'd that bastard do to me?"

"You're talkin' about MacKenzie? I expect he slipped somethin' into those drinks he kept feedin' you. You poured your undoin' right down your own gullet, Walters."

"You mean he . . . poisoned me? I'm dyin'?"

Breckinridge could easily believe that. He certainly felt like he was at death's door.

Rollins snorted and said, "Hell, no. He just gave you somethin' to knock you out. I've seen it done before. I thought at first he was just tryin' to get you so drunk you'd pass out, but then I realized there probably ain't enough liquor in this whole corner of Tennessee to do that, as big as you are. So he had to give you somethin' more powerful. Even then it took a while for the stuff to catch up to you. I think he expected to have you out cold sooner than he did."

"Sadie . . . she . . . she knew . . ."

"Wouldn't surprise me a bit if she did. She didn't seem shocked when you hit the floor."

Breckinridge groaned again. He wasn't sure which was worse, being so sick from the stuff MacKenzie had given him or knowing that Sadie had turned on him and cooperated with the gambler.

"Is she still here?" he asked, fearing that he already knew the answer to that question.

Rollins puffed on his pipe for a moment, then said, "No, she rode out with him when he left. On your horse, I might add."

That upset Breckinridge so much he pushed himself halfway upright again.

"She stole Hector?" he demanded.

"Yep. While you were still out, I walked down to the

livery and asked around. Seems the girl told him you'd sent her to fetch the horse. Ernie didn't have any reason to doubt it. Everybody in Cooter's Landin' knows that you and the girl rode in together."

Breckinridge managed to struggle to a sitting position. He put his head in his hands and held it for a few seconds, but that didn't help any. It hurt just as bad, and things still looked just as bleak.

Finally he raised his head to glare at Rollins and said, "You knew what was goin' on and didn't do a blessed thing to stop it."

Rollins took the pipe out of his mouth and spat.

"I suspected, but I didn't know," he said sharply. "Don't go blamin' me. A fella as big as you ought to know to look out for himself. Anyway, I don't owe you any favors. Hell, considerin' all that ruckus you caused earlier, you're lucky I didn't just cut your throat while you were passed out."

As angry as Breckinridge was, he also knew that Rollins was right. This disaster was his own damned fault. Obviously, something had been going on between Sadie and MacKenzie almost from the start. Breck was willing to bet that when MacKenzie brought the dress back to the tavern and gave it to Sadie, they had struck their bargain then and there. Breck could only hope that it had been MacKenzie's idea, that Sadie hadn't been the one to suggest that they double-cross him. Somehow that would have been even worse.

"Did they leave me anything? My rifle? My pistol?"

Slowly, Rollins shook his head.

"Reckon they cleaned you out, son. You got the clothes on your back, and that's it."

"Which way did they go?"

"South toward Chattanooga."

That answer didn't surprise Breckinridge, either. Sadie would have been eager to see what life was like in a bigger town. If MacKenzie had promised to show her, she would have gone along with whatever he wanted.

"If you're thinkin' about goin' after them," Rollins went on, "it'd be a waste of time. They've been gone for hours. You'd never catch up to 'em on foot."

"There are other horses in this place."

Rollins's voice hardened as he said, "If you go near any of them, you'll get yourself shot. We don't cotton to horse thieves around here."

"But you sat by and let me get robbed of everything I own in the world!"

"Like I said, that's your lookout," Rollins replied with a shrug.

Breckinridge could see that talking about the problem wasn't going to do any good. He had to figure out what he was going to do next, and he always thought better on his feet. Slowly, shakily, he climbed upright and spread his legs, planting his moccasins solidly on the ground to brace himself as everything whirled around him.

He stood there and waited for a couple of minutes while his iron constitution asserted itself and steadied him. When he thought he could walk without staggering—or worse, falling down—he started around the tavern.

"Where are you goin'?" Rollins called after him.

Breckinridge didn't reply.

He couldn't, because he didn't know the answer to that question.

* * *

The eastern sky held a faint grayish tinge. That told him it was probably an hour or so until dawn. He'd been unconscious most of the night. If Sadie and MacKenzie had kept moving all night—and there was no reason they shouldn't have, since the road was well marked and MacKenzie was familiar with the area—they would be in Chattanooga by now. MacKenzie probably knew plenty of places they could hole up. Breckinridge realized bitterly that he stood almost no chance of finding them.

Not only that, he wanted to avoid the larger settlements. That was why he had chosen the trail that brought them to Cooter's Landing, after all. The law in Chattanooga might have received word to be watching for somebody who matched his description. There was too great a risk in going there, not to mention the time he would waste by doing so.

No, like it or not, he had to accept the fact that Hector was gone, and so was Sadie. Under the circumstances he thought good riddance where the girl was concerned, but he keenly regretted the loss of his horse and the rest of his gear.

He walked down the street to the livery stable and blacksmith shop. Even at this early hour, a light burned in the shed-like living quarters in back. Breckinridge pounded on the door.

"*Ja, ja, wie gehts?*" came from inside. "Who is out there? What do you want?"

Ernie Muller opened the door. His bushy blond brows rose in surprise as candlelight spilled out onto Breckinridge.

"Herr Walters," Muller said. "I thought you left with the young lady last night."

Breckinridge guessed Rollins hadn't told the liveryman what had happened. He said harshly, "We're not travelin' together anymore. Do you have a horse I might have the loan of, Mr. Muller?"

A stern look came over Muller's beefy features. He said, "I don't loan horses, Herr Walters. I don't even rent them. I sell them. But if you need a mount, I have a few good ones."

"That won't do me any good. I don't have any money."

"A shame, that." Muller started to close the door. "I cannot help you."

"Wait a minute," Breckinridge said as he rested the palm of his hand against the door to stop it from closing. "Maybe I could work for you and earn a horse that way. I'm strong, and I've done a little blacksmith work in the past."

"Oh, *ja*?" The man's interest perked up. "We might be able to come to an arrangement."

"How long do you reckon it'd take me to work off the price of a decent mount?"

Muller frowned in thought for a couple of seconds, then said, "Three months, perhaps. No more than four."

Breckinridge's spirits plummeted yet again. He couldn't spend three or four months in Cooter's Landing. The law would catch up to him for sure in that amount of time and take him back to hang for Jasper Carlson's death.

For one wild second, he thought about walloping Muller and just taking a horse. The liveryman was good sized and muscular from the blacksmith work, but Breckinridge was confident he could knock out the older man with one good punch.

He was already a fugitive, after all. With a murder

charge already hanging over his head, what would it matter if he became a horse thief?

But it would matter to him, Breckinridge realized. No matter how he stood in the eyes of the law, he knew in his heart that he wasn't a murderer. But if he attacked Ernie Muller and took a horse, then he really would be a thief.

He heaved a sigh and said, "Sorry, Mr. Muller, I can't wait that long. Reckon I'll have to find some other way of getting out of here."

"Good luck to you then, young man. I'm not sure what happened, but I get the sense that life has not treated you fairly."

"You could sure say that again," Breckinridge agreed.

In the dim light, he trudged on down the street toward the ferry landing. As he walked, he started to frown at his feet. If it came right down to brass tacks, he could continue his flight to the west by walking. That would slow him down, but he might not have any other choice. And at least he would still be moving in the direction he wanted to go. Something else might turn up along the way.

Cooter's shack was dark. Breckinridge sat down on a stool outside the door and waited. The sky gradually grew lighter.

Finally, not long after the sun came up, the door of the shack opened and Cooter stepped out, yawning and hooking his thumbs in his suspenders. He jumped a little when he saw Breckinridge sitting there.

"What in tarnation, boy?" he demanded. "How

come you to be lurkin' around outside my place like this?"

"I need to get across the river," Breckinridge said as he got to his feet. He couldn't explain it, but he felt somehow that he would be safer if he could just put the Tennessee River behind him.

"I told you, the capstan's seized up. I'm gonna try to get it workin' today, but there ain't no tellin' if I will or not."

"Ain't there any other way?"

A dry bark of laughter came from the ferryman. He said, "I reckon you could try to swim it. I wouldn't suggest it, though. That river's more treacherous than it looks. Got currents in it you wouldn't expect. Less'n you swim like a fish, chances are you'd drown."

Breckinridge was a good swimmer, but the river was too wide and daunting. Cooter was right: if he gave out part of the way across, that would be the end of him.

But another thought came to him as he looked at the ferry. The thick rope attached to it ran all the way across the river and was anchored on the other side. It sagged a little in the middle but still hung several feet above the water.

"How about if I use that rope to get across?" he asked.

Cooter stared at him.

"You mean go hand over hand across it?" the ferryman asked. "That's plumb crazy! You couldn't do that."

"I'm thinkin' maybe I could."

"You'll fall in the river, for sure."

"Maybe not. Anyway, I told you, I got to get across."

That might just be sheer stubbornness on his part, but the challenge had grown to acquire large proportions. Logical or not, Breckinridge felt as if a lot were depending on him crossing the river.

"I can't pay you . . ." he went on.

Cooter snorted and waved a hand at the rope.

"If you want to try such a damn fool stunt and get yourself kilt, you go right on ahead. I ain't gonna stop you."

Breckinridge was nervous but determined. He nodded and said, "All right. One more thing first, if that's all right. You have a knife I can borrow?"

"Sure." Cooter stepped into the shack and came back out with a hunting knife. "What do you want it for?"

"Reckon I don't need anything extra weighin' me down," Breckinridge said as he took the knife in one hand and gathered up his long red hair in the other.

He sawed off as much of the hair as he could, making a crude but effective job of it and letting the shorn tresses fall around his feet. He couldn't do anything about his size or the color of his hair, but at least he could change how long it was. He didn't really think that would throw off any pursuers if they followed him to Cooter's Landing, but it was something to try, anyway.

He handed the knife back to Cooter and said, "Much obliged." Then he rubbed his hands on his buckskin trousers and stepped over to the posts where the rope was anchored on this side. He leaned out as far as he could, got a firm grip on the rope, and then swung under it, raising his legs to wrap them around the rope, too. By doing it that way, he didn't put as much weight on his hands, arms, and shoulders.

"You done lost your mind, son," Cooter called to him. "Folks got to see this."

The ferryman turned and broke into a loose-jointed trot toward the buildings.

Breckinridge pulled himself along one hand at a time, his legs sliding on the rope. His muscles began to ache almost immediately from supporting his weight. He didn't care if they hurt, as long as they didn't cramp up and cause him to lose his grip.

He was above the river now. He didn't try to turn his head and look down at the water. Instead he concentrated on the rope. He made sure his grip was secure before he let go with one hand and reached behind him. Now was not the time to get in a hurry, he told himself . . . but the longer he was out here the more likely it was his strength would give out.

He was vaguely aware that a crowd had gathered at the ferry landing, summoned by the excited Cooter. Breckinridge heard men calling bets back and forth to each other and realized that they were wagering on whether or not he would make it to the other side.

They were betting on whether he lived or died.

That angered him, but he tamped it down. He couldn't afford to lose his temper right now. He was fifty or sixty feet from shore, still close enough to get back in if he fell, but with each foot that he pulled himself along the rope, he was that much farther from safety.

His muscles burned, but he ignored the pain. Steady, steady, he told himself. Reach, pull, tighten his grip, take a breath, reach, pull . . .

Time had no meaning, only distance. He felt water against the back of his head and knew he was at the point where the rope sagged the most. He had reached the middle of the river.

From now on, every foot he managed to negotiate along the rope meant he was that much closer to the other shore.

He heard faint cheering from the crowd at the landing as he moved on. It was a little harder now because the rope angled up slightly and also because he was more tired. The strain of hanging on was really starting to take its toll. But he had come this far and he was damned if he was going to be defeated now.

He wasn't sure how far he had come when his fading strength finally betrayed him. His hands slipped on the rope, and when he tried to tighten his grip his fingers cramped and he lost his hold entirely. His body swung down and his head went under the water. His legs twisted around the rope but couldn't hold him up in that awkward position. He went into the river with a great splash.

Breckinridge thrashed, and as he did he felt mud under his hands. He pushed against it and came up out of the water. His feet went down and found the bottom. Realizing he had landed in about three feet of water, he stood up.

More cheering drifted to him from across the river. He couldn't help grinning as he lifted both arms and waved them over his head to signal that he was all right. Then with water streaming off his clothing he turned and trudged out of the river onto the bank.

His arms, shoulders, and back were a gigantic fiery ache. His legs were shaky. He knew he was still in danger, still a fugitive from the law, in worse shape than ever before because he didn't have a horse, a gun, a knife, or anything else except the buckskins he wore.

But he had made it across that damned river, by God!

With that exultant feeling coursing through him, he gave the people of Cooter's Landing one last wave and then turned to stride away from the stream, heading west again.

Chapter Twelve

Breckinridge had thought the stream at Cooter's Landing was big, but three weeks later he discovered what a big river really looked like.

He stood on a slight hill and gazed at what had to be the Mississippi. It was more than half a mile wide, he estimated, a giant, powerfully flowing monster of a river. On the surface it appeared placid, but with hundreds of miles of travel behind it that water must have built up a considerable current.

The river was empty at the moment as it flowed between grassy, gently rolling banks dotted with clumps of brush. Here and there trees grew. Breckinridge had heard stories about how much boat traffic was to be found on the Mississippi, but not today, not on this stretch of the river, anyway. He saw no sign of a settlement, no sign of civilization at all. The great river looked like it must have hundreds of years ago, he thought, before white men ever came to this part of the country.

The next thing to occur to him was to wonder how in the world he was going to get across.

Breckinridge sat down on the hillside to think. His shaggy hair, grown out some since he had hacked it off at Cooter's Landing, brushed the tops of his shoulders. He was a little leaner than he had been before Sadie Humboldt and Jack MacKenzie stole everything he had, but he hadn't gotten gaunt from hunger. He knew how to find roots and berries that were safe to eat, and he had been able to rig a snare and catch a rabbit. He'd found a rock sharp enough to make a cut in the animal's hide and had skinned it by the simple expedient of tearing the pelt off. Then he'd built a fire Indian-fashion, by rubbing sticks together, and roasted the hunks of rabbit meat. The meal wasn't very good, but it gave him strength.

Working with that sharp rock, he had fashioned a sling out of the creature's hide. With stones as ammunition, he had brought down several birds and another couple of rabbits as he continued his westward trek. Roots, berries, and some occasional half-raw meat weren't much to sustain a young man of his size, but they were the best he could do. He hadn't starved, anyway, and he was rather proud of that fact.

He had hoped he might run into some pilgrims headed west who would be willing to let him accompany them in return for helping out with the teams and doing chores around the camp at night. No such luck, however. Where was that great tide of immigrants he had heard folks talking about in the taverns back home? Not in southern Tennessee or northern Alabama and Mississippi, wherever the hell he was. That was for sure.

Now Breckinridge sat there and looked at the river and tried to decide whether he should go north or south as he followed the mighty stream. It had to be one or the other. Like it or not, he was going to have to find a town with a ferry or some other sort of boat to carry him to the western shore.

While he was sitting there, he heard a faint popping sound in the distance.

A frown creased Breckinridge's forehead. He knew gunshots when he heard them, and these came fast and frequent. Somebody in these parts was in trouble. That many shots meant men were firing at each other.

Breckinridge stood up and shaded his eyes with his hand as he looked out at the river. The Mississippi curved around a great bend to the south, Breck's left, and as he watched, several boats appeared, one larger vessel and a number of canoes.

The smaller boats were harrying the big one like a pack of wolves surrounding a potential meal. Men seated in the canoes wielded paddles and tried to drive them alongside the larger craft, which was propelled by a dozen oarsmen, six to a side, digging long oars into the water to force the boat against the current.

Several men knelt on top of a cabin in the center of the bigger boat and fired rifles and pistols at the men in the canoes. Those shots were returned and caused the men on the cabin to duck. There was no telling how long this running fight had been going on, Breckinridge thought.

His sympathies instinctively were with the men on the larger boat, even though he had no logical reason for feeling that way. Maybe he just didn't like to see anybody ganged up on because that had happened to him so many times while he was growing up. The other boys knew they couldn't defeat him alone because of his size, so they had swarmed him and tried to take him down that way.

Another man was fooling with something mounted at the front of the cabin. He turned it toward the nearest canoe, and suddenly a loud *boom!* rolled over the water and grayish-white smoke spurted. Breckinridge realized the weapon was a small cannon. The cannonball tore through the canoe and sent splinters flying into the air as well as dumping the craft's occupants into the river.

That didn't make the other attackers back off. They continued trying to close in as they skirmished with the defenders on top of the cabin.

One of the attackers lobbed a small dark object through the air. It landed on the bigger boat's deck and exploded. The man who had fired the cannon ran to the back of the cabin and grabbed the long sweep mounted there. Breckinridge wasn't very familiar with boats, but his mind was keen enough for him to figure out that the sweep was used for steering. The man threw his weight against it and swung it around, and the boat began to angle toward the shore on the side of the river where Breckinridge stood.

He started down the hill. Unarmed as he was, he didn't know what he could do to help the men on the larger boat, but that impulse drove him anyway.

He plunged into some brush, and as he thrashed his way through it he heard the cannon boom again. It would be a pretty formidable weapon against lightweight canoes, but it took time to load and the attackers' crafts were much more maneuverable.

Breckinridge burst out of the brush and saw that he was within a hundred yards of the river. The larger boat was still bound for shore with the smaller vessels swarming around it. The shooting on both sides continued. Nobody involved in this fracas was much of a marksman, Breck thought, or else they'd all be dead by now, as much powder as they'd burned.

His long legs carried him swiftly toward the river. As he ran, he realized that he wasn't completely un-armed after all. He had his sling and a good supply of rocks he'd picked up along the way and put in a pouch made from the hide of another rabbit he'd killed. Every time he came across a stone that looked like it would make good ammunition, he collected it.

He ran out onto a little point of ground that jutted a short distance into the water near the spot where the larger boat appeared to be bound. Fitting a rock into the sling, he began to whirl it by the cords he'd fashioned from rabbit guts. A man in one of the canoes pointed a rifle at the men on top of the boat's cabin, so Breckinridge took aim at him.

He let fly with the stone, which was roughly round and a little smaller than the palm of his hand. It whipped through the air and struck the rifleman square on the temple. The man reared up and then toppled over the side, either dead or unconscious.

Just like David and Goliath, Breckinridge thought, once again remembering his ma reading from the Good Book . . . although he was built more along the lines of Goliath, to be honest.

With all the commotion going on, no one seemed to have noticed Breckinridge yet, despite the fact that he was sort of hard to miss. The other attackers prob-ably thought the man who'd been knocked into the river had been clipped by a bullet fired from the bigger boat. Breck fitted another stone into his sling and again started whirling.

This time he hit one of the paddlers. The man dropped his paddle, gagged, clutched at his throat where the rock had struck him, and started thrashing around. Breckinridge figured the man's windpipe was crushed.

That finally got the attackers' attention. One of them yelled and pointed at the big youngster in buckskins standing on the shore. Breckinridge threw himself down as several rifles and pistols swung toward him and erupted in smoke and flame.

The cannon roared once more, followed by a splintering sound and howls of alarm and pain. Breckinridge figured another of the canoes had been blown out of the water. He raised his head to look and saw that was the case. Several men thrashed around in the river, obviously having abandoned the destroyed craft. A couple more paddlers floated facedown.

The rest of the canoes began veering away from the larger boat. The attackers had had enough from the looks of it. However, as Breckinridge started to stand up, one of the men turned and fired a pistol at him. Breck felt a jolt of pain as the ball burned along his upper left arm. The impact twisted him around and dropped him on his rear end. He stared angrily after the man who had shot him as the remaining canoes sped away across the river.

He wasn't likely to forget the man's lumpy, ugly face. The brutal features looked like they had been carved out of a rotting potato.

The cannon sent another shot whistling after the fleeing canoes, but the ball splashed into the river between two of the lightweight craft, rocking them but not doing any damage. Then the boat grounded against the shore and two men leaped to the bank holding thick ropes that they tied around nearby trees to keep the vessel from drifting away.

The fellow who'd been manning the cannon on top of the cabin jumped down to the walkway along the sides of the boat and then bounded ashore. He came over to Breckinridge and bent to grasp Breck's good arm and help him to his feet.

"*Merci, mon ami!*" the man said in a booming voice reminiscent of the sound the cannon made when it went off.

"You don't have to ask me for mercy," Breckinridge told him. "I'm on the same side as you fellas."

The man laughed and shook his head. He was tall and broad shouldered, although not as large and brawny as Breckinridge.

"*Non, non,*" he said. "That is not what I meant. *Merci* means thank you, and when I call you *mon ami* it means you are my friend."

Breckinridge realized what was going on now and recalled hearing the other language before on occasion. He said "You're talkin' French, ain't you?"

"*Oui.* Yes. My native tongue. I am Christophe Marchant."

He was striking looking, with his size, a shock of black hair, and a thin mustache that curled around at the ends.

"I'm Breckinridge Wallace," Breck introduced himself, giving his real name before he remembered that he'd been trying not to do that. The pain of his wounded arm must have distracted him, he thought.

He wasn't going to worry about it too much, though. Knoxville was hundreds of miles behind him now, and besides, he'd never liked lying, especially about who he was. Bill Walters was dead and could rest in peace as far as Breckinridge was concerned.

Christophe Marchant gripped Breck's hand and pumped it enthusiastically. Christophe said, "I am very pleased to meet you, *M'sieu* Wallace. You came to our aid, and for that I owe you a debt of gratitude."

"I just didn't cotton to the way those varmints were swarmin' around you like that," Breckinridge explained. "It always gets my dander up when I see somebody bein' ganged up on."

"*Oui*, I feel the same way. You risked your life by interceding on our behalf, though. You shed your own blood." Christophe gestured toward the crimson stain on Breckinridge's sleeve. "Come aboard the boat. One of my men is very clever when it comes to patching up such injuries."

"You're the cap'n of this boat?"

"*Oui*. She is the *Sophie*, the finest keelboat on all the mighty Mississipp'."

Christophe helped Breckinridge onto the boat and called, "Harry! We have a wounded man here."

A little man with a rat-like face under a knit cap hurried toward them. He said, "Can you take that shirt off, mister? Otherwise I got to cut the sleeve off to get at the wound, and you might not want that."

Breckinridge grimaced at the pain as he lifted his injured arm to peel the homespun shirt over his head. Harry, whose head didn't quite come up to the level of the wound on Breck's arm, looked at it and nodded.

"Not too bad," he declared. "Probably hurts like blazes, but it's just a graze. I'll fetch a jug of whiskey."

"I ain't much of a drinker," Breckinridge told him.

Harry snorted and said, "It ain't for drinkin'. Pour

whiskey on a wound and it stings like hell, but it's a lot less likely to fester. Don't ask me why. I just know it works."

While Harry had ducked into the cabin to fetch the liquor, Christophe asked one of the other men, "How much damage did that infernal bomb do, Andre?"

A man with a thin, dark, rather sinister face said, "We have a hole in the deck we'll have to repair and we lost one crate of cargo, but that's all, *mon capitaine.*"

"I was worried that it might have holed our hull," Christophe said. "We will stay here while we make the necessary repairs, eh?"

Andre nodded his agreement with that plan.

Harry came back with an earthen jug. He splashed whiskey directly on the wound on Breckinridge's arm. Breck's breath hissed between clenched teeth at the fiery pain, but it subsided quickly. Harry bound a strip of cloth around the wound and nodded in satisfaction.

"That'll do it," he said. "That arm will be stiff and sore for a few days, but it ought to heal all right."

"I'm much obliged to you," Breckinridge said. "I don't have any way to pay you for your help—"

"Pay us?" Christophe interrupted. "*Non,* that is the ridiculous notion. You came to our assistance. It is we who owe the debt to you."

"All I did was fling a couple of stones at those varmints."

"And you severely injured two of them. Don't think I did not notice. You are quite the excellent marksman with that sling."

Breckinridge grinned and said, "Here lately I've had to get good with it, or else I wouldn't have had anything to eat."

"You have no food, no other weapons?" Christophe asked. "No horse?"

"Nope," Breckinridge said as he pulled his shirt back on. "All I own in the world is what I'm wearin'."

"But you look like an American . . . what is the word . . . frontiersman."

"I reckon that's what I started out to be. I had a horse and plenty of gear. But I, ah, ran into some bad luck."

"The cards, eh? Or the dice?" Christophe raised his rather bushy eyebrows. "You are the gambler, no?"

"Not really. Somebody played a dirty trick on me, and I got robbed. They took everything I had."

"Was there a woman involved?"

Breckinridge frowned in surprise and asked, "How'd you know that?"

"Where there is trouble, my friend, *cherchez la femme* . . . look for the woman."

"Yeah, well, that's what happened, all right. There was this gal called Sadie . . ." Breckinridge's voice trailed off as he shook his head. "Aw, shoot, there ain't no point in talkin' about it. What's done is done. I just got to learn from it and go on."

"A very wise attitude. Most of the valuable lessons learned in life are accompanied by heartbreak and loss, or else we would not remember them."

Breckinridge didn't want to dwell on what had happened with Sadie and MacKenzie, so he looked around and asked, "What kind of boat is this, anyway?"

"The *Sophie* is a keelboat. We carry cargo of all sorts up and down the river between New Orleans and Saint Louis. At the moment we are on our way north with a load of cotton and tobacco."

"Who were those fellas who jumped you?"

Christophe clenched both hands into fists, shook them in front of him, and said, "Pirates! Damned river pirates after our cargo. Instead of doing honest work, they prefer to murder and steal. We have fought them off before. They are led by a man named Bolton, Asa Bolton." Christophe paused. "He was the one who shot you, friend Breckinridge."

"Big ugly fella?"

"*Oui*, that is him."

"I won't forget him any time soon," Breckinridge said. "If I ever run into him again, there's liable to be trouble. I don't cotton to bein' shot."

"A very understandable attitude. Be careful around Bolton, however. He is a very dangerous man."

"So am I," Breckinridge said, "when I get my dander up."

That brought a laugh from Christophe. He said, "You can worry about that another time, *mon ami*. For now, you will be our guest as we camp here tonight. We have plenty of food and wine and will be honored to have you join us."

Breckinridge wasn't that interested in the wine, but the prospect of an actual hot meal, something besides squirrel and rabbit and berries, made his mouth water. He nodded and said, "That sounds mighty good to me, Mr. Marchant."

"Please, call me Christophe. Here we are all comrades of the river, *voyageurs* of the mighty Mississipp'!"

Chapter Thirteen

After spending three weeks on the trail by himself, half-starved for both food and company, passing the evening with these rough keelboatmen was a very welcome change for Breckinridge. Of the ten-man crew, half were French, including Christophe Marchant, descendants of trappers and boatmen who had ventured into the American wilderness from Canada. Four of the others had been born and raised here, and the final member of the crew was a taciturn Englishman.

The salt pork, biscuits, and beans dished up at supper tasted mighty good to Breckinridge, as did the coffee with which he washed down the food. The coffee was different from any he had ever had, and Christophe explained that it had something called chicory in it.

"That is the way the Cajuns drink it in New Orleans and along the bayous down yonder in Louisiana," he said.

"What are Cajuns?" Breckinridge asked.

"French people who were driven down there by

their enemies from a place in Canada called Acadia. Cousins, I suppose you could say, of *voyageurs* such as myself." Christophe thumped his chest with a clenched fist as they sat on logs next to the campfire. "They live now mostly in the swamps, although some have settled in New Orleans."

Breckinridge shook his head and said, "There's a whole lot about this world I don't know, I reckon."

"You are a woodsman. You cannot be expected to know anything other than your homeland until you venture out away from it . . . as you are doing now," Christophe replied with a smile. "You will find that the world is bigger and more wondrous than you could ever imagine, *mon ami*. People are very different in the places you will go. Although in some respects they are always the same."

"Like there are some you can trust and some you can't," Breckinridge observed.

Christophe laughed and nodded.

"Exactly, my young friend. You have the beginnings of wisdom beyond your years."

After supper the Frenchmen all filled their cups with wine from a jug Christophe passed around, while the Americans and the Englishmen stuck to whiskey. Breckinridge was satisfied with the coffee. After a while he said to Christophe, "You're plannin' to post guards tonight in case those pirates come back, aren't you?"

"*Oui*. Although the likelihood of them attacking us on land is small. They prefer to carry out their thievery on the water."

"I'd be glad to take a turn, if you'd like," Breckinridge volunteered. He lowered his voice. "Some of these fellas might not be too alert later on, if you know what I mean."

"Not to worry. They all have a surprising capacity for intoxicants. However, I will take you up on your offer, *mon ami*. We have rifles and pistols with which you can arm yourself."

Breckinridge nodded and said with a sigh, "It'll be good to hold a gun again."

"I would make a gift of the weapons to you, but we may need them. This river, she is a dangerous place at times, and not just because of the currents and snags."

"I wouldn't take your guns," Breckinridge said. "There is one favor you fellas might could do for me, though."

"Name it, and if it is within our power to accomplish, it is yours."

"Once you get your boat patched up, if you could take me across to the other side of the river I'd be mighty obliged."

"But of course! You wish to continue traveling west, I take it?"

"Yep. Got places to go." Breckinridge didn't mention the Rocky Mountains, but they were always in the back of his mind these days.

He was going to have to figure out some way to outfit himself, though, if he was ever going to make it to the Rockies. He couldn't survive out there the way he had been doing these past few weeks.

Christophe hadn't asked him where he had come from or where he was going, but Breckinridge had a hunch the Frenchman was smart enough to have figured out that he was fleeing from something. Breck appreciated the fact that Christophe hadn't pried in his affairs.

Now Christophe echoed what Breckinridge had just been thinking. He said, "You will need weapons, supplies, perhaps a sturdy mount. I will be glad to deliver you to the other side of the river, but why not go where you can earn the things you will need to continue your journey?"

"Where would that be?"

"Saint Louis," Christophe said. "Come with us the rest of the way. If you are willing to work, I can pay you a small wage. That will be a start on what you need. And we will have the pleasure of your company for the remainder of this voyage."

Ever since leaving home, Breckinridge had been moving west as much as possible, putting more and more distance between himself and that unjust murder charge. The idea of traveling north, maybe even backtracking a little, worried him.

But there was no denying that Christophe was right. He'd have a better chance of making it to the mountains if he had the right gear.

"What do you say?" the captain prodded after Breckinridge had sat there frowning into the fire in thought for a few moments.

"Well, I sort of feel like you're just takin' pity on me—"

"Not at all! Using the oars to drive *Sophie* against the river's current requires great strength. It is obvious you have that in abundance."

Breckinridge nodded and said, "All right, you've got a deal. I'll come with you to Saint Louis."

"*Bon!* It will be to your advantage. Besides, you will have a chance to see the biggest city here on your American frontier."

That was sort of intriguing, all right, Breckinridge

had to admit. But the idea made him nervous, too. There was no telling what might be waiting for him in St. Louis. He would do his best to blend in with the crowds while he was there, but with his size and his flaming red hair, that might not be easy to do.

Christophe lifted his cup of wine and said with a grin, "To our new friend Breckinridge and his adventures!"

The others echoed the toast in two different languages, and as Breckinridge returned their salutes with his coffee cup, he felt the warmth of their companionship. It was something he hadn't experienced in too long a time.

Breckinridge took a turn standing guard duty, but Christophe was right about Asa Bolton's gang of river pirates not bothering them. The night passed peacefully, and the next morning the crew finished the job of repairing the deck where the bomb had blown a hole.

Christophe explained to Breck that such explosives were fashioned by forming a hollow ball out of dried clay, then filling it with black powder and inserting a fuse into it. A devilish instrument, Christophe called it.

By midmorning the *Sophie* was headed upriver again. Despite his injured arm, Breckinridge insisted on taking his place at one of the oars.

At first he was clumsy at handling the long, heavy object, but with his natural athletic ability he soon got the hang of it. After that it was more a question of reining in his great strength a little so that his efforts wouldn't overpower those of the man opposite him. That might cause the keelboat to veer to the side.

Blisters soon developed on his hands, but stubbornly he didn't say anything about them. Nor did he complain about the stiffness in his arm from the slight wound. He figured the best way to handle such problems was to keep working. He would bull through the pain the same way he had with most obstacles he had ever encountered.

After a while, though, his hands started slipping on the oar because of the blood that coated them. Christophe noticed that from the top of the cabin and exclaimed, "*Sacre bleu!* What have you done to yourself, Breckinridge?"

"Just a few little blisters," Breckinridge said.

"A few little—Harry! Bind up Breckinridge's hands."

"I want to carry my share of the load," Breckinridge insisted.

"You will. Once Harry has bandaged your poor hands, you can come up here and I will show you how to handle the sweep."

That was the start of Breckinridge's education in how to be a keelboatman. The place where he had encountered the *Sophie* was about halfway between New Orleans and St. Louis, so it would take several more days for the boat to reach its destination. Christophe liked to talk, and Breck listened closely and learned as much as he could about life on the mighty river.

They passed a big settlement on some bluffs overlooking the Mississippi, but Christophe didn't stop. He nodded toward the buildings and said, "That is Memphis. A rough place, my young friend. Not as bad as Natchez, mind you. That's downriver from where we picked you up, and it can be worth your life to go ashore at what they call Natchez-Under-the-Hill. But Memphis is bad enough, and a place where an unwary man can get in serious trouble in a hurry. I prefer to avoid it."

"I'm sure not lookin' for trouble," Breckinridge said.

"But sometimes it comes looking for you, eh?" Christophe asked with a twinkle in his eyes.

"Well, yeah," Breckinridge admitted. "I do seem to wind up in scrapes pretty regular-like."

"That tells me you are a man who will not sit back and allow the world to dictate to him. Instead you try to impose your will on the world. Unfortunately, such efforts are often doomed to failure, but if no one ever made them, how would things ever change? A man must take some risks to accomplish anything worthwhile."

Breckinridge wasn't sure his father would agree with that, or his brothers. Robert Wallace and his other offspring tended to chart the safest course possible through life, and they seemed satisfied with doing that.

His path might bring him nothing but misery, but Breckinridge knew he could never be that way.

When they were several miles above Memphis, Christophe turned the sweep tiller over to Breckinridge again and sat nearby on a crate, smoking a pipe as he pointed out landmarks on both banks.

"A man needs to know where he is all the time," the Frenchman said. "The river, she is a changeable creature. Snags and sandbars come and go. But if you know that on the last voyage there was a snag just past the spot where those three trees grow so close together"—he pointed to the trees he meant—"then you know to look and see if the snag is still there. See the little riffles in the water?"

"I see 'em," Breckinridge said.

"They mark the location of the snag. Send us past them well to port."

"That's left."

"Correct."

Breckinridge leaned on the sweep the way Christophe had taught him. As the *Sophie* began to veer to the left—or port, as Christophe called it—Breck spotted something in some other trees along the bank. He saw a flash as the sunlight reflected off of something . . .

Instinct made him lunge harder against the sweep. He saw a puff of smoke from the trees. The keelboat began to swing around even more. Christophe had time to exclaim, "*Mon dieu*, what are you—"

Then a rifle ball struck the sweep and chewed splinters from it.

"Bushwhackers!" Breckinridge yelled. He was out in the open, a perfect target on top of the cabin, and he didn't like it.

"Get down!" Christophe ordered as he leaped up off the crate and started toward Breckinridge. He had taken only a step when there was an ugly thud and he fell in an ungainly sprawl.

"Pull hard!" Breckinridge bellowed at the oarsmen, not even thinking about the fact that he had no right to give orders here. It just came natural to him. "Keep us movin' as fast as you can!"

He dropped to a knee next to Christophe, who was struggling to sit up.

"Get behind the cabin," the captain told Breckinridge. "We are too far from the other shore for them to have riflemen there."

Another rifle ball struck the cabin and threw up wood chips. Breckinridge got hold of Christophe and surged to his feet.

"I ain't leavin' you out here to be a sittin' duck," he said as he hurried toward the edge of the cabin roof.

A shot hummed past his head. He ignored it and dropped to the walkway on the far side of the boat. He and Christophe were both big men, and their combined weight landing like that rocked the vessel for a second.

He lowered the wounded man to the planks and told him, "You ought to be safe here."

"To hell with safety!" Christophe protested. "I can still fire a rifle. Lean me against the cabin wall and give me a gun! Andre, bring me a rifle!"

The lean, dark Frenchman, who was Christophe's second-in-command, ducked into the cabin and came back with a rifle. He handed it to Christophe, who now balanced on his good leg as he leaned against the cabin where Breckinridge had helped him get in place.

"It's Bolton and his men, I will wager a new *chapeau*," Christophe said. "Look, even now they come out of hiding in their canoes!"

It was true, Breckinridge saw. Four of the light-weight craft arrowed across the river toward the keelboat as the fusillade from the shore continued. Breck saw the pirates' strategy: keep the keelboatmen from fighting back by peppering the cabin with rifle fire and give the men in the canoes time to get close enough to leap on board and continue the fight hand to hand. It was very much like the previous attack, but having the riflemen on shore this time was a new wrinkle. Their shots would be more accurate than if they were firing from moving canoes.

Breckinridge spotted Asa Bolton himself in the first canoe. The pirate chief sat in the back shouting encouragement to the two men in front of him who were paddling hard toward the keelboat. Bolton gripped a pistol in each hand and clearly was ready to board the *Sophie* and carry the fight to its crew.

Breckinridge wasn't going to let that happen if he could stop it. He said to Christophe, "Is that cannon ready to fire?"

"Yes, and a man might be able to touch it off once without getting killed, if he was quick enough," the Frenchman replied. "But reloading would be worth his life. The men on shore would pick him off, *certainment.*"

"Maybe, maybe not. How do I fire the blasted thing?"

"You really wish to risk it?"

Breckinridge nodded and said, "I do."

With a grim look on his face, Christophe said, "Very well. Andre, fetch a punk."

Andre went into the cabin again and came back with a smoldering bit of wood from the fire that was kept burning in the stove below. He handed it to Breckinridge and said something in French that Breck didn't understand. He figured that Andre had just wished him luck, so he nodded and said, "Much obliged."

Then he put his free hand on the cabin top and vaulted onto it. Rifle balls hummed around him as he rolled over and lunged up next to the cannon.

He turned the weapon so that it pointed toward

the oncoming canoes and touched the punk to the hole where the powder charge was waiting to be detonated. The cannon roared as Breckinridge felt a shot pluck at his shirt.

He'd hoped to blow Bolton to hell, but as the smoke cleared he saw that the cannonball had gone over the first canoe and struck one of the craft behind it, which was now a mass of floating splinters and chunks of jagged wood. Pirates were in the water, but Breckinridge couldn't tell how badly they were hurt.

He had looked at the cannon enough in the past to know how it was attached to its swivel mount. He pulled the pins that fastened it in place and lifted it out of its cradle, a task that normally took two men to perform. The barrel was pretty warm from just being fired, but Breckinridge ignored that and cradled the weapon in his arms. He turned as another rifle ball whipped past his ear and jumped off the cabin onto the deck.

"*Mon dieu!*" Christophe exclaimed when he saw what Breckinridge had done. "Andre, we need powder and shot! Quickly!"

Andre and another man rushed to reload the cannon while Breckinridge stood there holding it. When it was ready to fire again, he said, "Somebody else'll have to touch it off. I can't do that and hang on to it, too."

"Such a thing is madness!" Christophe cried. "The cannon, she is not meant to be fired that way!"

"It's the best chance we got," Breckinridge said. "Come on, Andre."

The lean, dark-faced Frenchman nodded. He had the punk Breckinridge had dropped, and he held it ready as Breck stepped out into the open at the end of the cabin and turned so that the cannon he held with both hands braced against his hip was pointed toward the attackers. The pirates wouldn't be expecting that.

"Let 'er rip!" he shouted.

Andre touched off the powder charge. As the cannon roared, its recoil picked up Breckinridge and flung him backward. He felt himself flying through the air, and then he hit the river and the water closed over him.

He cursed himself bitterly as he sank deeper into the Mississippi. The cannon had been torn from his hands, and he knew it would sink to the bottom. Maybe they could recover it later . . . if they were still alive.

He oriented himself, then kicked and stroked for the surface. He broke out into the open air and gulped down a welcome breath. From here he couldn't see the pirates anymore, but then one of the canoes hove into view around the keelboat's bow. It was the one carrying Asa Bolton.

That man had the luck of the devil, Breckinridge thought. Breck started swimming toward the *Sophie* as Bolton leaped from the canoe, landed on the keelboat's deck, and charged toward Christophe with both pistols thrust in front of him, ready to blow the captain's lights out.

Chapter Fourteen

Christophe tried to turn to meet Bolton's charge, but his wounded leg betrayed him, folding up under him and dropping him to the walkway in an ungainly sprawl. The rifle Andre had given him earlier slipped out of his hands.

Bolton hadn't even glanced in Breckinridge's direction, so Breck put everything he had into one final lunge through the water toward the boat. He reached up, clamped a hand around Bolton's ankle, and heaved.

Taken by surprise, the leader of the pirates had no chance to maintain his balance. With a startled yell, he pitched forward. Both pistols blasted as he involuntarily jerked the triggers. The balls smacked into the deck between him and Christophe.

Breckinridge grabbed the edge of the deck with both hands and hauled himself out of the river. As water streamed from his clothes, he started toward Bolton. As a rule, Breck didn't believe in kicking a man while he was down—but he would make an exception for the pirate.

Instead, he was the one on the receiving end of a kick as Bolton rolled over and drove his boot heel into Breckinridge's belly. Breck doubled over as all the air was forced from his lungs and pain filled his midsection.

Since he was already falling forward, he let himself go all the way and landed on top of Bolton. Doing his best to ignore the sickness in his belly, Breckinridge hammered a fist to Bolton's lumpy face. He wanted to pound it even more out of shape.

Bolton struck at Breckinridge's head with one of the empty pistols. Breck jerked aside so that the weapon only scraped along slightly above his ear. The blow hurt but didn't do any real damage. Breck grabbed Bolton's throat with his right hand and hit him twice in the face, swift and hard, with the left.

Bolton bucked up from the planks and threw Breckinridge to the side. He wasn't as big as Breck, but his muscles were like corded cables under the skin. He twisted and brought the point of his elbow down in Breck's belly, inflicting more suffering to that already tender area. As Breck curled around the pain, Bolton seized Breck by the throat and banged his head against the deck.

Breckinridge realized that he was up against maybe the most vicious, dangerous fighter he had ever faced. Certainly this was the most perilous scrap he had been involved in since he'd run into those four Chickasaw renegades in the woods back home. Like the Indians, Bolton was fighting to the death.

That knowledge allowed Breckinridge to summon every bit of strength he could dredge up from deep inside him. He thrust his arms between Bolton's and broke the pirate's hold on his throat. Then he grabbed the front of Bolton's shirt and flung the man to the side. Bolton crashed against the cabin in the center of the keelboat and bounced off. When he landed on the deck he looked stunned.

He was at least partially shamming, though, because when Breckinridge went after him to finish him off, Bolton rolled over and slashed upward with a knife he had pulled from a sheath at his waist. Breck caught himself and jerked back just in time to prevent his aching belly from being ripped open. He locked both hands around the wrist of Bolton's hand that held the knife and twisted it around as he left himself drop on top of the pirate. His great weight forced the blade down. Bolton's eyes bulged out in pain and shock as his own knife went deep into his chest.

Then those eyes rolled back in their sockets and a grotesque rattle came from Bolton's throat. His body went slack as death claimed him.

Breckinridge figured he didn't have time to savor his triumph. He wrapped his hand around the knife's handle and ripped it free of Bolton's body as he pushed himself to his feet. He looked around for the next enemy who wanted to attack him.

Instead he saw that the keelboat had come to a halt in the river, except for the fact that it was drifting slowly back downstream. Only one of the canoes was still intact, and it was empty. Bodies floated facedown in the river, and more dead pirates littered the deck.

Christophe limped toward him, supported on one side by Andre. The captain exclaimed, "Never have I seen such a fight! It was a veritable clash of the Titans!"

Breckinridge rubbed his stomach and said, "I'm a Titan with a sore belly, that's for sure. Are all the rest of those varmints dead?"

"Dead or taken off for the hills," Christophe replied. "The men on shore abandoned their comrades after you blew two canoes out of the water with one shot, *mon ami!*"

"How in blazes did I manage to do that?"

"The cannonball's, how do you say, trajectory, she was lower than usual since you fired it from the deck. It went through one canoe and then struck the one behind it! It was the most superb artillery shot of all time!"

"The luckiest shot, that's for dang sure," Breckinridge muttered. "All I did was point the blasted thing in their general direction."

"In war, results are all that matter," Andre said. "And we have won this war with the pirates."

"We beat Bolton and his bunch. What if there are more up ahead?"

Christophe shook his head and said, "Word will get around that we destroyed most of his gang, and any other brigands will think twice about attacking the *Sophie*, mark my words. No one will dare make a move against us as long as have this young, redheaded Hercules with us!"

"Yeah, well, I'm only goin' as far as Saint Louis with the boat," Breckinridge pointed out.

"I hope to change your mind about that," Christophe said with a grin. "But if I cannot, I cannot." His shoulders rose and fell in an eloquent shrug. "For the time being, we are pleased to have you with us, young Breckinridge. By the way, where is the cannon?"

Breckinridge sighed and said, "On the bottom of the river, I reckon. I couldn't hang on to it when it knocked me off the boat."

A look of alarm appeared on Christophe's face for

a moment, but then he shrugged again and said, "We will just have to recover it. It will be good as new once we have cleaned the mud from it. Now, we must do something about these bodies . . ."

"The river is as good a place as any for them," Andre said.

It bothered Breckinridge a little, dumping the corpses overboard like that. Sure, the dead men had been pirates who would have killed Breck and all the other men on the keelboat without blinking an eye, but if it had been up to him he would have given them a decent burial anyway. None of the *Sophie*'s crew seemed interested in doing that, however, so he didn't argue with them.

Before any of the bodies were rolled overboard, Christophe insisted that Breckinridge should go through their belongings and claim any weapons he wanted. Any money the pirates had on them would be added together and split up evenly among the crew.

Breckinridge took Asa Bolton's knife and pistols. The knife was a good one, a heavy-bladed Bowie with a razor-sharp edge, a brass guard, and a handle wrapped with strips of leather. The pistols were equally fine and, as the tools of Bolton's killing trade, obviously well cared for.

None of the dead men had had rifles with them, so Breckinridge still had to get himself a long gun when he reached St. Louis. Now he had the funds to do so, however, once Christophe had apportioned the coins found on the pirates.

One member of the crew, the little Englishman named Sinclair, had been killed in the fighting. A burial party took him ashore and laid him to rest while Andre, the best diver in the group, stripped down to the bottom half of a pair of long underwear and searched under the water for the lost cannon.

It took several dives, but Andre located the cannon and secured ropes to it. Then Breckinridge and a couple of other men hauled it up onto the boat and laid it wet and muddy on the planks.

With all that going on, it was too late in the day to push on toward St. Louis, so they tied up the *Sophie* and made camp on the shore. Breckinridge had a huge bruise on his belly where Bolton had kicked and elbowed him, but other than that he was all right. Christophe gave him the night off from guard duty and told him to rest. Breck was more than happy to obey.

Three days later they reached their destination. The bruise on Breckinridge's stomach was starting to fade, and he had suffered no lasting ill effects from the battle with Asa Bolton. He was taking his turn at the oars, and as the big settlement sprawled on the western bank of the river came into view, he had to stare at it. He had never seen so many buildings in one place before, or so many wharves and docks. St. Louis was ten times bigger than Knoxville, he thought. No, a hundred times bigger!

That might be an exaggeration, he realized, but still, this was far and away the largest town he had ever seen. He felt excitement coursing through him at the prospect of visiting it, while at the same time the idea made him a little nervous. He wasn't sure he knew how to act around that many people at once.

Christophe's wounded leg didn't keep him from standing at the tiller and working the long sweep.

With an ease born of long practice, he steered the *Sophie* perfectly into position next to one of the docks. A couple of the crewmen jumped onto the dock and tied the keelboat to the sturdy pilings.

A stocky man in a brown beaver hat came along the dock toward the boat. He appeared to have been waiting for the *Sophie*'s arrival. When he stopped next to the vessel, he called up to Christophe, "I expected you yesterday, Marchant, or even the day before."

"We ran into some unexpected trouble, *M'sieu* Skelton," Christophe replied.

"You didn't lose any of my cargo, I hope," the man said with a worried frown.

"One bale of cotton, that is all. And I will make good the loss."

"Damn right you will," Skelton groused. "What happened?"

"Pirates. Asa Bolton's gang."

"Bolton! That son of a bitch is the scourge of the river."

"No more," Christophe said with a big grin. "Bolton will never attack another keelboat, thanks to my giant young friend there."

He leaned on the tiller and waved a hand at Breckinridge, who would have just as soon Christophe hadn't called any attention to him. Surely the authorities in a town as big as St. Louis would be in communication with the law back east. They might know he was wanted for murder. At least Christophe had been discreet enough not to call him by name.

Skelton squinted at Breckinridge and said, "Who's that? New man, ain't he?"

"Indeed. This is his first trip upriver. I have been trying to persuade him to become a permanent member of my crew, but it seems he has his heart set on adventuring."

Skelton grunted. He seemed to have lost interest in Breckinridge already, and Breck thought that was a good thing. The businessman went on, "I'll send my men with wagons to unload the cargo and take it to my warehouse. Once I've checked it over, we'll meet at Red Mike's and settle up, as usual?"

"*Certainment*," Christophe replied.

Skelton bustled off. Christophe leaned on a cane Andre had fashioned from a tree branch and climbed down from the cabin roof to join the other members of the crew.

"You are all free to go except for two men who will stay here and guard the cargo until *M'sieu* Skelton's men take charge of it," he said. "Any volunteers?"

"I'll do it," Breckinridge said. He was still nervous about venturing into the city, so the longer he could postpone that, the better.

"So will I," rat-faced Harry added.

Christophe nodded and said, "We will all meet at Red Mike's tonight, and after Skelton has paid me I shall distribute your wages."

One of the other men asked, "When are you headin' back to New Orleans, Cap'n?"

"Bright and early tomorrow morning, I hope, if I can secure a cargo tonight as I fully expect to do." Christophe grinned. "So enjoy your evening ashore, gentlemen. With any luck, tomorrow we will all be back to work!" He looked at Breckinridge. "With the exception of you, *mon ami*. Are you certain I cannot convince you to remain a riverman?"

"I reckon not," Breckinridge said. "I've sort of got my heart set on seein' me some real mountains."

No one tried to bother the cargo while Breckinridge and Harry waited for Skelton's men to come and get it. The sight of Breck sitting on a keg with a big Bowie knife and a brace of pistols tucked in his belt probably discouraged anybody who might have given a thought to stealing anything.

Once the cargo had been unloaded, Harry asked, "What are you gonna do now, Breck?"

"Well, it's a while yet before we're all supposed to get together at this Red Mike's place. Thought I might go see about buyin' a rifle and maybe look at some horses. Red Mike's, that's a tavern, right?"

"Yeah. Follow the waterfront. You can't miss it. How are all those bumps and bruises you picked up on the trip?"

"Just about gone," Breckinridge said.

Harry grunted and shook his head.

"You heal up faster'n anybody I ever saw. It's almost like there's somethin' supernatural about it."

"Nah," Breckinridge said with a grin. "Just good clean livin', that's all."

"Maybe so. Or maybe the cap'n was right when he referred to you as Hercules. Maybe you're one of those old-time gods come down to walk among mortal men."

That idea made Breckinridge throw back his head and guffaw with laughter. He shook his head and said, "Not hardly!"

"Well, maybe I'll come with you while you look

around," Harry offered. "You don't know your way about Saint Louis, and I've been here plenty of times."

"I'd sure be obliged to you for that, Harry."

The two men stepped ashore, and Harry led Breckinridge along the wharf and into a street paved with cobblestones. Breck had never seen such a thing before, even back in Knoxville.

Harry guided him to a general mercantile store so big it took up an entire block. A sign over the double doors at the entrance proclaimed it to be CRANSTON'S EMPORIUM. Harry said, "Whatever you need, you ought to be able to find it here. I've heard that all the mountain men outfit at Cranston's."

"That sounds like just what I need. I aim to be one of them mountain men."

Harry shook his head and said, "I can't even imagine it. I don't know why anybody would want to go way out there in the middle of nowhere with nothin' around but savage redskins and wild animals."

"You fight pirates on the river," Breckinridge pointed out. "They're pretty doggone savage."

"Yeah, but that's different."

Breckinridge grinned. He didn't see any point in arguing the matter with Harry. Instead he clapped a big hand on the smaller man's back and said, "Let's go see about gettin' what I need for the trip."

Cranston's Emporium was bigger than several stores back in Knoxville put together, Breckinridge thought as he explored it for the next hour with Harry. Food, clothing, trapping supplies, guns, knives, coffeepots, skillets, tools, powder and shot, saddles, packs . . . Harry was right: everything a man might need to survive in the wilderness could be found here. Breck could have spent plenty of money, if only he'd had it.

Until he collected his wages from Christophe, all he had was his share of the money taken from the dead pirates. He had hoped that would be enough to buy a rifle, but he quickly saw that wasn't the case. He was going to need a lot more than what Christophe owed him to purchase enough supplies for a trip to the mountains. That meant he would have to find a job here in St. Louis and save up his wages for a while.

That was disheartening, especially when Breckinridge looked longingly at the rifles hung on pegs on the wall behind one of the store's counters. One gun in particular was a real beauty, with a charging ram engraved in vivid detail on one side of the stock and a gleaming brass patchbox on the other. The brass fittings continued on the breech.

"I never saw anything so pretty," Breckinridge said with a sigh as he gazed at the rifle. "Well, other than a gal or two."

Harry chuckled and said, "I'm glad to hear you say that. But remember, a woman will let you down. Take good care of a gun and it never will."

"I just wish I could afford it."

Harry hesitated, then said, "If you put my money together with yours, you could, I reckon."

Breckinridge shook his head.

"I couldn't do that, Harry. I couldn't ask you to be so generous."

"You ain't askin', you blamed fool. I'm offerin'. There's a big difference."

"Well, maybe . . ."

Harry snorted and said, "No maybes about it. We're

buyin' that gun, and you're takin' it to the Rockies with you. Shoot one of them grizzle bears with it for me, and we'll call it square."

"If you're sure—"

"I wouldn't have offered if I wasn't sure."

Grinning, Breckinridge waved one of the clerks over. The man handed him the rifle, which he examined closely. Satisfied that it was as fine a weapon as it appeared to be, he haggled briefly over the price before making a deal. The clerk threw in a powder horn and a shot pouch to sweeten the bargain.

"I'll pay you back," Breckinridge said as he and Harry left the store. He had the new rifle cradled in the crook of his left arm.

"Like Hades you will. That money was a gift, Breck. There's a good chance we wouldn't have been able to fight off Bolton's gang if it hadn't been for you. We all might have wound up dead. Hell, if you ask me, you deserved all the loot we got out of their pockets." Harry grinned. "Anyway, it was found money. I was never countin' on it, and I'll still get my wages from Christophe. Just remember me once you get out there in the wilderness."

"I ain't likely to forget you, Harry," Breckinridge promised.

It was late enough now they could head for Red Mike's. As they approached the tavern Harry pointed out a painted sign hanging over the entrance that depicted a black ship with black sails.

"Mike's an old sea dog who's sailed all over the world," Harry explained. "Don't ask me how he wound up runnin' a tavern in Saint Louis. He named this place The Black Ship, but everybody just calls it Red Mike's. He gets all the rivermen, but the fur trappers like to drink here, too. The two bunches get to brawlin' sometimes, so watch yourself."

"Reckon I'm in both camps, or soon will be," Breckinridge observed. "Anyway, I'm not lookin' for trouble."

They went into the smoky, dimly lit tavern, which reminded Breckinridge of such places back home. He supposed that no matter where you went in the world, one tavern was pretty much like another. They all smelled the same, that was for sure, a mixture of pipe smoke, spilled beer and whiskey, unwashed human flesh, and bodily wastes. The aroma wasn't what anybody would call pleasant, but it was oddly comforting.

The place was busy despite the early hour. Most of the tables were occupied by men drinking or playing cards or both. More men lined the bar and nursed buckets of beer or threw back shots of whiskey. Breckinridge saw a few women, all of them hard-faced serving girls with coarse hair and expressions that said they had seen it all, more times than they cared to remember.

Then a flash of honey-colored hair caught his eye and he turned his head to look closer. His breath froze in his throat as he saw the man and woman sitting at one of the tables where a poker game was going on. Neither of them had seen him yet.

Sadie and MacKenzie must not have stayed in Chattanooga for very long, because here they were, now, in St. Louis.

BOOK FOUR

Chapter Fifteen

Breckinridge's mind was a riot of emotions. First and foremost among them was anger. He wanted to charge across the room, grab Jack MacKenzie, pull the gambler up out of his chair, and smash a fist in his face a few times. MacKenzie was a no-good thief and deserved nothing less.

Breckinridge was mad at Sadie, too, but he still wanted to believe that MacKenzie had talked her into double-crossing him. Anyway, he wasn't the sort who would ever lay hands on a woman in anger, no matter how treacherous she was.

At the same time, a part of him wanted to wheel around and get the hell out of Red Mike's place before either of them noticed him. That would certainly simplify matters. He could find Christophe later and get the money the keelboat captain owed him. If he waited at the *Sophie*, he was sure Christophe would show up sooner or later.

Harry noticed how Breckinridge had stopped short and started to say, "Hey, what—"

At that moment, Breckinridge knew he had delayed

too long. Sadie glanced up, and across the room their gazes met. Breck couldn't hear it over the hubbub in the tavern, but he saw her mouth open and knew she had just gasped in surprise at seeing him.

Her hand shot out and her fingers closed, claw-like, on MacKenzie's arm. Angrily, the gambler tried to shake her off, but she spoke rapidly to him. His head jerked up. He saw Breckinridge, too, and his other hand made an instinctive move toward his coat. Breck figured MacKenzie had a pistol under there. MacKenzie hesitated, probably waiting to see what Breck was going to do.

"You go ahead and find any of the other fellas who are here, Harry," Breckinridge said. "I see some old friends over there."

"Are you sure? You looked pretty shaken up there for a second, Breck."

"I'm sure," Breckinridge said. He started across the room toward the table where Sadie and MacKenzie sat, keeping his walk to a slow, deliberate pace. He didn't want to spook MacKenzie into pulling a gun and firing in this crowded room.

As Breckinridge came up to the table, MacKenzie threw his cards in and said, "Sorry, gents, I'm out of the game."

"Wait a minute," one of the other players objected. "I believe you owe me quite a bit of money. I was willing to extend you credit and give you a chance to win it back, but if you're going to walk away, you'll have to pay up first."

MacKenzie's lips tightened into a thin line. He said, "I don't have that much money, Rory. You know that."

The other man leaned back in his chair and gave him a mocking smile.

"In that case you'll have to pay with some other currency," Rory said. He turned his insolent gaze on Sadie. "I can think of something that will do quite nicely."

She flushed in anger or embarrassment or both as she said, "Don't let him talk like that, Jack."

Rory leaned forward and said, "He doesn't have any choice but to let me do whatever I want. He's in the hole to me, remember?"

Breckinridge moved a little closer to the table. As his shadow loomed over it, Rory turned his head to glare up at him.

"What do you want, you lunkhead?" the expensively dressed young man demanded.

Breckinridge never would have dreamed that if he ever saw Sadie and MacKenzie again, he would be put in the position of defending them. He disliked the man called Rory on sight, however. The card player was no riverman or fur trapper. His fancy clothes and soft hands were proof of that. They bespoke wealth. Breck had a hunch Rory was one of those well-to-do fellas who liked to associate with working men so he could feel superior to them. Breck despised that arrogant breed.

"Like to have a word with my friends here," Breckinridge said in reply to Rory's question. He nodded toward Sadie and MacKenzie.

"You can talk to them when I've finished my business with them," Rory snapped. "Until then, go away."

"Nope, I've got to see 'em now," Breckinridge said stubbornly. "They can deal with you later."

Rory stiffened. The other men at the table began sliding their chairs back carefully and getting up.

A hush radiated out from this confrontation and spread across the room.

"Do you know who I am?" Rory demanded.

"Nope, and I don't care, either," Breckinridge answered honestly.

"I'm Rory Ducharme."

"Sorry, that don't mean a thing to me."

"It will, you ignorant oaf!"

With that, Rory lunged up out of his chair. His hand darted under his coat and came out clutching a derringer. The little gun flashed up toward Breckinridge's face. At this range, even the small-caliber ball fired by such a weapon could be fatal, Breck knew. He swung his new rifle, and the barrel cracked down hard against Rory's wrist. The derringer popped, but the ball smacked harmlessly into the table, scattering cards and coins.

Breckinridge launched a straight, hard punch that crashed into the middle of Rory's face. He felt Rory's nose flatten under the blow, and he thought maybe some bones broke there, too. Rory probably wouldn't be as handsome once he recovered.

As Rory fell unconscious to the sawdust-littered floor, several men charged toward the table from the bar. Breckinridge realized that Rory probably wouldn't venture into a rough place like this without a few hired bodyguards to keep him safe. They hadn't done their job, but now they would come after the man who had struck down their employer and try to even the score.

Breckinridge was willing to fight the men, but Sadie grabbed his arm and MacKenzie brandished a pistol and barked, "Let's get out of here!"

Harry yelled, "All you rivermen, on your feet! It's a brawl!"

Indeed it was. In a matter of seconds a swirling melee filled the tavern. Behind the bar, a brawny, red-headed Irishman who had to be Red Mike shouted at the combatants, who blatantly ignored him as they flailed and pounded at each other.

Sadie tugged Breckinridge toward the door as she urged, "Come on, Bill!"

That reminded him she didn't know his real name. He would set her straight on that if he got the chance. He would set her straight on a lot of things.

But first they had to get out of the middle of this ruckus. Even though it galled him to turn his back on a fight, Breckinridge wanted to confront Sadie and MacKenzie more than he wanted to stay there and wallop Rory Ducharme's bodyguards.

The three of them bulled their way through the crowd toward the door. As they passed Harry, Breckinridge caught the eye of the little rat-like man, who waved them on with a cheerful grin and called, "Go on, get outta here! See you later at the boat!"

Then Harry leaped on the back of a larger man and started to choke him.

Breckinridge, Sadie, and MacKenzie stumbled out of the tavern. Night had fallen, and the shadows along the waterfront were thick. MacKenzie said, "Down here," and led them away from Red Mike's Black Ship.

Breckinridge was soon lost, but MacKenzie seemed to know where he was going. The gambler finally stopped near a pier where water lapped softly against the pilings.

MacKenzie laughed and said, "It seems fate has cast

us as allies again, Bill. Why is it that hell always seems to start popping as soon as you come around?"

"My name ain't Bill. It's Breckinridge Wallace, and don't start talkin' about us bein' allies. I ain't forgotten that you drugged me and robbed me, Jack."

"Oh, Bill—I mean Breckinridge," Sadie said. "I'm sorry about that—"

"Don't listen to her," MacKenzie said. "She was perfectly willing to go along with the idea as soon as I suggested it."

Breckinridge's hands tightened on the rifle he held. He said, "So it *was* your idea, not hers."

MacKenzie shrugged.

"I've never minded owning up to whatever I've done," he said. "I don't live my life making apologies, and I won't start now. Yes, I slipped something in your drinks to knock you out. I suggested that we take your horse and your gear. But I could have killed you, and I didn't. Not only that, I also told Rollins that if he hurt you, I'd come back and kill *him.* So you see, in one way of looking at it, I probably saved your life. Rollins is a vicious, spiteful bastard."

Breckinridge kept a tight rein on his temper. It wasn't easy. He said, "How'd the two of you come to be here in Saint Louis?"

"I thought my luck would have changed when we returned to Chattanooga. It hadn't. I deemed it wise to make a change of scenery."

"In other words, you made a run for it out of town so you wouldn't have to pay off your gamblin' debts." Breckinridge didn't bother trying to hide the disgust he felt. "Do you ever pay up . . . or do you keep some pretty gal with you and make her square things for you?"

Sadie sniffed and said, "You don't have to be crude about it." She paused, then added, "But at least you called me pretty."

"You are pretty," Breckinridge said. "I don't reckon I'd ever trust you again, though."

"That's fine," she said, and now there was a touch of anger in her voice. "We'll just go our separate ways—"

The sudden roar of a gunshot interrupted her. Breckinridge jerked around toward the sound and spotted Rory Ducharme standing about half a block away with his right arm extended and smoke curling from the barrel of the pistol he held. He had another pistol in his left hand, and as he started to bring it up, Breckinridge's instincts took over. Earlier, after buying the rifle, he had loaded and primed it, so all he had to do as he brought the weapon smoothly to his shoulder was cock it. He pressed the trigger and the flintlock snapped down, sparking and detonating the powder charge. The rifle boomed and kicked against his shoulder.

Rory Ducharme flew backward like he'd been punched by a giant fist.

As the echoes of the shots faded, Breckinridge heard shouting. It was still several blocks away but coming closer. MacKenzie grabbed his arm.

"That'll be Ducharme's men trying to catch up to him," he said. "We have to get out of here."

Rory hadn't moved since he'd fallen. Breckinridge was reasonably sure the man was dead. He'd aimed for the heart, and even in bad light he was a good shot.

He and MacKenzie turned at the same time, and the gambler let out a choked exclamation at the sight of Sadie lying crumpled on the ground. He sprang to her side, knelt there, and lifted her. Breckinridge felt something twist inside him at the sight of the large dark stain on the front of her dress.

Rory's single shot hadn't missed completely after all.

MacKenzie seemed genuinely grief-stricken as he clutched Sadie's limp form to his chest. Breckinridge's throat felt pretty tight, too. He and Sadie had never been as close as she had wanted, and in the end she had gone along with betraying him, whether it had been her idea or not. But even so, he hadn't wished for any real harm to come to her.

After a long moment, MacKenzie heaved a sigh. He looked up at Breckinridge and said, "You should go. Ducharme's bodyguards will be here any minute. Once they find out he's dead, they'll come after you. They'll know that if they don't bring your head back to his father, it'll be their own lives at stake."

"His father . . . ?"

"Otto Ducharme. One of the wealthiest—and most evil—men in this part of the country. He only loves one thing: his son. And you've killed him."

"He shot at me first," Breckinridge said.

"That won't matter. Ducharme will have you hunted down and killed. You'd better get out of Saint Louis as quickly as you can, any way you can." MacKenzie paused. "Whichever way you go, I'll tell them you went the opposite direction. I'll give them that phony name you were using as well."

"Why would you do that for me?"

MacKenzie looked down at Sadie's face, which was still and peaceful now in the moonlight. Without lifting his head, he said, "Believe it or not, she still had a soft spot for you. She was sorry about what we did to you. I don't think she'd want anything else to happen to you."

"What happened to my horse?"

"I sold him in Memphis to pay for our passage on the riverboat that brought us here."

Breckinridge sighed. It looked like he would never see Hector again. He wondered if the horse had been there in Memphis when the *Sophie* had gone by without stopping. It seemed entirely possible.

The shouts were louder now. Breckinridge knew he was just about out of time. He wondered if he dared go back to the keelboat and wait for Christophe. It didn't seem like a very good idea. Otto Ducharme's men might track him there. He wasn't going to bring trouble down on the heads of Christophe, Andre, and his other friends from the keelboat.

"I'm sorry about what happened, Jack. I truly am."

MacKenzie stroked Sadie's cheek and whispered, "Just go."

Breckinridge went.

He ran through the night, carrying the rifle at a slant in front of his chest. He didn't know where he was going, but he put the river at his back and headed away from it. That took him west, the direction he'd wanted to go all along. He ran through dark streets, between buildings that loomed like slouching beasts. The cobblestones gave way to hard-packed dirt. The shouts faded far behind him.

He had a rifle, a couple of pistols, powder and shot, and a good knife, he thought as he left the settlement and entered open country. No money, but where he was going there wasn't really anything to buy. He could have been a lot worse off, he told himself. He had been a lot worse off when he woke up behind the tavern at Cooter's Landing. Then he'd had nothing but the clothes on his back.

He didn't know how far away the Rocky Mountains were, but it seemed unlikely he could walk that far. He wouldn't have to, he decided. Something would come up. It always did.

Finally, after he had been running for what seemed like hours, weariness caught up to him and he slowed to a walk. He looked back over his shoulder. He couldn't see the lights of St. Louis anymore. The only lights in the whole universe were the stars above his head, and a thin sliver of moon that hung low in the sky.

Breckinridge had never felt quite so alone, and in his solitude the sorrow he felt over Sadie's death stabbed even deeper inside him.

He wondered if MacKenzie had been telling the truth. Would the gambler really mislead the pursuers and send them in the wrong direction? Or would he tell them Breckinridge's true name and point in the exact direction he had gone? Breck didn't know, but he figured time would give him the answers.

He wondered as well if he was destined to spend the rest of his life running away from first one thing and then another. He didn't like the feeling.

This was easy country to travel through, mostly flat and covered with knee-high grass. Some folks called this the Great American Desert, but these plains seemed pretty lush to Breckinridge. He strode along for what seemed like scores of miles, although he was sure he hadn't really covered that much distance. The eastern sky was gray behind him. He thought that when it got light, he would look for some game to shoot for his breakfast.

The smell of coffee drifting to his nose came as a complete surprise.

Somebody else was out there in that vast emptiness. Breckinridge supposed he shouldn't have been surprised. He'd heard about immigrants crossing the plains, following something called the Oregon Trail. Maybe there was a wagon train up ahead somewhere. All he had to do was follow his nose. Maybe they would be the hospitable sort of folks who would offer him a cup of coffee and some breakfast. They might even let him travel along with them for a ways. He was a good hunter. He could help provide fresh meat for all the pilgrims headed for the promised land . . .

All the thoughts and plans that sprang unexpectedly into his mind must have distracted him, because he didn't know anybody else was in the vicinity until he heard hammers being cocked all around him and an order was issued sharply in a crisp, clear voice.

"Don't move, mister, or we'll shoot."

Chapter Sixteen

Breckinridge knew from the sounds there were at least four guns pointed at him, so he didn't move. As the shapes of men materialized out of the predawn gloom, he said, "Take it easy, fellas. I don't mean you any harm."

"He sounds like a white man, Lieutenant, not an Injun," one of the figures said.

One of the other men replied, "I didn't expect to run into Indians this early in our trip, Private Hampton." He added dryly, "We only left Saint Louis yesterday, remember."

The figures surrounding him were oddly shaped, and after a moment Breckinridge realized why. They were wearing tall hats that made their heads look unnatural. That fact, along with the way the men referred to each other, told Breckinridge what he needed to know about them.

"You fellas are soldiers," he said.

One of the men came closer to him. The gray light was getting stronger, and Breckinridge was able to make out the man's dark coat, lighter trousers, and the hat with some sort of plume on it. He held a rifle with a bayonet attached to the end of the barrel. The weapon pointed down now, but even in the gloom Breck could tell that the man was alert and was ready to lift the rifle and use it in a hurry if he needed to.

"Who are you?" the soldier asked.

Breckinridge hesitated before answering. He had never heard of the army hunting down wanted criminals before. That was a job for the civilian authorities.

Anyway, out here on the plains miles west of St. Louis, it was highly unlikely these soldiers would have heard of him and know he was wanted for murder back in Tennessee.

"My name's Breckinridge Wallace," he said.

"What are you doing out here?" the soldier who seemed to be the spokesman asked. "Are you an immigrant?"

Breckinridge thought about it and replied, "I reckon you could say that."

"Where's your wagon train? Did you wander off from it?"

"No wagon train," Breckinridge said. "I'm, uh, travelin' by myself."

"What about your saddle horse? Your pack animal?"

Breckinridge couldn't help grinning ruefully as he said, "I reckon what I'm wearin' and carryin' is all I got to my name."

"Good Lord, man! Have you lost your mind? Setting out across the plains alone, with no mount and no supplies? You won't last a week!"

Breckinridge didn't like having his abilities disparaged like that. His voice held a trace of anger as he said, "You might be surprised, mister. If you'll just let me go on my way, we'll just see who lasts and who don't."

One of the other soldiers said, "Better let him go, Lieutenant. He's probably one of those crazy mountain men. There's no telling what he'll do."

"May I remind you, Private, we have a responsibility to protect civilians, even from themselves," the lieutenant said crisply. "If this man isn't right in his, ah, mental state, I can't just allow him to wander off to certain death."

"I'm standin' right here," Breckinridge said. "And I don't take kindly to bein' called touched in the head."

"Then come back to our camp with us," the lieutenant said. "If you can convince me that I should allow you to proceed, then so be it." He paused. "But in the meantime you can have a cup of coffee and something to eat."

The smell of food and coffee still hung in the air and made Breckinridge's mouth water. He wasn't sure it would be a good idea for him to get mixed up with a bunch of soldiers, but he supposed having some breakfast with them wouldn't hurt anything.

"All right," he said. "I reckon I can do that." He looked around and added, "You think you could tell those other fellas to stop pointin' their rifles at me?"

That request brought a chuckle from the lieutenant. He said, "At ease, men. I don't think Mr. Wallace represents a significant threat to us."

"I dunno, Lieutenant," one of the soldiers said dubiously. "He's about as big as a buffalo."

"And sort of wild and shaggy like one of 'em, too," another man put in.

The soldiers obeyed their officer's order, though,

and lowered their weapons. The lieutenant motioned for Breckinridge to fall in alongside him and started walking across the prairie. The rest of the soldiers followed them.

"I'm Lieutenant John Francis Mallory of the Army Corps of Topographical Engineers, Mr. Wallace," the officer introduced himself. Breckinridge could see now that the lieutenant was young, probably in his early twenties. Of course, that was older than he was, Breck thought, but after everything that had happened in the past couple of months, he felt like he had grown up in a hurry.

"What are top . . . topographical engineers?" Breckinridge asked, stumbling a little over the word. He felt confident his brother Edward would have known without having to ask, but Breck was still learning about things.

"We're responsible for exploring the areas of the country that haven't been documented yet," Lieutenant Mallory explained. "It's our job to survey and prepare maps of those unexplored areas. There are a few trails already established across the plains, but most of the region is, well, a vast unknown."

"Fur trappers have been goin' to the mountains for twenty years or more," Breckinridge said. "I've heard talk about 'em."

"Yes, but nearly all of them stick to the Missouri River and follow it all the way to the Yellowstone country and beyond into the mountains. Then there's the Oregon Trail to the Pacific northwest that the immigrants use, and the Santa Fe Trail into the Spanish southwest, but other than that . . ." Mallory shrugged. "We don't really know what's out here. There may be even better routes that no one has discovered yet."

"And it's the army's job to find 'em?"

"That's what we're here for. There's a great deal at stake. The entire western half of the continent can't be settled and developed properly unless there are safe trails that can be used by civilians."

Breckinridge wasn't sure the western half of the continent really needed to be "settled and developed properly." It seemed to him that the land had been getting along pretty well the way it was. But he supposed that was what governments did, otherwise they wouldn't have had much of an excuse for existing.

A few minutes later the group came to a campsite on the bank of a small stream. The camp was coming alive for the day as at least two dozen men attended to a variety of chores. Some were cooking, others took care of picketed horses, and still others were taking down tents and packing them for the day's journey. It was a busy place, bustling with activity.

But all of the soldiers stopped what they were doing to stare at the giant redheaded stranger with Lieutenant Mallory and the other members of the patrol. The attention made Breckinridge feel a little like a freak.

One of the men, a short, grizzled veteran, asked, "Who's this, Lieutenant?"

"Allow me to present Mr. Breckinridge Wallace, Sergeant Falk," Mallory said. He added dryly, "Evidently Mr. Wallace is immigrating to the west but traveling very light."

Falk looked Breckinridge up and down with a skeptical eye.

"Where's his gear?"

"That's it," Mallory said. "Just what you see."

Falk's disgusted snort made it clear what he thought about that.

Breckinridge said, "Well, I ain't a soldier. I can get by without havin' to tote all the comforts of home around with me."

"All the comforts of home, is it?" Falk snapped. The scrappy little non-com took a step toward Breckinridge, who was almost twice as tall as he was. "I'll show you comforts of home, you big—"

"That's quite enough, Sergeant," Mallory said. "I've invited Mr. Wallace to have breakfast with us while I speak with him, and I expect him to be treated in a hospitable fashion."

"Of course . . . sir," Falk replied with obvious reluctance.

"Come with me, Mr. Wallace," Mallory said. He gestured for Breckinridge to have a seat next to one of the cook fires. Breck lowered himself to the ground and sat with crossed legs. Mallory used a piece of leather to lift the pot from the edge of the flames and poured coffee into tin cups for each of them. Breck took an appreciative sip of the hot, black brew, then accepted a tin plate of bacon and flapjacks from one of the other soldiers.

The food was good, and Breckinridge ate with gusto. During his time on the keelboat, he had started to regain some of the weight he had lost on his near-starvation trek across Tennessee, but even under the best of circumstances his appetite was prodigious.

Lieutenant Mallory watched him and said with a smile, "You're just a growing boy, aren't you, Mr. Wallace?"

Because of his size, most folks took Breckinridge for several years older than he really was, but evidently

Mallory had done a better job of guessing his age. However, it often came in handy to be thought older than he was, so Breck said guardedly, "I don't know what you're talkin' about."

Quietly, Mallory replied, "I daresay you're younger than I am . . . and Sergeant Falk never misses an opportunity to remind me of just how wet behind the ears I am."

"I'm old enough to be out here. Let's just let it go at that."

"Of course. It's really none of my affair, anyway." Breckinridge agreed.

As they continued eating and the sky grew rosy above them with the approach of dawn, Mallory asked, "Are you bound for any place in particular, or just heading west in general?"

"I thought I'd go to the Rocky Mountains," Breckinridge said. "I plan to be a fur trapper."

"The Rocky Mountains take in a great deal of area. In fact, they stretch from up in Canada all the way down into northern Mexico. They may not be referred to as the Rockies that far south, but they're all really part of the same chain, or at least that's what I believe from studying the available maps."

"Well, wherever they have the best trappin', I suppose that's where I'll go."

Mallory shook his head and said, "The fur industry isn't what it once was, you know. I'm told that back east men have started wearing silk hats instead of beaver."

"I reckon there'll always be a market for beaver pelts," Breckinridge said, although in truth he really didn't know much about that subject just yet. He'd figured he would educate himself when he got to the mountains.

"Well, for your sake, I hope you're right." A wistful note came into Mallory's voice. "You know, I wouldn't mind seeing the mountains myself. I come from Illinois. It's mostly flat there. Farming country. Not nearly as adventurous as trapping and fighting Indians and mountain lions."

"Don't forget the grizzle bears," Breckinridge said, thinking about what Harry had said to him the day before, back in St. Louis. He looked down at the rifle lying on the ground beside him, the rifle he had bought with Harry's help.

Hard to believe that had happened less than twenty-four hours earlier. Sadie's death was even more recent. And yet to Breckinridge, that part of his life was already receding into the past. It seemed to him that his life always took violent, dramatic lurches from one path to another. There was never anything gradual. He never knew when he was going to be thrown completely off balance.

There was a stir on the other side of camp. A man in a broad-brimmed felt hat and a fringed and beaded buckskin jacket strode toward Breckinridge and Mallory. His lined face looked like it had been carved out of hardwood, and the white beard he sported made his permanent tan seem even darker.

Mallory stood up to greet the newcomer, and for some reason Breckinridge got to his feet, too.

"How does it look up ahead, Tom?" the lieutenant asked.

"Clear sailin' for the most part," the older man replied. "There's a good-sized herd of buffler a couple miles farther on. We'd best give them a wide berth.

You don't want to be anywhere around a bunch of buffs if they take it in their heads to run. That's the quickest way in the world to get yourself stomped flat."

"No Indian sign?"

"Nope. I don't expect to cut any for a few more days, either. We ain't gotten to their huntin' grounds yet." The man looked at Breckinridge. "Who's this big galoot?"

Breckinridge stuck his hand out and said, "Breckinridge Wallace."

"Tom Lang," the bearded man replied as he shook Breckinridge's hand.

"Tom is our civilian scout," Mallory explained. "Tom, Mr. Wallace is a traveler who's joining us for breakfast."

Tom Lang grunted and said, "Eatin' some of our rations, is what you mean."

"I'd be willin' to do a little huntin' in exchange for the food," Breckinridge said. "Maybe help your party get some fresh meat."

Lang bristled at that. He said, "You don't think I can hunt well enough to keep these soldiers well supplied with meat? That's one reason the army hired me to come along on this here expedition."

"I never said that—"

"Well, it sure sounded like it to me."

"Maybe I'd better be movin' on—" Breckinridge began.

"Nonsense," Mallory said. "Our conversation has convinced me that you're sane, Mr. Wallace. I won't try to stop you from continuing on your way. But since you're going west . . . and we're going west . . . there's no real reason we shouldn't travel together for a time, is there?"

Breckinridge hesitated. Earlier he had thought about the possibility of joining up with a wagon train if he came across one. This army surveying party wasn't the same thing, but Breck had to admit to himself that he wouldn't mind the company.

While Breckinridge was considering the proposition, Tom Lang spoke up, saying, "No disrespect, Lieutenant, but we don't need this big ol' farm boy slowin' us down. He's a greenhorn, never been west of the Mississippi before."

"I might remind you that neither have I, Tom," Mallory said.

"Yeah, but that's different. It's your job to be out here now. Anyway, you got me to guide you and show you what's what. I don't reckon Wallace here could contribute much. He'd just be a drain on our supplies."

Listening to Lang got Breckinridge's dander up enough for him to say hotly, "If you're worried about your provisions, Lieutenant, we'll just say that I won't eat nothin' I didn't shoot my own self."

"I don't think we need to go that far," Mallory said. "I believe we have more than enough for an additional member of the party."

"One other thing you ain't considered," Lang argued. "You don't know this fella. He could be a cutthroat, a highwayman. Could be the law's after him."

That was hitting too close to home, Breckinridge thought, at least the part about being a fugitive. He thought it was safe to assume that by now Otto Ducharme knew his son was dead. He might even know who had killed Rory. If Ducharme was as rich as Jack MacKenzie had said, the authorities would be eager to do whatever he wanted, including tracking down the man who'd killed his son.

"That's a good point, Tom," Mallory agreed. A smile tugged at his mouth as he looked at Breckinridge and asked, "Are you a murderer and a thief, Mr. Wallace?"

"No, sir, I sure ain't," Breckinridge replied honestly. "I never murdered anybody, and my ma raised me better than to be a thief."

"If I'm any judge of character, I believe you're telling the truth. My invitation to join us still stands."

Tom Lang looked disgusted and shook his head, but he didn't say anything else.

Breckinridge was suddenly wary. He asked, "I don't have to enlist in the army to come along, do I?"

Mallory laughed and said, "No, we'll carry you on the rolls as a civilian volunteer."

"Well, in that case . . ." Breckinridge hesitated one last time, then said, "I reckon I'll meander along with you fellas for a while."

Mallory clapped a hand on his shoulder.

"Excellent! I think you'll be a fine addition to our company, Mr. Wallace."

"If I'm one of the bunch now, you better call me Breckinridge, or Breck."

"All right, Breckinridge," Mallory said. "Military discipline requires that you refer to me by my rank."

"That's fine, Lieutenant."

Mallory looked around. The sun was peeking over the horizon. He said, "We should have broken camp and been ready to move out by now. Let's get busy, men." He glanced at Breckinridge. "That includes you. Can you handle horses?"

"Yes, sir."

"We have a number of spare mounts, but no extra saddles, I'm afraid."

"If you've got an extra saddle blanket, that'll do," Breckinridge said.

"I think we can manage that. Pick out a horse for yourself, Breck, and get ready to ride." Mallory turned his head to look to the west. "The great unknown awaits."

Chapter Seventeen

For the next couple of weeks, Breckinridge traveled with the surveying party. He spent most of his time with Lieutenant Mallory, who seemed to enjoy trying to teach him about surveying and mapmaking. Most of what Mallory said didn't make much sense to Breck, but he listened carefully and picked up a few things. He discovered that the best maps were the ones he drew inside his own head. Once he had been to a place, walked the ground, studied the landmarks, he knew somehow that he would never forget it.

Breckinridge also went on some scouting and hunting trips with Tom Lang. The guide remained gruff and not overly friendly, but Breck told himself that was just Tom's way. And whether he liked Breck or not, Lang expressed his admiration when the young man made a difficult rifle shot and brought down an antelope a couple of hundred yards away.

"We'll have antelope steaks tonight!" Lang said eagerly as the echoes of Breckinridge's shot rolled away across the plains. Then he frowned a little and added, "I hope there ain't nobody out there to hear that shot. We're gettin' into Osage country."

"Are they hostile?" Breckinridge asked.

"Any Injun can be hostile if he takes it into his head to be. Best way is to figure that until one of 'em proves he's friendly, you better assume that he ain't."

While they were skinning and butchering the antelope, Breckinridge said, "Have you seen any Indian sign?"

"Not yet." Lang gazed off into the distance. "But it's only a matter o' time now before we run across 'em. They got bad redskins back where you come from?"

Breckinridge thought about his encounter with the Chickasaw renegades in the Blue Ridge foothills.

"A few," he replied.

That evening while they were sitting by the campfire after supper, Breckinridge mentioned Tom Lang's comments about the Osage to Lietenant Mallory.

"Tom seems to think you're gonna be in for a fight sooner or later," Breckinridge added.

Mallory sighed and nodded.

"I know, and I'm afraid he's right. The Indians may not be educated as we think of the word, but they're smart enough to look at the situation and see what's happening. They've been living in certain ways for hundreds of years, and that's about to change. Once civilization has swept all the way across the country from the Atlantic to the Pacific, there won't be room for them anymore. They'll have to live like white men . . . or not live at all."

"That don't hardly seem fair."

"The politicians in Washington call it Manifest Destiny, and fairness has nothing to do with it."

Breckinridge gazed off into the night and said, "As big as the country is, seems like there ought to be room here and there for folks like that to live the way they've always lived."

"You're an enlightened thinker, Breckinridge. Or at least you don't think like a politician."

Breckinridge snorted and replied, "I reckon that's one of the best things anybody ever said about me."

Mallory lowered his voice and said, "To be honest, I have a few misgivings myself about what we're doing. Don't misunderstand. I believe the country should be civilized. I love the surveying and the cartography. Seeing all this new territory is wonderful. But I worry that inevitably it's going to lead to war. Blood will be spilled partially because of the work that I'm doing."

"You don't have to be part of the army to go out and see new places," Breckinridge pointed out. "Look at me. I'm settin' off for the mountains, and I ain't got to answer to nobody."

"And I envy you that freedom," Mallory said with a sigh. "But my father and his father before that were in the army. My grandfather served under George Washington during the Revolution. It was expected that I uphold the tradition, even though my own interests run more toward the sciences. The Corps of Topographical Engineers is just about the only place I fit into the military."

"Your enlistment will be up one of these days, won't it?" Breckinridge asked.

"I suppose it will."

"Then when it is, you come out here and hunt me up. By then I'll know the mountains backwards and forwards. We'll go fur trappin' together."

Mallory laughed and thumped a hand against

Breckinridge's shoulder. He said, "I think I'd like that. You have a deal, my friend. We'll be mountain men."

Breckinridge nodded. The suggestion had been a spur of the moment thing, but he didn't regret it. Mallory was a decent sort, and smart as a whip, no doubt about that. It might be a good thing for both of them if they partnered up, somewhere down the line.

The party pushed on into the west. The Oregon Trail was to the north of them, Mallory explained to Breckinridge, and the Santa Fe Trail was to the south. Their goal was to discover if there was a middle route equal to those two great immigrant trails. Breck was no expert on the subject, but as far as he could see, there wasn't.

The terrain was easy enough for traveling, mostly flat and grassy with occasional rolling hills or a clump of brush or scrubby trees to break up the monotony. Wagons would be able to make it through country like this without much trouble.

The problem was water. The expedition came across a number of small creeks that allowed them to water their horses and fill their canteens, but the supply wasn't abundant enough for a wagon train with several hundred people and even more livestock. There was a good reason why the main trails followed rivers for the most part. As the party penetrated farther into the plains, Breckinridge began to understand why some folks called this the Great American Desert. It would seem that way to anybody accustomed to the woodlands back east.

Breckinridge had already stayed with the group longer than he'd intended when he accepted Lieutenant Mallory's invitation to join them. But he and Mallory had become friends, and besides, Breck was still headed west, the way he wanted. Mallory assured him the mountains were up there ahead of them. Hundreds of miles away, to be sure, but Breck was confident he would get there sooner or later.

The expedition was three weeks out of St. Louis, far from the bounds of civilization, when the Indians jumped them. They were riding along the southern bank of one of those little streams, Mallory and Breckinridge in front, the dragoons strung out behind them, and Sergeant Falk bringing up the rear. Tom Lang was out scouting somewhere ahead of the party.

Suddenly, figures stood up in the tall grass across the creek. They had been invisible until now. The movement caught Breckinridge's eye, and when he turned his head to look he caught a glimpse of the Indians before they opened fire with old-fashioned muskets and bows and arrows. The savages were tall, most of them more than six feet, and the topknots of hair on their otherwise shaved heads made them appear even taller.

Osage! Breckinridge thought, remembering Tom Lang's description of the people through whose hunting grounds they were passing.

Then men began to cry out and topple from their saddles. Arrows had skewered some of them, and others fell when struck by the heavy lead balls from the muskets. Instantly, the air was full of chaos: screams, booming gunshots, the ugly thud of lead against flesh, the whinnying of spooked horses, angry shouts from the soldiers, shrill war cries from the Indians.

Breckinridge whipped his rifle to his shoulder as a musket ball hummed past his ear. He drew a bead on one of the Osage ambushers and fired. The warrior jerked backward as the ball punched into his bare chest. His knees folded up and dropped him back into the tall grass.

"Forward!" Lieutenant Mallory shouted. "Forward!"

Breckinridge knew what the lieutenant intended. He wanted his men to gallop straight ahead along the creek in the hope that it would take them out of the line of fire. But as the dragoons who were still mounted surged forward, more Indians appeared, this time on the same side of the creek. The warriors grabbed the soldiers and dragged some of them off their horses. Other Indians carried long lances that they thrust upward so that unfortunate soldiers rode right into the sharp weapons and were run through. This battle was quickly turning into a massacre.

Two of the Osage warriors charged toward Breckinridge. They must have believed it would take both of them to pull him off his horse.

Breckinridge didn't give them a chance to find out if they were right. He jerked out his pair of flintlock pistols, leveled them, and fired them simultaneously. The Indians went over backward as if they'd been slapped down by a giant hand.

Another warrior came at him with a lance. Breckinridge grabbed it, wrenched it out of the man's hands, and banged his heels against his horse's sides. The animal leaped forward as Breck spun the lance around. With his own strength and the horse's weight behind it, the lance went all the way through the Osage's body so that the bloody point stood out a couple of feet from his back.

Breckinridge shoved the dead man out of the way and kept the horse moving. He wanted to reach Mallory's side. The lieutenant had drawn his saber and was slashing back and forth with it as the Indians closed in around him. Mallory's tall hat fell off and was trampled underfoot by the warriors.

Breckinridge kicked one of the Indians in the head as he charged past the man. The warrior's neck snapped and he dropped as every muscle in his body went limp. Another Osage fired an arrow at Breck, but he saw it coming in time to duck. He felt the feathers on the arrow's shaft brush his cheek as it went past.

Breckinridge had almost reached Mallory when one of the Indians shoved a lance into the belly of the lieutenant's horse. The animal screamed. Its front legs buckled, and Mallory was thrown forward out of the saddle. Breck made a grab for him but wasn't in time to catch him.

Mallory managed to hang on to his saber as he hit the ground and rolled over. He came up fighting, but as he swung the saber, one of the Indians fired a musket at him. The ball hit Mallory in the right arm, shattering his elbow. He cried out in agony as the saber flew out of suddenly nerveless fingers.

Another of the Indians drove a lance into the lieutenant's back. He staggered forward, obviously fighting to stay on his feet.

"John Francis!" Breckinridge bellowed. That was the first time he had called Mallory anything other than lieutenant, as Mallory had requested. But Breck felt like they had become friends, and rage filled him as he saw Mallory struck down.

Breckinridge spread his arms and dived off his horse. He tackled two of the Indians closing in on Mallory. As they all went to the ground, Breck wrapped his hands around their necks from behind and slammed their heads together as hard as he could. Bone crunched as the impact shattered their skulls.

One of the downed warriors had been carrying a lance. Breckinridge snatched it off the ground where the Indian had dropped it and came up swinging. He laid around him with the lance like it was a flail. The weapon was fairly lightweight, but with Breck's strength behind it, it was deadly. More bones broke. The Indians fell back as Breck cleared an area around the fallen officer.

Breckinridge stood there with his chest heaving as Sergeant Falk and several more of the dragoons fought their way through the chaos and joined him to form a defensive ring around Mallory. Blood dripped from a long gash on Falk's forehead, but other than that he seemed to be all right.

Breckinridge did a quick count. Twelve men were still on their feet, out of a company of more than twice that many. The other soldiers all sprawled on the ground, some dead, some seriously wounded.

The brave enlisted men were outnumbered, Breck realized. The two groups of Osage had joined forces, and now there were at least twenty warriors surrounding the soldiers. Breckinridge figured he and his companions would give a good account of themselves, but their odds of surviving this fight were pretty low.

A rifle cracked somewhere nearby, and one of the warriors fell with a good chunk of his head blown away. That made the Osage scatter. The warriors didn't know where the shot had come from or how many men were coming to the soldiers' aid. As the Indians disappeared across the grassy prairie, Breckinridge watched them go in stunned disbelief. He'd been certain he was about to die, but now it appeared that the attackers had had enough.

"What the hell just happened?" Breckinridge muttered.

"Once an Injun's spooked, he's done fightin'," Sergeant Falk said. "He thinks his medicine's gone bad. His luck's turned. Doesn't matter whether there's any truth to that or not. He thinks it, so it is."

Breckinridge accepted Falk's explanation. He knew the sergeant had fought Indians a number of times before as a member of army details escorting wagon trains on both the Oregon and Santa Fe Trails. Falk knew what he was talking about.

A groan made Breckinridge look around. Mallory was still alive, although his uniform was sodden with blood and his ruined arm lay limply at his side.

Breckinridge dropped to a knee next to his friend. He looked up at Falk and said, "We got to do somethin' to help him!"

"There's nothing we can do for him," Falk said grimly. "He's stabbed through and through, and between that and his arm, he's lost too much blood."

"Damn it—"

"Breck . . ."

The whispered name interrupted him. He looked down at Mallory and saw the lieutenant struggling to speak. Mallory's eyes were open, but he seemed to be having trouble focusing on anything. Breckinridge leaned closer and said, "I'm right here."

Mallory looked at him then and said, "You've got to . . . promise me something."

"Whatever you want," Breckinridge said, and he meant it.

"You've got to swear . . . you'll go on to the mountains . . . and live a life of adventure . . . for me, too. When you get there . . . when you're looking at all those things . . . you've never seen before . . . you'll be looking at them . . . with my eyes as well."

"Sure, John Francis. I'll do it. You'll be right there with me."

"In . . . spirit . . ." Mallory grimaced. "One more . . . thing . . . My maps . . . they have to get back. I can't . . . finish my mission . . . but what I've done . . . has to be delivered."

Breckinridge didn't see why. As best he could tell, this expedition hadn't accomplished a damned thing. Mallory hadn't found a better trail to the west. He hadn't even found a route as good as the ones that had already been established. His death, the deaths of the other soldiers who had been killed, were all a waste.

But his duty was important to him, whether it wound up serving a point or not. Breckinridge knew that from the conversations they'd shared. If Mallory wanted the maps he had made on the trip so far to be taken back and turned over to his superiors, then Breck intended to see that was done.

"I'll take 'em back," he vowed. "I'll do it myself."

Mallory lifted his left arm and reached across his body with a trembling hand. It closed for a moment around Breckinridge's arm as Mallory whispered, "Thank . . . you . . ."

Then his arm fell away and his head sagged to the side, and Breckinridge knew he was gone.

"Damn shame," Falk said. "For a greenhorn officer, he wasn't a bad sort. At least he was willin' to listen and learn. Most of 'em aren't."

Breckinridge's face was bleak as he stood up. He saw that Tom Lang had reappeared, cradling his long rifle in the crook of his arm. Breck asked, "You fired the shot that dropped that Osage when they had us surrounded?"

"Aye," the scout replied. "When I heard the shootin', I got back as quick as I could, but I didn't get here in time to help much. From the looks of it, the red-skinned varmints slipped in behind me after I'd gone by and set up their ambush."

"You spooked them and made them run off," Falk said. "If you hadn't, we'd probably all be dead by now."

Tom Lang shrugged, clearly upset. He said, "If I'd done my job better, maybe none of you would be dead."

Breckinridge turned to Falk and said, "Are you turnin' around and goin' back to Saint Louis?"

"There's nothing else we can do," Falk replied. "The lieutenant was the only one who knew anything about makin' maps. The rest of us were just along to keep him safe." A bitter note came into the sergeant's voice as he added, "We did a mighty poor job of that, didn't we?"

"We were outnumbered, Sergeant," one of the dragoons said. "And they took us by surprise."

"Aye, they did. I don't want them to do the same thing again."

Breckinridge was worried about the same thing. He

picked up the rifle and pistols he had dropped during the battle, reloaded them, and then said, "I'm gonna take a look around, just to make sure those Osage are really gone."

"I'll come with you," Tom Lang said.

"We'll make camp here," Falk said. "We've got wounded to tend to and dead to bury. Also, we need to round up as many of the horses as we can. They scattered pretty good, but I think we can find some of them. That'll make it a lot easier to get back."

Breckinridge and Lang left the others where they were and trotted across the prairie, making a large circle around their position to insure that the Indians weren't trying to double back and spring another ambush. Breck was hardly what one would call experienced where these plains tribes were concerned—today was his first encounter with them—but he had a keen eye and the confidence to take care of himself in the wilderness.

The Osage were well and truly gone, Breckinridge and Lang discovered. Breck said, "I don't hardly see how they could have disappeared that fast."

"That's the way they do," Lang said. "Ain't nobody better'n an Injun when it comes to blendin' into the landscape. If you don't have a keen eye and a lot of experience, sometimes you might walk right past one of 'em, close enough to touch, and never see him."

"That'd be a handy skill to have. Can white men learn it?"

"Very few. Only one I ever heard tell of who was the equal of an Injun is an old fella called Preacher. He's supposed to be the best that ever was. Not even the redskins can see him if he don't want them to."

"I'd like to meet him someday," Breckinridge said.

"Traipse around the mountains long enough and you're likely to."

When they got back to the camp, they told Falk what they'd found. The sergeant said, "I reckon we'll stay here tonight, then start back in the morning. By the way, Wallace, that promise you made to the lieutenant about takin' his maps back . . . you don't have to worry about that. We'll see to it. Anyway, you're a civilian. Those maps are the property and responsibility of the United States Army."

"Maybe so, but I gave Lieutenant Mallory my word. I was brought up to keep the promises I made. I reckon you can take charge of the map cases, Sergeant, but I intend to see to it that you and them all make it back safe and sound."

Falk shrugged and said, "Suit yourself. I know you were headed west, and I thought you might want to keep on going that way."

Breckinridge did, but he didn't see any way he could continue his journey right now without breaking his promise to Mallory, and he didn't want to do that. For the first time since leaving home, he had to turn around and go back in the other direction.

Back to St. Louis, where he was no doubt wanted for the murder of Rory Ducharme.

Chapter Eighteen

The soldiers rounded up enough of the surviving saddle mounts and packhorses so that everyone in the party was able to ride as they started out the next morning, leaving more than a dozen freshly filled graves behind them.

The burial sites were unmarked—there were no trees nearby to furnish branches for crosses—and it wouldn't have mattered anyway, Breckinridge knew. The elements would soon claim anything left behind.

More graves would be dug along the way. Several of the wounded men succumbed to their injuries during the journey.

Since there was no mapmaking going on anymore, the trip back proceeded at a slightly faster pace than the expedition had been making before. They didn't see any more Indians, but Tom Lang said it was likely the Osage were watching them.

"There's a good chance they'll leave us alone now," the scout told Breckinridge and Sergeant Falk. "They can see for themselves that we're goin' back where we came from. That's all the Injuns really want, for us to leave 'em alone and stop crowdin' in on 'em."

"It won't be that way once we have enough soldiers out here," Falk said. "We'll teach those savages they can't stand in the way of progress."

"Mebbe so," Lang mused, "but it's gonna be a bloody lesson on both sides."

Based on what Breckinridge had seen so far, he didn't doubt that a bit.

With Sergeant Falk in command, the group followed a slightly different route on the return trip, angling more to the north. Falk intended to stop at Independence, Missouri, the jumping-off point for the Oregon Trail.

"There's a garrison there," he explained. "I'd like to get those maps off my hands as soon as possible. I don't know if they're worth anything to the army or not, but I know if I lose 'em, I'll be in trouble."

That decision set well with Breckinridge. He knew it would be dangerous for him to return to St. Louis. He was willing to do it, to keep his promise to Lieutenant Mallory, but if there was a way of fulfilling that pledge without putting himself in harm's way, he was in favor of that.

Tom Lang and Sergeant Falk had both been over the Oregon Trail and told Breckinridge about the wonderful country that waited at the end of that exodus for settlers. It didn't interest Breck one bit. If he had wanted to remain a farmer, he could have stayed back in Tennessee. Well, he could have, he thought to himself, if the law hadn't been after him for killing Jasper Carlson.

First Jasper, then Rory Ducharme, Breckinridge

mused. In both cases, he had been defending himself. The accusations leveled against him were unjust. But in the eyes of the law, all that mattered was that the two dead men had wealthy, powerful fathers.

It wouldn't be like that in the mountains, Breck thought. Out there in the wilderness, a man's survival would depend only on his own strength, skill, and cunning.

He looked forward to the day when he could pit himself against that world.

In the meantime, the surviving members of the mapmaking expedition reached Independence sixteen days after the battle with the Osage. Only a couple of years earlier, the settlement had been a sleepy little village on the Missouri River, but all that had changed with the opening of the Oregon Trail and the large number of immigrants who had poured into the place to outfit themselves for the six-month-long journey ahead of them. Independence was now a bustling town with wagon trains departing almost every week—sometimes several in a week.

There was also a garrison of soldiers, as Sergeant Falk had said. The non-com led the way to a cluster of tents around a parade ground. The place was too small and primitive to call it a fort.

A heavyset officer with a lot of gold braid on his jacket emerged from the largest tent to greet them. Breckinridge didn't know what all the decorations meant, but as he and Tom Lang sat on their horses, the scout told him quietly, "That's Colonel Lansing. He's the hellfire-and-brimstone sort. He'll probably chew Falk up one way and down t'other for comin' back without the lieutenant."

The fat, red-faced, side-whiskered colonel did exactly that, launching into a tirade when he learned that Lieutenant Mallory had been killed and the expedition cut short. He seemed slightly mollified when Falk turned the map cases over to him, but then he got wound up again.

Tom Lang lifted his reins and started to turn his horse away.

"Come on," he said to Breckinridge. "Ain't no reason for us to listen to this, and I need to wet my whistle."

That sounded good to Breckinridge. He had seen Falk hand over the maps, so he considered his pledge to Mallory carried out. He had no other business with the army.

Tom Lang led the way to a tavern. It was called the Red Buffalo, and a sign with a buffalo painted that color hung over the door. Lang and Breckinridge dismounted, tied their reins at a hitch rail, and went inside.

The last time he had gone into a tavern, Breckinridge reflected, he had found Sadie Humboldt and Jack MacKenzie inside. Before that evening was over he had killed a man and made himself even more of a fugitive. Understandably, he felt a little wary as he stepped into the dim, smoky room and looked around, halfway expecting to see more trouble waiting for him.

Instead, as far as he could tell, everybody in the place was a stranger to him. Breckinridge relaxed a little. That was the way he liked it these days.

The Red Buffalo was crowded, but the crowd hadn't yet formed that could stand up to Breckinridge

Wallace when he wanted through. He wasn't rough or rude about it, just inexorable. People naturally moved aside from him as they would have scurried out of the path of a moving mountain. Tom Lang followed along in his wake.

When they reached the bar, Lang ordered whiskey and Breckinridge told the aproned barman to bring him a bucket of beer, though he wasn't sure how he'd pay for it. Breckinridge looked around again and saw that most of the folks in here were men, and there were all sorts, from fresh-faced youngsters much like himself—only smaller, of course—to white-bearded old-timers like Tom Lang.

Several women appeared to work here, but they weren't serving drinks. Instead they led men through a curtained doorway and into and out of doorless rooms on either side of a hallway lit by a guttering candle in a wall sconce at the far end.

Seeing Breckinridge watching them, Tom Lang laughed and said, "You need to go pay a visit to one o' them calico cats, boy?"

"They're doin' a boomin' business," Breckinridge said without answering Lang's question.

"Of course they are! Independence is full of fellas who are about to leave for the Oregon country. That means they're facin' six months of no towns and no places like this. They know there's a chance they might not make it that far, too. It's a hard trip, and there's a thousand ways to die between here and there. So this is sort of their last hoo-rah, I reckon you could say. The last chance to have a little sweetness in your life for a long time . . . maybe ever."

Breckinridge nodded. What Tom Lang said made

sense. And Breck felt a powerful stirring when he looked at the women. He was no more immune to their appeal than any other man.

But he thought about Maureen Grantham and hesitated. He didn't have some foolish notion about being faithful to her or anything like that. She didn't have any claim on him, or he on her. He knew, though, that if he went with one of those tavern gals, he might think of Maureen while he was with her, and that seemed disrespectful.

Thankfully, he didn't have to worry about making that decision. It had already been made for him by his empty pockets.

So when Tom Lang prodded him by saying, "How about it, son?" Breckinridge shook his head.

"I don't have any money, remember?"

Lang threw back his head and laughed.

"Oh, hell, is that your only problem?" He reached in one of the pockets of his fancy buckskin jacket and slapped a silver dollar on the bar. As he pushed it toward Breckinridge, he said, "It's on me. Go ahead, take it."

"I couldn't do that," Breckinridge said. "You might want to use it for yourself. I mean, to get you one of . . . one of . . ."

Lang laughed again and said, "Good Lord, I'm too old to be cavortin' with some harlot. For me, the pleasures of the flesh mean a good drink, a pipe full of fine smokin' tobacco, and a nice comfortable place to sit and rest my feet. Young fella like you, though, all full o' piss and vinegar, needs to do somethin' about it. Take the money and find a gal. In a place like this, a dollar ought to buy you a pretty good one."

Still Breckinridge hesitated. Then a soft hand touched his arm, and he turned his head to look down into a smiling face surrounded by chestnut hair.

"Hello," the girl said. "My, you're a big one, ain't you?"

Breckinridge figured she had spotted the coin Tom Lang was urging on him and had swooped in, hawk-like, to try to get her hands on it. A girl in a profession like hers had to have some predatory instincts.

Yet she somehow managed to retain a trace of innocence about her. Maybe it was that smattering of freckles across the bridge of her nose, or the shyness— real or feigned—in her green eyes.

"What's your name?" she went on.

"Breckinridge," he replied, and as he said it his fingers closed around the coin on the bar. He ignored the cackle of victory from Tom Lang. "What's yours?"

"Laura," she said.

"Just Laura?"

Her expression hardened slightly as she said, "I didn't ask you for a second name, did I?"

"No, ma'am, you sure didn't," Breckinridge admitted hastily. "I beg your pardon for bein' rude."

Her smile came back as she said, "Oh, don't worry about it, Breckinridge." She leaned her head toward the hallway. "Would you like to come back to my room for a little while?"

He took a deep breath and said, "Yes, ma'am, I believe I would."

* * *

The experience was a new one for Breckinridge. He had been with gals before, back home, but there had never been any payment involved. Laura had made sure she had that silver dollar before she slipped out of her dress.

Once she did, however, things were much like Breck remembered. And she seemed to enjoy it as much as he did, just like the girls back in Tennessee. She enjoyed it so much, in fact, that he was too busy to think of Maureen even once.

When it was over, she didn't rush him to get dressed and leave, but rather stayed curled in the circle of his brawny arms for a while, muttering something about how Dooley would kill her for wasting time, but she didn't care.

Breckinridge figured Dooley was the fella who owned the Red Buffalo. He wanted to promise Laura that he would take care of her, that he wouldn't let Dooley or anybody else hurt her.

He kept his mouth shut. Promises like that tended to backfire on him.

Finally she said they couldn't stay there any longer, no matter how much she wanted to. She squeezed her arms around him, kissed his cheek, and said, "You almost make me believe in things again, Breckinridge."

"Shoot, everybody believes in things, don't they?"

Her smile was sad as she said, "Not always. Sometimes, after being disappointed long enough, often enough, believing in things just makes you hurt. So you stop. But then somebody like you comes along . . ." She sighed and slipped out of bed. "Get those buckskins back on. It's time to go."

Breckinridge got dressed. He and Laura left the room and went back to the tavern's main room.

The bartender must have been watching for them. He came out from behind the bar and stalked toward them, scowling. He was a tall, angular man with a pockmarked, hatchet-like face and a shock of dark hair.

"You were back there too long," he accused Laura. "You'd better have got some extra money out of it."

She lifted her chin, and Breckinridge sensed that such defiance was unusual in her.

"You got to let us have a little extra time now and then, Dooley," she said. "A girl gets worn out—"

"I don't care about that. You know the rules. You don't get your cut for the rest of the night. That'll square it."

"Mister, it's my fault," Breckinridge began. "You shouldn't—"

"Shut up and get out," Dooley snapped. "This is none of your business."

Breckinridge was starting to get mad himself. He didn't like the way this fella talked to Laura, and he wasn't going to allow Dooley to mistreat her. His hands clenched into fists and he started to take a step that would put him between Dooley and Laura.

She clutched at his arm in fear and said, "Breckinridge, no! Look around."

Breckinridge looked. He saw men sitting on stools in the corners of the room. Each of them held a pistol. The tavern's other customers, recognizing the impending trouble, were moving out of the line of fire.

"I don't allow any brawling in my place," Dooley

said with an arrogant smile. "Just like I don't let trollops tell me my business." The smile went away and was replaced by a puzzled frown. "Wait a minute. Did she just call you Breckinridge?"

"That's my name," Breckinridge said, suddenly worried that Dooley somehow knew about the trouble he was in with the law.

"Breckinridge Wallace?"

Now it was Breckinridge's turn to be surprised, even a little thunderstruck.

"What if I am?" he asked cautiously.

"I've got a letter for you."

How in the world . . . ?

"You can have it," Dooley went on, "for five dollars."

Breckinridge sighed and said, "Well, that's a shame, because I don't have five dollars."

"I do," Tom Lang said as he stepped up to them. "I've been listenin', and I'll ransom that there letter from you, Dooley. You got to promise you'll let this little gal off the hook for that extra money you think she owes you, though."

Dooley frowned. He said, "I don't like to let nobody tell me how to run my own business—"

"You know me, Dooley Simmons," Lang said in a hard voice. "You know I don't tolerate no foolishness. My word carries some weight in this town, too. If I tell folks they ought to steer clear of the Red Buffalo, what do you think they'll do?"

"You wouldn't do that," Dooley blustered.

"Don't try me."

The bartender rolled his eyes, shook his head, and sighed. He muttered, "All right, all right. Laura, you go on and tend to your business. Forget what I said earlier."

"Thanks, Dooley." Laura came up on her toes, and Breckinridge bent down so she could kiss his cheek again. "And thank you, Breckinridge. Thank you for making me believe in something again for a few minutes . . . and damn you for it, too."

With that she slipped off into the crowd before Breckinridge could say or do anything else.

Tom Lang took out a five-dollar gold piece and said, "Where's that letter?"

"Behind the bar." Dooley jerked his head in that direction. "Come on over and I'll get it."

Lang pointed and said, "Bring it to that table."

Dooley nodded his agreement.

When Breckinridge and Lang were sitting down, Breck said, "Thanks for steppin' in like that, Tom."

"Aw, hell, don't mention it. I admit, I didn't like you much at first, son. Never have cottoned to big galoots like you. But you've sort of growed on me these past few weeks. Plus I talked to Sergeant Falk enough to know that you was a holy terror during that fracas with the Osage. I can't help but respect a good fightin' man."

"I wasn't good enough to save Lieutenant Mallory's life."

"Well, that's just it. No matter how good you are, you ain't gonna win every battle. You ain't gonna save ever'body who needs savin'. The important part is to keep fightin' until you die. That's the way to make the world sit up and take notice of you, son."

Breckinridge nodded. He would try to remember

the things that Tom Lang told him, because he knew that trouble would come to him again. It always did.

Dooley brought over a piece of paper that had been folded and sealed with wax. He handed it to Breckinridge, but not until Tom Lang had given him the gold piece.

"The man who gave that to me said to watch for a young fella with bright red hair who was as big as a mountain," the bartender explained. "He gave me your name, too: Breckinridge Wallace."

"What did he look like?" Breckinridge asked.

"Good-sized gent with dark hair. Not nearly as big as you, of course." Dooley frowned. "It's been more than a month since he was here, so I could be remembering wrong, but I'd swear there was a little resemblance between the two of you."

Breckinridge felt his heart slug harder in his chest. The man Dooley described could have been one of his brothers. He asked, "Did he say why he was leavin' a letter for me with you?"

Dooley laughed.

"Hell, he didn't just leave one with me. He left 'em all over town, in the taverns and the stores and any place else you might come in. Said he'd been looking for you and it was mighty important he get in touch with you. Don't ask me why, though. That's all I know."

Tom Lang suggested, "Reckon if you open that letter, you might find out."

Breckinridge nodded. He pried the wax seal loose while Dooley went back to the bar. Then he unfolded the letter and leaned forward to read it, squinting a little because of the dim light in the tavern.

As he read, he felt his jaw sagging. Tom Lang must have seen the shock and amazement on Breckinridge's face, because he asked anxiously, "Good Lord, Breck, what's wrong?"

"Wrong?" Breckinridge echoed. He shook his head. "Nothin's wrong. Nothin' at all." He looked up. "I'm goin' home, Tom. I'm goin' home."

BOOK FIVE

Chapter Nineteen

The letter was from Breckinridge's brother Edward.
It read:

Dear Breckinridge—
   *This letter is one of many I have written in hopes
of establishing communication with you. I intend to
continue writing them and leaving them in places
where you may turn up. I hoped to locate you in St.
Louis, but since that effort proved a failure I have
moved on to other settlements here in Missouri.*
   *The most important thing for you to know is
this: while you no doubt consider yourself to be a
fugitive from the authorities, there are no charges
levied against you in the matter of Jasper Carlson's
death. One of the young men who was a companion
of Jasper's and Richard Aylesworth's on the night
in question recanted the account he gave originally
to the sheriff and instead told the truth of what
occurred. Once that happened, several others in
the group agreed with his testimony in order not
to get in trouble with the law themselves. Jasper's*

father was incensed, as was Richard, but there was
nothing they could do. All charges against you were
dismissed.

This means it is now safe for you to return home
to Tennessee. With the blessing of Father and Mother
I have journeyed west to deliver this good word to
you. I will continue my travels until I have found
you, or until I have exhausted all the places to
search. In the meantime, if this letter reaches you,
please come home, and in due course of time I will
see you there. We are all very grateful that you no
longer have anything to fear from the law, and we
look forward to sharing your fraternal
companionship once more.

> *With warmest wishes,*
> *Your brother,*
> *Edward Wallace*

Breckinridge must have read that letter a hundred
times during the months it took him to get back to
Knoxville. At first he had a hard time following some
of Edward's formal, fussy sentences, but he understood the important part. He could go home without
having to worry about being arrested, tried, and
hanged for killing Jasper Carlson.

That didn't change the fact that he was probably
wanted by the authorities in St. Louis for Rory
Ducharme's death. But they didn't know his name
or where he was from. Somebody in Red Mike's place
might have heard Sadie call him Bill, but that wouldn't
help anybody find him. Breckinridge believed that if
he steered well clear of St. Louis, he didn't have much
to worry about from the law.

The real question was . . . did he really *want* to go home?

Since leaving Tennessee, he had gone through considerable hardship and tragedy. He had seen people who meant something to him die suddenly and violently. He had come within a hair's breadth of death himself on numerous occasions. He had been forced to kill to defend himself and others. Just on the surface of it, that didn't sound like a life anyone would want. Anyone who wasn't crazy, anyway.

But thinking about all the bad things that had happened didn't mean he had forgotten about the good times, like traveling up the Mississippi River and feeling the great power of the Father of Waters, or waking up before dawn and watching the glory of the sun rising over the prairie. Even though he had barely begun to explore the frontier, Breckinridge had already had the experience of laying eyes on places that few white men had ever seen before. That feeling couldn't be duplicated in Tennessee; it hadn't been untouched wilderness for a couple of hundred years.

Breckinridge had explained what was in the letter as he and Tom Lang sat in the Red Buffalo drinking beer. He said, "Here's the thing . . . I ain't sure I want to go back."

The old scout nodded solemnly and said, "I knew that was what you were about to say 'fore the words ever came outta your mouth, son. You don't have to tell me about how the frontier gets under a fella's skin. I come out here from Pennsylvania nigh on to thirty years ago, and I never could bring myself to go back. Had a wife and a family and ever'thing. I missed 'em, I reckon, but I couldn't live a tame life again. I was ruint."

"You abandoned your family?" Breckinridge said.

"Well, I felt bad about it," Lang replied defensively. "But I sent 'em money right along, and I got a fella who could write to write my wife a letter and tell her I wouldn't be comin' back. Shoot, for all I know she told ever'body I was dead and married herself a new husband. I hope she did. She wasn't a bad sort."

Breckinridge told himself not to pass judgment on Tom Lang. Every man was responsible for his own actions, and while he might believe he knew how he would react in a certain situation, there was no way of being sure that was right until the time came.

One thing he knew, though, was that he didn't like the way things had been left with his family, running off like that in the middle of the night with everybody worried that they would never see him again. Even if he didn't stay, he could spend some time with his parents and brothers.

He could even see Maureen again.

That thought sent a flush of embarrassment through him. He had spent time alone on the trail with Sadie, even though nothing had really happened between them. He had done more than spend time with Laura. Those things probably made him unfit company for a proper young lady like Maureen Grantham. True, she wouldn't know what he had done . . . but *he* would know.

He would figure out what to do about Maureen when he got there, he decided. For now he knew he wanted to see his family. He said as much to Tom Lang.

The old scout had nodded and said, "Sure, you go pay 'em a visit. But you'll be back out here on the frontier, Breck. Mark my words. Sooner or later, you'll be back."

* * *

All the mounts used by the mapmaking expedition belonged to the U.S. Army, of course, so Breckinridge had to turn his horse over to Sergeant Falk before he left Independence. He told Falk about his plan to return home for a visit, and the gruff non-com said, "When you're done with that, why don't you give some thought to enlisting in the army? We could use a man like you, Wallace. You're a ring-tailed devil in a fight."

"I appreciate that, Sergeant, but I reckon I ain't cut out to be a soldier."

"Don't like taking orders, eh?"

"Or givin' 'em, neither," Breckinridge replied with a grin. "I'd rather just go along and sort of just let every fella do what he thinks is best."

"That way lies anarchy, Wallace."

"You could be right, Sergeant," Breckinridge said, since he wasn't exactly sure what that two-bit word meant.

"How are you going to get where you're going without a horse?"

Breckinridge had been careful not to mention just where "home" was. Over the past few months he had developed a natural caution and believed that it was usually better not to tell people any more about him than they had to know.

"Shank's mare, I reckon," he said as he glanced down at his feet. It was going to be a long walk to Tennessee, but he had done most of it before and could do it again, he supposed.

Falk frowned and said, "There's a dispatch rider heading for Washington tomorrow. He'll have a small escort with him. I might be able to persuade Colonel Lansing to assign a civilian scout to the detail. I doubt if the colonel will approve the added expense of wages, but he might go along with providing a horse and supplies."

"Sergeant, that'd be a mighty nice thing for you to do. A group like that headin' east don't really need a scout, though, do they? It ain't like they'll be headin' into Indian territory."

"No, but there's always the danger of cutthroats and highwaymen—"

"Who'd have to be plumb crazy to tackle an army detail."

"Blast it, Wallace, do you want me to do you this favor or not?" Falk demanded.

Breckinridge grinned again. He said, "I sure do, Sergeant, and like I said, I'm mighty thankful to you."

Falk's efforts paid off, and Breckinridge was assigned to the dispatch rider's escort. That gave him a horse for the trip across Missouri. He left the group before it reached St. Louis, however, and struck out southeast on foot.

When he came to a small town with a landing on the Mississippi River, he stayed there until he was able to land a job on a keelboat heading south to New Orleans. The captain, a bushy-browed, hawk-nosed old-timer named Dunstan, was acquainted with Christophe Marchant, and when he heard that Breckinridge had worked on the *Sophie*, he was glad to take him on as a member of the crew.

"I'll be leavin' when we get down to Memphis, though," Breckinridge warned the captain. "I can't go all the way to New Orleans."

"That's all right," Dunstan said. "I've got a man laid

up with a bum knee, but he ought to be better by then. You'll be taking his place."

That was agreeable to Breckinridge. His luck generally seemed to work out in little things like that, as if he had a guardian angel watching over him.

But he had a guardian devil, too, who took great delight in smacking him down every time he least expected it.

The trip downriver was uneventful. Dunstan's boat, which bore the ungainly name of the *Mudhen*, put in at Memphis just long enough to let Breckinridge off. Breck recalled Christophe talking about what a tough town Memphis was, but he also remembered that Jack MacKenzie had traded away Hector here. Breck didn't expect to be lucky enough to find the horse and be reunited with him . . . but stranger things had happened in his life.

That particular stroke of good fortune wasn't to be. Breckinridge never saw Hector during the time he spent in Memphis, which was only a week. He stayed out of Blufftown, the roughest part of the settlement, and did some blacksmith work to earn enough money to buy some supplies. He figured he would do some hunting along the way and stretch the provisions out just as long as he possibly could.

The walk across Tennessee was less arduous than the one in the other direction had been, more than six months earlier. Breckinridge didn't have to survive on roots and whatever small animals he could snare this time, but he still had some cold, hungry nights along the way. Winter was looming, so he kept moving at as fast a pace as he could manage. He wanted to be home before the worst of the weather arrived.

And now, finally, he was here, having circled

around Knoxville. He trusted what Edward had told him in the letter, but that wariness was still with him. He stood on a hilltop, tall, leaner than he had been when he left but still massively powerful, with a fine rifle and a pair of pistols and a keen-edged knife he used to trim his beard and hack off some of the wild, blazing thicket of hair. He looked down at his father's farm and watched the members of his family moving around in the late afternoon, finishing the day's chores. The sky was overcast with thick gray clouds blown by a chilly wind. But the windows of the farm house glowed yellow with light and warmth and beckoned Breckinridge to come down and allow himself to be enfolded by all that he had left behind.

Fear struck through him. What if they realized he was different now? What if all the blood he had spilled had changed him, rendered him unfit for the companionship of normal people, even his own family? For a long moment Breckinridge was struck by the powerful impulse to turn and walk away, to go back to the new life he had started to make for himself on the frontier. Maybe that would be best for everyone concerned.

But he knew he couldn't do that. Not after coming this far. That would be the cowardly thing to do. With his mind made up, he squared his shoulders, drew in a deep breath, and then started down the hill toward his home.

The dogs knew he was coming before anyone else did. Giant, long-haired Sammy bounded up the slope toward him, barking a raucous welcome. Ancient Max toddled along behind, taking it slow because he didn't see well anymore. He raised his voice in barks of greeting, too, even though he might not have known who he was barking at. Breckinridge knelt to embrace both dogs as they eagerly licked his face.

Robert Wallace stepped out of the barn holding a pitchfork, tense and wary as if expecting possible trouble. He called, "Is somebody there? Who—Good Lord! Breckinridge? Is it really you?"

Thomas and Henry came out of the barn behind their father. Henry let out a whoop and charged toward Breckinridge.

"Breck!"

That shout drew Jeremiah and Samantha from the house. In seconds, Breckinridge's brothers surrounded him, hugging him and pounding him on the back. He greeted them almost as boisterously, holding back slightly because he was bigger than all of them. Then he shook hands with his father and turned to his mother, who stared at him with disbelief in her eyes.

"I told myself I'd never see you again, so I wouldn't be disappointed when that happened," Samantha said. "I convinced myself of it. But now . . . here you are."

"He's come home," Robert said. "Our boy's come home."

There was a finality to his tone, as if he expected Breckinridge to stay here forever now that he was back. Breck didn't want to ruin this reunion by speculating about what he might do in the future, so he remained silent. He just put his arms around his mother and cradled her gently against him.

After a moment, Samantha stepped back, looking a little flustered, and said, "I have to go cook some more food. That supper I've got waiting won't be nearly enough now that you're here, Breckinridge."

That made his brothers laugh. As they all trooped

toward the house, Breckinridge said, "Edward's not here?"

"He's still out there somewhere on the frontier looking for you," Robert explained. "We got a letter from him the other day, though, saying that he'd be starting home soon, so he'll get here before winter sets in."

"Don't worry, you'll see him when he gets back," Thomas added.

Breckinridge hoped so. But he couldn't guarantee how long he would be here. That would depend on how the visit went, he supposed.

For now, he was just going to enjoy being home.

Chapter Twenty

The meal was the best Breckinridge had had in months, just as he expected. His mother stayed busy cooking all evening. She set plate after plate of food in front of Breck, and he emptied each of them in turn while his father and brothers looked on in amazement. Finally Robert said, "I see it's true what they say about some things never changing."

"I didn't eat this good the whole time I was gone," Breckinridge said around a mouthful of biscuit and molasses.

"Yeah, you're skinnier than you used to be," Henry said. "I'll bet I could whip you at arm-wrestlin' now."

Breckinridge just grunted to show how unlikely he considered that possibility.

After a while, he asked, "How are things in Knoxville? How's Maureen Grantham?"

He tried to make the questions sound casual, but he wasn't sure how well he succeeded. Evidently not very well, judging by the sudden wary looks that appeared on his family's faces.

They all hesitated for a few seconds, then Robert

said, "She's not Maureen Grantham anymore, Breckinridge. She's Maureen Aylesworth now. She married the Aylesworth boy a couple of months after you left."

That news went through Breckinridge like a physical blow. He knew that Richard Aylesworth had intended to marry Maureen, but Richard himself had said that he was going to wait a couple more years.

Obviously, he had changed his mind.

The marriage wasn't the only bit of unwelcome news. Breckinridge's mother said, "There's talk that Maureen is in the family way."

"She's expectin'?" Breckinridge said, jolted and a little sickened by the idea of Maureen having Richard Aylesworth's baby. That just wasn't right.

"Aye," Robert said heavily. "So if you had any thoughts in your head about that girl, son, you might as well forget 'em. She's a married woman now. You'd do well to stay as far away from her as you can."

Breckinridge knew his father was right, but at the same time he had been yearning to see Maureen again ever since he had turned his steps back toward home. Many of those cold, lonely nights on the trail, he had clung to his memories of her, conjuring up her beautiful image in his mind's eye and drawing warmth and hope from it. She had kept him going, and now he had a hard time accepting the fact that she belonged to someone else.

Because Richard would regard her as a possession, like a fine rifle or a good hunting dog. Breckinridge was sure of that. That was just the sort of man Richard Aylesworth was.

Robert leaned forward and asked, "Did you hear

me, Breck? I said you need to stay away from Maureen Grantham . . . I mean, Maureen Aylesworth."

"I hear you, Pa," Breckinridge said.

But he didn't promise he would do as his father advised. He was going to have to think about that for a while before he made up his mind.

For a couple of days, Breckinridge worked hard around the farm. There were jobs he could do because of his great strength that it took two of his brothers to accomplish. He counted on that strenuous labor to keep his mind off Maureen. The tactic didn't really work very well, however, as she continued stealing into his thoughts.

Maybe if he paid her a visit and saw with his own eyes that she was happy, that marriage to Richard Aylesworth was what she really wanted, then he would be able to put her out of his mind and go on with his life.

The only other alternative was to leave for the frontier immediately, where the daily struggle to stay alive might prove to be a sufficient distraction.

Breckinridge had given his family a highly edited version of his adventures since he'd left. He didn't want any of them, especially his mother, to know just how dangerous some of those times had been. But even leaving out a lot of things, the stories were still exciting enough to stir up some wanderlust in his brothers. He saw it in their eyes as he was talking, and he hoped he wouldn't be the cause of more disruption in the family. The last thing his folks needed was to have more sons run off to see the vast frontier for themselves.

On the other hand, he asked himself, who was he to deny his brothers that experience if it was what they really wanted?

With all that turbulence going on in Breckinridge's mind, it was no wonder that he quickly found himself growing restless. He longed for the simplicity of the wilderness. Tom Lang had sure been right: the West got into a man's blood and didn't want to let go.

By the time almost a week had gone by, Breckinridge knew it was no use. He had to see Maureen and say a final good-bye to her. That was the only way he could stop being haunted by thoughts of her.

After the midday meal, he went to the creek for a bucket of water and started washing up. His father saw him and got a worried look on his face.

"You're going to see the Grantham girl, aren't you?" Robert asked.

"I just want to talk to her one last time, Pa," Breckinridge replied. "If I don't, it's liable to be eatin' away at me the rest of my life."

"What do you think is going to happen?" Robert asked angrily. "You think she's going to decide she made a mistake marrying Richard Aylesworth and run away with you? She's with child, Breckinridge! She's not going to abandon her husband."

"I don't expect her to. I just want to see for myself that she's all right and tell her good-bye. I never got a chance to that other time."

"Maybe she doesn't want to see you. Did you ever think about that?"

Breckinridge frowned. He said, "If she tells me to go, then I'll go. But at least it'll be settled."

Robert snorted in disgust.

"I'd say it was pretty well settled when she told Aylesworth, 'I do.'"

Breckinridge dumped the bucket of water over his head, shook out his long red hair, and pulled on a buckskin shirt.

"Are you gonna stop me, Pa?" he asked.

"You know I can't do that. I wouldn't, even if I could. Sometimes a man's got to make his own damn-fool mistakes, or else he's never going to learn anything."

At least his father had just referred to him as a man, Breckinridge thought. To the best of his memory, that was the first time his pa had acknowledged the fact.

He put a saddle on one of the horses and was about to ride away when he stopped and looked around at his father.

"I just remembered, I don't know where they live," he said.

"I shouldn't tell you," Robert said, "but you'd just ask somebody in Knoxville and find out that way. The boy's father bought them a house." He told Breckinridge where to find the place, then added, "Don't lose that horse this time."

Breckinridge nodded ruefully. He had told his family that Hector had been stolen, which certainly was true as far as it went. He merely left out the part about how he'd been drugged and double-crossed by a gambler and a runaway girl.

The ride to Knoxville didn't take long. It was a cool, late autumn afternoon, with small patches of blue sky peeking through a gray overcast.

Breckinridge found the house without any trouble and tied the horse to a post beside the gate in the picket fence around the yard. The house was large and comfortable looking, sitting under tall trees that were mostly bare at this time of year. A couple of stately evergreens flanked the flagstone path leading up to the verandah, though.

Breckinridge stood there looking at the house for a moment, then took a deep breath and opened the gate. As he approached the house, he thought he saw a curtain move a little at one of the windows on the second floor.

Was Maureen behind that curtain, looking out at him? Was she shocked to see him? Happy? Angry?

A maid answered Breckinridge's knock on the door. He said, "I'd like to speak to . . . Mrs. Aylesworth . . . please."

He hated the way those words sounded in his mouth. They were so wrong they made his skin crawl.

The maid told him to wait and closed the door. As Breckinridge stood there, the wind picked up a little. It felt chillier now than it had when he was riding into town, Breck thought.

The maid opened the door again and said, "The missus says you should come on in."

She led Breckinridge into a well-appointed parlor and told him to have a seat. All the chairs looked a little spindly to Breck, so he lowered himself onto a divan instead, worrying slightly about its even being able to support his weight.

He didn't have to sit there for very long. Maureen appeared in the parlor's arched doorway. Breckinridge caught his breath at the sight of her.

She was as beautiful as ever, wearing a dark blue, high-necked dress. Her hair was pulled to the back of her head and fastened there. As she came toward

Breckinridge, he saw the rounded belly. She was in the family way, all right. Richard must have gotten her like that not long after their marriage.

"Breckinridge," she said softly as she held out both hands toward him. "You shouldn't have come here."

He stood up and clasped her hands. No power on earth could have prevented him from doing so. As usual, he towered over her, so she had to tip her head back to look up at him.

His father had been right about one thing: she wasn't a girl anymore. Even though less than a year had passed since he last saw her, she had changed dramatically. She was a woman now . . . with a woman's burdens haunting her dark eyes.

"Maureen . . ." he said as he struggled to come up with the right words and cursed himself for being so tongue-tied. Finally he went on, "I had to see you again."

"And it's good to see you," she said as she managed to put a small, sad smile on her face. The smile went away as she added, "But Richard wouldn't like it if he knew you were here."

Breckinridge saw something flare in her eyes as she mentioned her husband. He thought at first that it was worry, then realized it was more than that.

She was afraid.

His hands tightened on hers, although he was careful not to grip them too hard. He said, "Maureen, what's wrong? Are you scared of that—"

"Scared?" she broke in. "Of my own husband?" She let out a little laugh that didn't convince Breckinridge at all. "Why would I be afraid of Richard? He loves me." She hurried on, "Please, sit down. I told the maid to bring us some tea. We'll have a nice visit, but then you'll have to go. Richard is at the store now, but he'll be home directly."

"He works in his father's store, does he?"

"He runs it now. The elder Mr. Aylesworth was struck down by apoplexy several months ago. He survived the attack, but he can't work anymore."

So Aylesworth had taken over his pa's store. That came as no surprise to Breckinridge. A lot of fellas went into the family business. Breck, however, wasn't one of them.

Breckinridge sat down on the divan again. Maureen sat, too, keeping a proper distance between them. Breck wished he could take her in his arms and give her a kiss, just one kiss, but he knew that would be wrong. He wouldn't be able to forget that she was carrying Aylesworth's baby, either.

"So tell me," Maureen said with that forced brightness again, "where have you been? What have you been doing while you were gone?"

Breckinridge condensed the tale even more for her than he had for his parents and brothers. He gave a brief account of how he had worked on a keelboat on the Mississippi, then joined a military surveying expedition out onto the prairie. He purposely didn't mention river pirates or Indians or bloody death.

"That sounds very exciting," Maureen said. "With all that going on, what brings you back to Knoxville?"

"I got a letter from my brother Edward. It said I wasn't, uh, wanted by the law anymore."

Maureen's face grew solemn as she nodded.

"Yes, that was all terribly unfortunate," she said. "Richard told me that you misunderstood the situation and were afraid you'd be blamed for the tragedy.

He tried to find you to let you know that you didn't need to leave, but he was too late."

In other words, thought Breckinridge, Aylesworth had spun a whole passel of bald-faced lies, and Maureen had swallowed each and every one of them.

Or maybe she just pretended to believe them. Maybe she was even pretending to herself. That might be easier than accepting the truth about the man she had married.

The maid brought cups of tea on a fancy silver tray. Breckinridge felt awkward as he held the dainty china cup in his big hand. He worried that he would crush it without meaning to, so he was careful as he sipped the tea.

"What made you decide to marry Richard?" he asked, then thought that the question was too blunt. It was too late to take it back, though.

"Why, he said that he loved me and proposed to me," she replied.

And that was all it took, Breckinridge thought bitterly.

"My father was opposed to the idea at first," she went on. "He said that I was too young to be married. But Richard swore his devotion to me, and that won Father over, I suppose. It was quite a fine wedding. I . . . I wish you could have been there, Breckinridge."

Somehow he doubted that she was being sincere. He knew good and well that *he* wouldn't have wanted to be there to see her united for life with a no-good scoundrel like Richard Aylesworth.

He looked down into the tea cup and said, "And now the two of you are startin' a family."

"Yes," Maureen said. When he glanced at her he saw that her face was pink and knew he shouldn't have brought up the subject. He'd embarrassed her. She went on, "I hope to have many children."

"Well, I hope you get what you want." He drained the cup and leaned forward to set it on a table. "I reckon I'd better be goin'—"

She surprised him by reaching toward him and resting her hand on his arm.

"Breckinridge," she said, "why did you really come to see me today? What have you heard?"

Her voice held a tone of urgency. She was upset about something again. He said, "Why, I just wanted to say howdy and find out how you're doin'. I'd like to think that we were friends."

She smiled again.

"We were. We *are* friends, Breckinridge."

"And I, uh, wanted a chance to say so long to you. I never got to tell you good-bye when I left before."

"Are you leaving again?" Suddenly she looked worried. "You haven't come home to stay?"

"No, I reckon not." He hadn't told his family yet, but he knew there was no doubt in his mind. He'd be going back to the frontier, probably before winter set in.

"Oh, I wish you would. I'd really like to see you every now and then. As long as . . . as long as you don't pay any attention to any crazy stories you might hear . . ."

There it was again, her worry about something he might have heard. Breckinridge was baffled about what she was referring to, but he didn't want to admit that.

"Well, I won't be leavin' right away," he said. "I think it might be a good idea if I didn't come back by, though—"

A heavy footstep on the porch interrupted the conversation. Maureen's head jerked sharply in that direction as her eyes widened.

"Richard . . . !" she breathed.

Breckinridge came to his feet as the front door opened and the footsteps continued into the foyer. They stopped short as Richard Aylesworth appeared in the entrance to the parlor, looking as dapper as ever. He stared at Breck, apparently as shocked as he would have been if he'd come into his home and found a grizzly bear sitting in the parlor sipping tea.

For a moment Aylesworth struggled to get any words out of his mouth. Then he said with utter venom, "Wallace!"

"That's right," Breckinridge said. "I've come home, Aylesworth . . . no thanks to you."

Aylesworth's surprised expression turned to one of anger as his gaze darted toward his wife. He said, "Maureen, what's this oaf doing here? How could you allow him into our home?"

Maureen's hands fluttered helplessly in front of her as she stood up and said, "Please, Richard, there's no need for an unpleasant scene. Breckinridge simply came by to say hello. He and I are old friends—"

"A man's wife has no need for male friends, old or otherwise," Aylesworth said coldly. He looked at Breckinridge again. "I'll thank you to get out, Wallace."

"I was just goin'," Breckinridge said. He took a step toward the door. If Aylesworth didn't get out of his way, he was prepared to walk right over the varmint.

Maureen reached out and clutched at his sleeve, stopping him.

"Breck, please—" she began.

"Let him go, darling," Aylesworth said, and despite the affectionate term, the words were as cold and flinty as if he'd been giving an order to a servant.

Breckinridge turned to look at Maureen. Her hand fell away from his arm and her eyes turned toward the floor. She murmured, "Of course, Richard," and stepped back so that she was standing with her legs against the divan.

"Good-bye, Mrs. Aylesworth," Breckinridge forced himself to say. "I hope you have a long, happy life."

Maureen flinched slightly, as if he had just slapped her instead of wishing her the best. Maybe that was really the way he'd meant it. Breckinridge didn't know.

Aylesworth stepped aside and came over to Maureen as Breckinridge stalked out. From the corner of his eye he saw her pull away from him slightly as he grasped her arm. He wasn't rough about it, though, so Breck didn't see any reason to stop.

She had made her own bed, as the old saying went. Her life was no longer any of his business, not by any stretch of the imagination.

Despite that, as he rode away a thought nagged at the back of his brain.

He wished he knew what she'd meant by that comment about things he might have heard.

Chapter Twenty-one

The patches of blue sky had gone away and the afternoon had turned blustery. By the time Breckinridge made it back to the farm, a cold rain was falling. As usual, he hadn't worn a hat, so his head was soaked when he came in. He didn't really feel any discomfort, though. His mind was still reeling from the encounter with Maureen and Aylesworth.

"Land's sake, you're as soaked as an old wet hen," Samantha Wallace exclaimed when she saw him. "Go on over by the fire and dry out for a while."

"Where are Pa and the boys?" Breckinridge asked as he did what his mother told him. He had to admit that he was a mite chilled. The warmth felt good as he stretched his hands out toward the flames dancing in the fireplace.

"They're in the barn," Samantha replied. "One of the cows is calving, and your pa said it might be a difficult birth. He expected they'd be out there all afternoon. I'm sure if you want to join them it would be all right. Put on a hat first, though, for goodness' sake."

Breckinridge had no desire to help with the calving.

He had done enough work like that in his life. Anyway, he had something else on his mind.

"Ma, what have you heard about the marriage of Richard and Maureen Aylesworth?"

Her lips pinched together as she turned to regard him. After a moment she said, "Your father told me you planned to go see that girl. That was a mistake, Breckinridge. You've no right to intrude on someone else's marriage."

"But what have you heard?" Breckinridge insisted. "Does he treat her badly?"

"What goes on behind the closed doors of a man's house is no business of anyone else."

"You don't really believe that."

She snorted and said, "Indeed I do! And I *don't* indulge in gossip."

"So there's something to gossip about," Breckinridge said.

His mother threw her hands up in exasperation.

"I'm glad you're back, son, but Lord, you'd pester a person to death! I'm telling you, forget about Maureen Grantham. You'll cause nothing but trouble if you insist on poking your nose in where you have no business."

Breckinridge saw the stubborn determination on her face and knew he wasn't going to find out anything from her. He nodded and said, "All right, Ma. I understand."

"Do you really, or are you just saying that to placate me?"

"I understand," Breckinridge said again, and as far as he was concerned, that was true.

He understood that something was wrong between Maureen and Aylesworth, and he couldn't just ride away and head back to the frontier without finding out if there was anything he could do to help her.

He let things lie for a few days while he pondered the best course of action. Although he had plenty of suspicions, he didn't actually *know* anything about what went on between Maureen and Aylesworth. He supposed it was possible he had read all the signs wrong, so he decided to find out more before he proceeded any further.

He went to the blacksmith shop in Knoxville to talk to Phineas Cobb, who shoed horses for just about everyone in town. Because of that, Cobb knew what was going on with most of them. He liked to talk, too, and he had a fierce streak of independence that made him unafraid to share what he knew.

Also, Breckinridge thought with a grin as he rode up to the blacksmith shop, Cobb was a natural-born busybody who could put most old women to shame when it came to gossiping.

"Breckinridge Wallace!" the blacksmith greeted him. Cobb was a short man, almost as broad as he was tall, with massively muscled arms from swinging a hammer. He was bald except for two tufts of white hair that stuck out above his ears. "I heard you was back in these parts. What can I do for you?"

"Horse needs a new shoe," Breckinridge said. That was true enough. When Breck's father had mentioned the problem, he had volunteered right away to take the animal into town and have the chore attended to, because he knew that getting information out of Cobb wouldn't take much effort.

"Well, let me take a look. You're lucky I can get right on this job. Not very busy this afternoon."

Cobb led the horse into the shop and started examining the animal's shoes, probably checking to see if he could justify replacing any of the others, Breckinridge mused.

"I wondered if you'd ever hear that it was safe for you to come back here," the blacksmith said as he worked. "Things looked mighty bad for you for a while there. Old Junius Carlson wanted your hide after you killed his boy."

"That was an accident," Breckinridge said. "I didn't like Jasper, but I wish it hadn't happened. Who was it broke down and told the law what really happened?"

"That was the Copeland boy, William," Cobb said as he pried off the shoe that needed to be replaced. "But then the rest of the bunch went along with him. Afraid of windin' up in jail for lyin' to the law, I reckon. All but Richard Aylesworth. He kept insistin' that you jumped them and started the whole thing. Way I heard it, his pa finally pulled him aside and ordered him to tell the truth. Richard did, but you could tell he didn't like it. He made out like it was all a mistake, a misunderstandin', that he never said what ever'body knew he really did."

"Everybody but his wife," Breckinridge said. "She must've believed him."

The blacksmith shot a glance at him and then nodded.

"She wasn't his wife then, but they got married not long after that. Yeah, Mrs. Aylesworth wants to believe him, I suppose, but I bet deep down she don't. She's bound to know by now what sort of polecat Richard Aylesworth really is, the way he treats her."

Cobb couldn't be cooperating any better, Breckinridge thought. He felt anger bubbling up inside him, but he tamped it down and said apparently casually, "Mistreats her, does he?"

Cobb's beefy shoulders rose and fell in a shrug as he said, "I wouldn't go so far as to say he beats her . . . but I wouldn't say he doesn't, either. 'Course, any woman's got to be kept in line by her husband if he's worth his salt, but hell, the Aylesworth boy's always had a habit of carryin' things too far, if you know what I mean."

Breckinridge knew. All too well, in fact.

"Reckon he probably treats her a mite more gentle now that she's expectin'," the garrulous blacksmith went on. "But that don't mean he's nice to her. Always talks to her real cold-like, he does, like he can't stand bein' around her. Can't see why any man'd feel like that. She's just as sweet and pretty as can be."

That was true, Breckinridge thought. Maureen was sweet and pretty . . . too sweet for her own good. Too sweet—and too scared—to stand up to Aylesworth.

But what he had heard here today had helped him make up his mind. He wanted to leave Tennessee and head back to the frontier, but he couldn't do that while Maureen was trapped in such a bad situation. He had sworn to himself that he wouldn't go back to her house, but he knew now he was going to have to break that vow. He had to offer her his help. If she wanted to get away from Aylesworth, he would help her do just that.

No matter how much trouble it caused.

* * *

He knew he might need to bide his time, but he didn't want to wait too long. Phineas Cobb seemed to think that Aylesworth wouldn't hurt Maureen because she was carrying his child, but Breckinridge didn't want to count on that. He had seen the way Aylesworth could fly into a rage and do crazy things. He wouldn't put anything past the man.

The next day, Breckinridge saddled one of the horses. His brother Henry saw him and wanted to know where he was going, but Breck dodged the question.

"Just goin' for a ride," he replied as casually as he could. "You know how restless I've always been."

"Yeah, I suppose so," Henry said. "How about if I come with you?" He looked around the barn to make sure their father wasn't within earshot, lowered his voice, and went on, "I could use a break from all these chores around here."

Breckinridge didn't want to hurt his brother's feelings, but he didn't need any company on this trip, either. He said, "I sort of got used to bein' alone while I was out yonder on the frontier, Henry. Maybe another time."

"All right," Henry said stiffly. "Sure, if that's the way you feel."

He walked off, and Breckinridge wanted to call him back and explain. But he knew he couldn't, not really. Nobody in his family would understand why he had to do this thing. They never had grasped exactly how he felt about Maureen.

Before Henry had a chance to tell anybody else that Breckinridge was going anywhere, Breck swung up into the saddle and galloped away from the farm. He thought he heard a couple of shouts behind him, but he didn't look back. He couldn't allow himself to be distracted from his purpose. He didn't want anything to weaken his resolve.

When he reached Knoxville, the first thing he did was to ride past the huge Aylesworth general store. It was busy, with several wagons pulled up at the store's front porch, which also served as its loading dock. Aproned clerks, along with customers, loaded supplies into the backs of those wagons. Breckinridge didn't see Richard Aylesworth, but since Aylesworth ran the store these days it was more likely he was inside.

Breckinridge rode on to Maureen's house. The same maid answered his knock. Her eyes widened, and for a second he thought she was going to close the door in his face. But then she gave him a sullen look and said, "I don't reckon Miz Maureen wants to see you, mister."

"Why don't you ask her that?" Breckinridge said.

"She don' need no big ol' fella like you comin' 'round here and makin' trouble. She a married woman. She don' need to be havin' no truck with some fella who ain't her husban'."

For all her fiery nature, the maid was a little bit of a thing, and Breckinridge was about to warn her that he would pick her up and set her aside if he had to, when Maureen's familiar voice asked from behind her, "Who is that at the door, Ophelia?"

The maid scowled at Breckinridge, then turned her head to say, "It ain't nobody, Miz Maureen, jus' some tramp—"

Maureen moved up alongside the woman, and

her face lit up with a smile as she said, "Breckinridge, it's you again." He could tell that reaction was her natural one, but it was quickly replaced as her smile vanished and she said, "I'm not sure you should be here . . ."

"That's what I been tellin' him, Miz Maureen," the maid insisted. "Or tryin' to, anyway."

"You never were very good at listening when you didn't want to hear, were you, Breckinridge?" Maureen said to him.

"I just want to talk to you for a minute," he said. "Once I've spoken my piece, if you want me to leave, I'll go without makin' any fuss about it, Maureen. You got my word on that."

For a long moment, Maureen hesitated. Her teeth caught her bottom lip between them for a second as she thought. Then she said, "All right, but I'm going to hold you to that, Breckinridge. Let him in, Ophelia."

The maid *ha-rumphed* to make it clear how she felt about Maureen's decision. But she stepped aside and let Breckinridge walk into the foyer.

"We'll be in the parlor, as before," Maureen went on.

"You want tea again?" Ophelia asked.

Maureen shook her head and said, "No, not this time. Mr. Wallace won't be here that long."

Breckinridge wasn't sure he liked the sound of that. But at least Maureen was willing to listen to him. She was going to give him a chance to win her over, to convince her that if she was truly afraid of Richard Aylesworth, she would be better off leaving him. Sure, there would be a terrible scandal, but that was better than staying with a scoundrel like Aylesworth.

Maureen led him into the parlor. She motioned for

Breckinridge to sit down on the divan, but she stayed on her feet this time instead of taking a seat next to him.

"What is it you want from me, Breckinridge?" she asked. "You know that there is really . . . nothing . . . I can give you."

"I don't want anything except to help you," he said.

"And how do you propose to do that? I have everything I could possibly need."

"How about a husband who loves you and treats you decent?"

She paled as she stared at him. Even with him sitting and her standing, their heads were almost on the same level.

"I told you not to believe any ridiculous gossip you might hear about me," she said. "Richard is madly in love with me and treats me like a princess."

"That's what you want everybody to believe."

"It's the truth!"

Breckinridge shook his head and said, "Everybody in Knoxville knows what sort of man Richard Aylesworth really is. He lied about what happened during that fight. He was a lot more responsible for Jasper Carlson dyin' than I was. I was just defendin' myself, but Jasper wouldn't have even been there if it wasn't for Richard. He lied to the law, whether you want to admit it or not."

Maureen's chin quivered a little as she said, "You're wrong. The whole thing was a tragic misunderstanding. An accident—"

"Richard and his friends figured on beatin' me within an inch of my life. Actually, I reckon Richard planned on killin' me—all because I'd had the audacity to come callin' on you. He had his sights set on you, and nobody was supposed to interfere with that."

Breckinridge sighed. "Well, it looks like he got you. But that don't mean he gets to keep you, not if you don't want to be here."

"But don't you see, I *do*. I do want to be here. Richard isn't . . . perfect. No man is. But I chose to marry him, and I'll not go back on my word."

"Your pride's more important to you than your life?" Breckinridge nodded toward her belly. "More important than your baby's life?"

"How dare you!" Maureen was trembling all over now. "Breck, you have no right . . . you can't just come charging in here like a bull and turn my life upside down . . . I have to honor my vows . . . I have to—"

She stopped short, moved closer to him, and without any more warning than that she threw her arms around his neck. Instinctively, Breckinridge came to his feet and bent his head to hers. His mouth found her lips and he drew her against him, cradling her gently against his massive bulk.

Breckinridge was so lost in the sensations washing through him that he barely heard the rapid footsteps in the foyer and the low-pitched cry of warning from Ophelia, the maid.

"Miz Maureen! Miz Maureen! It's Mist' Aylesworth, Miz Maureen! He—"

Breckinridge lifted his head and turned toward the door. He still had his hands on Maureen's shoulders as Richard Aylesworth charged through the foyer and into the parlor with a pistol clutched in his hand. He screamed filthy obscenities at Breck as he thrust the gun out. Breck pushed Maureen behind him, shielding her with his own body as smoke and flame gushed from the weapon's barrel.

Chapter Twenty-two

Breckinridge felt the impact of the pistol ball as it scraped along his side. The burning pain twisted him around. He caught his balance and charged toward Aylesworth, not giving him time to reload. Aylesworth slashed at Breck's head with the empty weapon, but Breck blocked the blow with a sweep of his left forearm that sent the pistol flying.

An instant later, his right fist crashed into Aylesworth's face and drove the other man backward into the foyer. Aylesworth couldn't keep his feet. He fell against a delicately made table on the other side of the entrance. It splintered under him, and he landed on the floor amidst the debris.

Breckinridge bellowed in rage as he charged into the foyer. He bent over, grabbed the lapels of Aylesworth's coat, and jerked him to his feet again. Breck pulled his fist back. Aylesworth had been begging for a good whipping for a long time, and Breck was just the fella to give it to him.

That blow never landed. Breckinridge froze at the sound of a scream.

He jerked his head around and saw the maid standing in the arched entrance of the parlor. The woman had her hands clapped to her cheeks as she stared in horror at Maureen, who lay crumpled on the floor. Breckinridge's heart felt like it was going to burst out of his chest when he saw the blood on her dress.

Instantly, he knew what had happened. The shot Aylesworth had fired had passed between Breck's arm and side, grazing him in the process but not stopping until it struck Maureen behind him.

He let go of Aylesworth, who was still stunned and dropped limply to the floor when Breckinridge released him. Wheeling around, Breck lunged past the maid into the parlor. He dropped to a knee beside Maureen and grasped her shoulders as gently as he could.

Her eyes were open. The lids fluttered wildly as she stared up at him. She said raggedly, "B-Breck . . . what . . . what happened?"

"You've been shot," he told her. "Just be still and I'll see how bad it is."

"My . . . my baby!"

"Shhh."

He had seen how Harry had dealt with gunshot wounds back on the *Sophie*. He opened Maureen's dress and moved aside her undergarments to reveal the puckered hole high in her midsection. There was a lot of blood, but he tried not to think about that right now. It was impossible to tell how deeply the ball had penetrated without feeling for it, so he gathered up his courage and stuck a finger into the wound.

Maureen cried out in pain and arched her back.

"What are you *doin'* to her?" the maid screeched.

Breckinridge didn't look around or explain. All of

his attention was focused on Maureen, and he kept it that way. He probed deeper and felt a surge of relief as his fingertip touched the lead ball. It hadn't gone very deep, only a couple of inches. Maureen whimpered in agony as he tried to work his finger around under the ball. He kept his other hand clamped on her shoulder to hold her still as he murmured, "I've got it, darlin', I've got it. Just a minute or two more . . ."

The ball moved. Carefully, Breckinridge worked it up toward the surface. A moment later, the bloody bit of lead popped free of the wound.

"There you go," Breckinridge said with a grin. "It's out now—"

Something crashed against his back with enough force to knock him forward. He barely got a hand on the floor in time to catch himself and keep his weight from coming down on Maureen.

"You son of a bitch!" Richard Aylesworth howled like a rabid wolf.

Breckinridge levered himself up, twisting to his feet as Aylesworth swung a leg of the chair he had just broken over Breck's back. Breck couldn't get completely out of the way. He took the blow on his left shoulder and felt pain shoot all the way down that arm.

His right hand flashed out and clamped around Aylesworth's throat. He swung Aylesworth toward the divan and let go of him. Out of control, Aylesworth landed on the piece of furniture and drove it against the wall. The impact made a picture hanging there leap off its nail and clatter to the floor.

"Get a cloth against that wound and stop the bleedin'," Breckinridge snapped at the maid. She seemed too horrified at first to comprehend what he was saying, but when he added, "*Now!*" she leaped to follow the order.

Aylesworth struggled up and charged Breckinridge again. Either he didn't know that his wife was hurt, or he just didn't care and was more interested in indulging his own fury. He threw a flurry of punches so swiftly that Breck couldn't block all of them. A couple of the blows landed, one on his jaw and one on his chest, but neither of them really rocked him. Aylesworth was too caught up in his crazy rage to put much power behind the punches.

Breckinridge weaved aside from a wild, looping right and landed a left jab of his own on the man's nose. Blood spurted hotly across Breck's knuckles as Aylesworth's nose flattened under the blow. Aylesworth reeled back, and Breck lifted a powerful right uppercut to his jaw.

That punch knocked Aylesworth off his feet again. He landed on his back, arms and legs outflung, and didn't move. He'd been knocked cold.

Breckinridge swung around to check on Maureen. Driven by fear for her, his pulse thundered inside his head. He saw Ophelia on her knees beside Maureen, holding a thick pad of cloth to the wounded girl's body.

"I don' think it's bleedin' as bad now, Mist' Wallace," the maid said, "but Miz Maureen, she gon' need a doctor mighty quick-like!"

"I'll go fetch one—" Breckinridge started to say as he took a step toward the door, but he stopped as a man hurried into the foyer, followed by several others.

Breckinridge recognized Parley Johnson, the sheriff. The men with him were some of his deputies.

Johnson was a stocky man with a thick gray mustache. His eyes, set deep in pits of gristle, took in the scene quickly. Breck didn't know what conclusions the sheriff drew, but they couldn't be good ones.

Johnson took a pistol from behind his belt, cocked it as he pointed it at Breckinridge, and barked, "Don't move, Wallace! When I got word of a shot being fired here, I should have known it was you. By God, what deviltry have you gotten up to now?" He answered his own question by exclaiming, "You've killed the Aylesworths!"

"Richard ain't dead," Breckinridge snapped. "I just had to knock him out because he was tryin' to kill me!" He waved a hand at Maureen and went on, "One of you men better fetch the doctor mighty quick. Maureen's been shot!"

"And I'll bet you're the one who shot her!" Johnson said. "You've always been a troublemaker, Wallace. You're under arrest until I find out what happened here."

"Damn it!" Breckinridge exploded. "I don't care what you do to me, just get some help for Maureen!"

The sheriff ignored that, turned to his deputies, and ordered, "You men take Wallace into custody."

The deputies looked pretty reluctant to follow that order, but they shuffled forward. In exasperation, Breckinridge said, "I surrender! You don't have to arrest me, Sheriff. I'll come along peacefully—as soon as you get the doctor for Miz Aylesworth!"

Johnson glared at him but said to one of the deputies, "Tim, go get the sawbones. Be quick about it, too!"

As the man rushed out of the house, Aylesworth

groaned and started struggling to sit up. He had regained consciousness but clearly didn't have his wits about him yet.

Johnson pointed a finger at Breckinridge and said, "Don't you move." Then he went over to help Aylesworth stand up.

Aylesworth clutched at the sheriff's arms as he climbed to his feet. He shook his head groggily, but then his entire body stiffened as he focused his gaze on Breckinridge.

"There he is, Sheriff!" Aylesworth gasped. "For God's sake, don't let him get away. He shot my wife!"

"I knew it," Johnson growled. "You deputies block the door!"

Breckinridge stood there, flat-footed and flabbergasted. He couldn't believe Aylesworth had just accused him of shooting Maureen.

And yet, that was exactly what he should have expected to happen, a little voice in the back of his head told him. Richard Aylesworth hated him beyond any reason. Maureen might be dying at this very moment, but Aylesworth was more concerned with seizing another opportunity to lie about Breckinridge.

A little moan from Maureen jerked Breckinridge's attention away from his own plight. Her eyes moved, looking around the room as if she were just realizing that it was full of people. She whispered, "R-Richard . . ."

The fact that she had called for Aylesworth was like a dagger in Breckinridge's heart, but again, he should have expected that, he told himself. Aylesworth was her husband, after all. The father of her child. A bitter, sour taste filled Breck's mouth. It was the taste of defeat. He had never stood a chance to convincing Maureen to leave Aylesworth. He knew that now.

But at least she could tell the sheriff that it had been Aylesworth who fired the shot, not him. He felt bad for thinking about his own plight at this moment, when she lay there injured, in danger of losing her child or even dying.

"Miz Maureen, you jus' lay still," Ophelia said. "You done lost a heap o' blood. You got to rest—"

"Richard," Maureen said again.

Aylesworth was steady on his feet now. He hurried across the room and knelt at her side. He took hold of her right hand in both of his.

"I'm here, darling," he said. "Hold on. The doctor is on his way." He looked around. "The sheriff is here, Maureen. You need to tell him how Wallace shot you when he was trying to kill me."

Breckinridge began, "That's a damned—"

The sheriff pointed the pistol at his face and said, "You shut up."

"Tell the sheriff," Aylesworth urged.

"I . . . I don't know," Maureen said in a weak voice. "It was all so . . . insane. It all happened . . . so fast . . . But you're right . . . Richard . . . you must be . . ."

Breckinridge's blood seemed to turn to ice in his veins. She was going along with Aylesworth's bald-faced lie! Again, he knew he shouldn't be surprised. She was so firmly under her husband's thumb she would agree with anything he said, no matter how much Breck wished it were otherwise.

He looked at Ophelia, wondering if she would speak up and reveal the truth. She had been in the foyer when Aylesworth burst in and took that shot at Breck. She had seen what happened.

But the maid's eyes met his, and her head went back and forth in the tiniest of shakes. She wasn't going to dispute the word of a man who held the power of life and death over her.

"I reckon if Miz Aylesworth or that baby dies, you'll hang for sure this time, Wallace," the sheriff said.

Breckinridge's heart slugged heavily in his chest. Once again life had taken one of those sudden lurches and yanked the world right out from under him.

Only this time it might be the trap door of a gallows falling out from under him, he thought.

"I know you gave me your word," Johnson went on, "but I'd feel better if your hands were tied—"

Breckinridge wasn't going to let that happen. If he went along meekly with the sheriff, he was doomed. He knew it, and he knew what he had to do next. Three deputies stood between him and the door. Normally he wouldn't worry about being able to plow right through three men.

But a couple of them had taken out pistols, and the sheriff was armed, too. If he made a move toward the door, they would shoot him down.

When he exploded into action, it was in another direction. He whirled around and one long stride brought him to the parlor's front window. The sheriff yelled, "Stop him!" and one of the pistols boomed. Breckinridge lowered his head and twisted so that he hit the window with his shoulder. The glass shattered and flew outward around him.

Two more shots roared, one after the other, but none of them found their target. At least, he didn't feel any of the balls strike him as he tumbled through the broken window onto the porch. Broken glass stung him, but he was able to ignore that as he rolled over and surged to his feet. As he leaped off the porch he saw the other deputy coming back into the yard with the doctor, and the part of his brain that wasn't frantic with the need to escape was glad of that. Now Maureen would get the help she needed. Maybe both she and the baby could be saved.

"Get him, damn it!" the sheriff bellowed from the window.

The deputy tried to get in Breckinridge's way, but Breck picked him up and threw him aside like a rag doll. He didn't bother with the gate. He vaulted over the fence and grabbed the reins of the horse he had ridden into town. One of the lawmen must have gotten his pistol reloaded, because another shot sounded as Breck swung up into the saddle.

Again the ball went wild. Breckinridge hauled the horse around and jabbed his heels into its flanks. The animal leaped forward into a gallop. Breck headed for the edge of town and the road that led to his family's farm.

Once again he was on the run from the law, and once again it was completely unjustified. He was getting damned sick and tired of that feeling.

He kept the horse at a gallop all the way to the farm. By the time they got there the animal was about done in. Breckinridge knew he would have to have a different mount. He hoped he could hang on to this one instead of losing it like Hector.

Sammy and Max set up a commotion as he approached, and that brought his father out of the barn and his mother out of the house. Breckinridge didn't see any of his brothers and took that to mean they were all working in the fields, getting a cover crop down for the coming winter.

Unless they came in quickly, he wouldn't have a chance to say good-bye to them. He regretted that, but it couldn't be helped. By now the sheriff would have organized a posse, and he'd be on his way out here to clap Breckinridge in irons and drag him back to jail.

"Good Lord, son, you're about to run that poor horse to death!" Robert said as Breckinridge reined in. "What's wrong?"

"The law's after me," Breckinridge said as he dismounted and started uncinching the saddle so he could throw it on another horse.

Samantha had come close enough to hear. She said, "Saints preserve us, what have you done now?"

Breckinridge felt a flash of anger. He could tell that both his parents assumed he was to blame for whatever trouble he had found. Seemed like they could give their own flesh and blood the benefit of the doubt just this once.

There wasn't time to worry about that, though. As he carried the saddle and blanket into the barn, he said over his shoulder, "Richard Aylesworth shot his wife."

"Merciful heavens!" Samantha said. "Is . . . is she . . . ?"

"She's alive, and I think she'll be all right. I ain't so sure about the baby she's carryin'."

"That poor girl."

Robert asked, "What's this got to do with you?"

"Aylesworth told the sheriff I was the one who did the shootin'. I said that was a bald-faced lie, but Maureen . . ." The words Breckinridge were about to say threatened to choke him, but he forced them out. "Maureen backed up his story. Even after what he did, she wouldn't turn against him. So the sheriff thinks I busted into their house, beat on Aylesworth, and tried to shoot him but hit Maureen instead."

"There's no one who can tell Sheriff Johnson the truth?"

Breckinridge thought about the maid Ophelia, then shook his head.

"Not this time, Pa. Not unless Maureen goes back on what she said. And I don't reckon I'll be gettin' lucky like that a second time."

Samantha moaned and hugged herself. A chilly wind blew through the barn, but Breckinridge didn't think the breeze was what caused his mother's reaction.

"It's not right," she said. "You shouldn't have to run for your life a second time. It's just not fair."

"Life don't seem to care about fair," Breckinridge said. "If it did, a lot more people would get what was comin' to them."

He didn't know if he was talking about Richard Aylesworth . . . or himself. It didn't really matter, he supposed.

"So you're leaving," his father said.

"I got to, Pa. The sheriff will be on his way with a posse."

Breckinridge's mother said, "I need to get you some food. Wait here."

"Make it fast, Ma. As soon as I get another horse saddled, I need to get out of here."

Samantha hurried toward the house while Robert said, "Take that big bay. He's a good sturdy mount. Not as good as Hector was, but . . ."

"I'll do my best to hang on to him," Breckinridge promised.

He would do that by never trusting anyone again,

the way he had trusted Sadie Humboldt and Jack MacKenzie.

"Which direction are you going?"

"I want to head back to the frontier, but I can't go west. That'd take me right into the posse. Reckon I'll head east this time, into the Blue Ridge. I know those hills pretty darn good. I think I can give the sheriff the slip, then swing around either north or south and work my way back west."

"Do you think you'll be able to come home again later, like you did this time?"

Breckinridge sighed and shook his head.

"I wouldn't count on it, Pa. Most fellas only get one miracle in their lives."

"You didn't even get to see Edward again," Robert said despairingly.

"I know. Maybe I'll run into him somewhere along the way while I'm headin' back to the frontier. If I don't . . . well, forever's a long time, Pa. No point in wastin' too much time thinkin' about what might or might not happen, because we just don't know."

"You're right, we don't," Robert agreed in a voice choked with emotion. He grasped his son's arm, then pulled him close and slapped him on the back as they roughly embraced. "Take care of yourself. Never forget that we love you."

"I won't, Pa. I give you my word on that."

Breckinridge's mother came hurrying back with a sack of food. Breck tied it to the saddle on the big bay horse his father had told him to take.

"Tell your mother good-bye while I fetch your guns," Robert said.

Breckinridge hugged Samantha. She said, "I can't

believe I'm telling you good-bye again. I thought you'd be around from now on."

That wouldn't have happened even without the tragic incident at the Aylesworth house, Breckinridge thought, but he didn't see any point in telling his mother that. Instead he hugged her and said, "I'll be all right, Ma. You know I can take care of myself."

"Maybe the best of all of us," she agreed. "But that won't stop me from worrying about you."

"I know. Reckon that's the way it's meant to be with parents and young'uns."

"I hope you get to find out for yourself someday. I hope you'll have a fine family."

Breckinridge sort of doubted that. He had been able to imagine himself married to Maureen and raising a whole passel of kids, but since that would never happen now, he figured it was unlikely he would ever find anybody else he'd want to settle down with. He would always carry that lost dream inside him.

Robert came back with Breckinridge's rifle, pistols, and knife, along with a full shot pouch and a couple of powder horns.

"You'll be armed for bear, or whatever else you might run into," he said as he handed over the weapons to his son.

"Thanks, Pa." Breckinridge hugged both his parents again, then put his foot in the stirrup and stepped up into the saddle. He turned the bay and lifted a hand to wave farewell. "Say so long to the boys!"

Before he could do anything else, he heard a swift rataplan of hoofbeats. A glance at the road showed him a group of at least half a dozen mounted men racing toward the farm. They were still several hundred yards away, so he lifted the reins and jammed his heels into the bay's flanks. The horse leaped into motion. Breckinridge's wave to his parents was a hasty one as he galloped away from the barn.

He didn't follow any road or trail as he departed. Instead he took off across country, racing through fields, jumping the bay over rock fences, weaving around clumps of trees. He thought he heard some shots behind him, but he couldn't be sure about that. If the members of the posse were shooting at him, they didn't hit him, and that was the only important thing.

The terrain began to slope upward into the foothills of the Blue Ridge Mountains. Breckinridge knew every foot of those hills. He was counting on that knowledge to help him escape. Also, it was only a couple of hours until dark, and he was certain that if he could elude the pursuit until night fell, they would never catch him.

Anyway, he didn't have much choice except to get away, he told himself.

There was nothing waiting for him back in Knoxville except a hangman's rope. No hope, no reversal of fortune, no miracle this time.

Only death.

A month later, Breckinridge led the bay onto a ferry. An early snowfall covered both banks of the Mississippi River, and an icy wind blew from the north. Breck wore a blanket capote over his buckskins and had a cap made from the skin of a raccoon on his head. He had never cared for hats, but when a cold wind blew, like today, the coonskin cap felt good. He had made it himself from an animal he shot during the westward journey.

The posse had clung stubbornly to his trail for a while, but Breckinridge got away from them just as he expected to. His natural skill in the woods gave him an advantage over the townsmen the sheriff had brought with him. Once he had circled wide around Knoxville and headed west, he was confident no one was after him.

He had taken a few odd jobs along the way— blacksmithing, unloading freight, splitting wood— and between the money he earned and the game he was able to shoot he hadn't gone hungry or wanting for other supplies. He hadn't socialized much with people, which was hard given his friendly nature, but he didn't want to get taken in the way he had been before.

Now he had reached the Mississippi at last, and he looked across the dark, grayish-blue surface of the river at St. Louis sprawled on the opposite shore. He would have preferred setting out for the mountains right away, as soon as he had procured some more supplies, but winter was the wrong time of year. He would run the risk of getting caught out in the open by a blizzard and freezing to death. Like it or not, the smartest thing to do would be to wait for spring.

St. Louis was a big town. He intended to lie low and not draw attention to himself . . . as much as that was possible with his size and his red hair.

Unlike the primitive, mule-drawn ferry at Cooter's Landing, this one had a steam engine, and when enough passengers had boarded, some on horseback and others in buggies and wagons, the vessel chugged across the river and came to a stop next to a wharf supported on thick pilings. Men waiting on the dock lowered a broad gangplank into place for the passengers to disembark.

Breckinridge led the bay off the ferry and looked around. He wasn't far from the Black Ship, he realized. Maybe he would pay a visit to Red Mike's place. He might see some familiar faces if he did, he thought.

For now, though, he was just glad to be west of the Mississippi River again. He knew he would miss his family, but he vowed that he would never set foot east of the mighty river again.

There was too much civilization over there.

And civilization was just too damned much trouble.

BOOK SIX

Chapter Twenty-three

Breckinridge groaned and rolled over. He bumped against something soft and warm. The girl called Sierra groaned, too. Like Breck, she had had too much to drink the night before. Under normal circumstances, he would have reached out to caress that inviting flesh, she would have responded, and they would have had themselves a fine old time.

Now their headaches were too bad to do anything except lie there and hope that the room would stop spinning soon. At least Breckinridge assumed that was the way Sierra was feeling. It sure described his own current state.

Finally the call of nature became too urgent to ignore, so Breckinridge was forced to get up and dig the chamber pot from under the bed. When he managed to accomplish his business without falling down, he decided he might as well go over to the window and get a little fresh air. That might help clear his head even more.

He swept the threadbare curtain aside and pushed

up the windowpane, ignoring the fact that he was naked as a jaybird. Sierra's room, where he'd been staying for the past few weeks, was on the second floor of the less-than-respectable boardinghouse, so it wasn't like there were any passersby right outside the window. As for anybody who might be across the street, Breckinridge didn't give a damn.

Then, as sometimes happened at the most inopportune moments, he recalled that he hadn't been raised to be such a degenerate. His current circumstances—hungover and living with a soiled dove—would have appalled his mother. Even his pa, who wasn't as stiff necked as the woman he'd married, probably would have been disappointed in him, Breckinridge thought. Scowling, he turned away from the window, grabbed the bottom half of a pair of long underwear from the back of the chair where he had thrown them the night before, and pulled them on.

Then he returned to the window to drag in some more air. It was chilly, but nothing like the frigid winter just past. Spring had come to St. Louis.

Soon it would be time to go.

That thought did more than anything else to drive the cobwebs out of Breckinridge's brain.

He left the window open but pulled the curtain back across it. He needed only a few minutes to get dressed. When he had pulled on the high-topped moccasins, he stepped over to the bed and slapped the enticing curve of Sierra's rump through the sheet.

"Hey, get up," he told her. "I want to go get something to eat."

She let out a pitiful moan and buried her head with its wild mass of curly black hair deeper in the pillow.

"Eat?" she repeated in a trembling voice. "How can you even think about eating *now?*"

"I was feelin' a mite puny when I woke up, but some fresh air took care of it."

"We don't all have your iron constitution, Breckinridge. I'm not crawling out of this bed until the sun has gone down."

With her Mexican accent, when she said his name it came out *Breckinreedge.* Her father had come from down there below the border, she had explained one night. He had shipped out from Vera Cruz, wound up in New Orleans, worked his way north to St. Louis, and married a half-Cherokee whore. Sierra was the result of that union, so named because her pa missed the mountains of Mexico where he was born and raised. The mixture of blood had produced a honey-skinned beauty who had followed her mother into the world's oldest profession.

Breckinridge had met her at the Black Ship and the two of them were drawn to each other at first sight. Within a week they were living together. Sierra couldn't replace Maureen in Breckinridge's affections, of course—she certainly wasn't the sort of gal he could ever dream of marrying—but they had a mighty good time together and she probably didn't take whatever was between them any more seriously than he did.

Soon he would be leaving, though, and they would have to say good-bye. As much as Breckinridge was looking forward to heading for the mountains, he had to admit he was going to be sad to bid farewell to Sierra.

"Suit yourself," he told her. "After I get something to eat, I have to go meet Tom. He said he'd introduce me to Colonel Baxter today."

"Good luck," she said, her voice muffled by the pillow.

Breckinridge tucked his pistols behind the broad belt he wore, settled the coonskin cap on his head, and left the boardinghouse, saying howdy to the landlady as she did the same. She had run a brothel in the past, Sierra had explained to Breck, but decided to go into a slightly less scandalous enterprise. She rented rooms to soiled doves, but they didn't conduct business here.

A stack of flapjacks and three cups of coffee at a nearby hash house made him feel almost human again. When he left the café, he judged by the sky that it was the middle of the afternoon. Tom Lang and Colonel Baxter might already be at Red Mike's place. Breckinridge hoped he hadn't kept them waiting too long.

He'd been very pleased but not all that surprised when he ran into Tom Lang at the Black Ship a while back. The old scout was wintering in St. Louis, too, before heading out again. Tom didn't have any firm plans for the spring, but he had promised that if he ran across anything good, he would let Breckinridge know.

Tom honored that pledge a few days earlier. Over buckets of beer, he had explained, "This fella Baxter, he fancies himself a colonel. I don't know if it's a real rank or just one he gave himself, but the important thing is, he's got money to pay for outfittin' a group of trappers to go up the Missouri."

"I thought most trappers worked on their own," Breckinridge had said.

"That's the way it used to be," Tom Lang agreed. "Either that or they worked for the American Fur Company. But the company ain't as big and powerful as it used to be, and the market for pelts ain't as strong, neither."

Breckinridge recalled John Francis Mallory telling him the same thing. That hadn't stopped the young lieutenant from wanting to become a trapper and explore the Rocky Mountains himself, a dream that had been wiped out by an Osage lance.

"Fellas have taken to bandin' together into their own little fur-trappin' companies," Tom went on. "Somebody like Colonel Baxter puts up the money and gets a share, and everybody else does, too. That means you might not make as much, but you don't run the risk of windin' up flat broke."

"I'd sort of figured on goin' out to the mountains by myself," Breckinridge had said with a frown.

"Won't nobody stop you from doin' that . . . but the redskins are gettin' more touchy all the time. Startin' out, some of the tribes was friendly to the white man. They figured there was plenty of room for ever'body and that a few white men wouldn't fill things up too bad. But now they've watched the wagon trains and the army and seen how the white men just keep comin' and comin' and comin' . . . and they've figured out that if things keep goin' like that, sooner or later they're gonna be crowded out. So even the Injuns that used to be friendly are lookin' to take a fella's hair now if they get the chance. We saw that last year with them damned Osage."

"So you're sayin' it'd be a lot safer if I joined this Colonel Baxter's party," Breckinridge said.

Tom's shoulders rose and fell in a shrug.

"I'm sayin' you do what you want to," he told Breckinridge. "But word is, the colonel's lookin' for a scout, and I intend to sign on for that job if he'll have me."

Breckinridge had pondered long and hard after that conversation, and finally he came to the decision that what Tom Lang said made a lot of sense. Besides, even if he went west with Baxter's group, he could always split off on his own if he couldn't get along with the others.

Now as he went into Red Mike's, he immediately spotted Tom's white beard and hair at a large round table in one of the rear corners. Two men sat with the old scout. Both of them were well dressed, especially compared to the rough trappers' and rivermen's garb worn by most of the tavern's patrons. One had hair and side whiskers as white as Tom's. The other stranger was younger, with tightly curled brown hair and a slightly rounded face.

Tom lifted a hand in greeting and said, "There he is," to the other two men. As Breckinridge came up to the table, he went on, "We were gettin' worried about you, Breck."

"Sorry. I'm runnin' a little behind today." Breckinridge pulled out one of the empty chairs and sat down.

"Punctuality is an important quality," the younger of the two strangers said.

"I reckon that's right," Breckinridge said, "but from what I've heard there ain't no clocks in the mountains."

The man's mouth tightened. Before he could respond, Tom leaned forward and said, "Colonel, this here is Breckinridge Wallace, the fella I told you about. As fine a fightin' man as you'll find west of that big river out there."

"Based on the sheer size of him, I don't doubt it." The well-dressed white-haired man extended his hand across the table to Breckinridge. "I'm Colonel Benjamin Baxter, Mr. Wallace. This is my son Morgan."

Breckinridge shook hands with the man and said, "Pleased to meet you, Colonel." The younger man hadn't made any move to put his hand out, so Breck just nodded to him and added, "Morgan."

"That's Mr. Baxter to you," Morgan snapped.

"Sure," Breckinridge said easily. "I was brought up to respect my elders."

Morgan Baxter flushed. He was older than Breckinridge, certainly, probably in his mid-twenties. But they could have passed for roughly the same age, Breck knew.

The colonel said, "I'm sure Tom has told you about our joint venture, Mr. Wallace."

"Call me Breckinridge. Mr. Wallace will always be my pa. And yeah, Tom said you were outfittin' a bunch to go to the mountains and do some trappin'."

"Exactly. I'm convinced that this depression in the market for furs is only temporary, but it's been enough to weaken the stranglehold that the American Fur Company has had on the industry. When the market comes roaring back as it's bound to do, I intend to be in a position to capture the lion's share of it."

"That's ambitious," Breckinridge said, nodding slowly.

"Of course, as with any enterprise we're going to have to start small and grow steadily. Hence this inaugural expedition up the Missouri."

Breckinridge thought he understood what Baxter was saying. He kept nodding as if he did, anyway. Truthfully, business didn't interest him in the slightest. To him it was all just a bunch of squinty-eyed gents bending over ledgers in a dim, airless room. Hell, in other words.

"You understand that we're going to be working on a basis of shares?" Baxter asked.

"Yes, sir. Tom told me about it."

"And that's agreeable to you?"

Breckinridge hesitated. He was committing himself to something here, at least for a while. But everything about it made sense as far as he could tell, so he nodded and said, "Yes, sir, it is."

"Splendid! I'm glad to hear that you're going to be one of us."

Breckinridge frowned slightly and said, "When you say 'one of us,' you mean the bunch that you'll be sendin' to the Rockies."

"I mean the group that I'll be *leading* to the Rockies," Baxter said with a smile. "Such an expedition needs an experienced commander."

"I thought that Tom—"

"Mr. Lang is our scout," Baxter said. "But I'll be in charge, just as I was during my military career."

Breckinridge looked at Tom. The old-timer seemed a little uncomfortable. He didn't meet Breck's eyes. Breck figured Tom had known about this and had chosen not to say anything.

"So you're comin' along, Colonel?" Breckinridge asked.

"Of course I am," Baxter answered. "I'm in the habit of keeping a close eye on my investments, and as I said, I'm an experienced commander."

"I'm coming along, too," Morgan added.

Breckinridge liked the sound of that even less. He didn't know where and when Colonel Baxter had served in the army, but he looked soft now, as did his son. Neither of them seemed like the sort of fella who would handle the hardships of the frontier particularly well.

Baxter had put his finger on an important point, though. It was his money funding this trip, so Breckinridge supposed he had the right to do whatever he wanted. Breck had continued to do odd jobs over the winter and had saved up enough to purchase some supplies, but if he started to the mountains alone he would be setting out with the bare minimum he needed and no margin for error. By signing on with Baxter at least he was assured of being better supplied.

"Do you have a problem with this arrangement, Mr. Wallace?" the colonel asked, and now there was a slightly chilly note in his voice.

"No, sir," Breckinridge answered right away with a shake of his head. "You're the boss."

"He's the colonel," Morgan said, "and I'm his lieutenant."

The message behind those words was clear to Breckinridge. *You'll follow my orders, too,* Morgan was saying. Breck was more reluctant to go along with that, but he managed to nod again.

"Very well," Baxter said, brisk now that the business had been concluded. "We'll be leaving from the docks in three days, weather permitting. You'll have to make your mark on an enlistment paper before we go."

"I can write my name," Breckinridge said. "I've had some schoolin', and my ma taught me even more."

"That's good. An education is always a good thing, even in the wilderness."

"This enlistment business . . . that ain't like signin' up to be in the army, is it?"

"Not exactly. It just sets out the scope of our agreement."

Breckinridge nodded. As long as the paper didn't say he was bound to stay with them whether he wanted to or not, he was all right with that.

Anyway, even if it did, he didn't see how they could enforce it, hundreds of miles away from civilization.

Baxter stood up and shook hands with him again. Morgan still didn't offer his hand. As the two men left the tavern, Breckinridge leaned back in his chair and sighed.

"I'm sorry, Breck—" Tom Lang began.

"You knew, didn't you? About those two goin' along, I mean."

"Well, sure, that was part of the deal from the first. But it's the colonel's money. You know how it works. If you've got the money, you get to do whatever you want."

"Yeah," Breckinridge mused. He understood how the world worked.

But he also understood that all the money in the world wouldn't mean a damned thing to a bloodthirsty Indian or a charging grizzly bear.

Chapter Twenty-four

Breckinridge barely had time to dodge the half-full whiskey bottle that came flying at his head. He caught a glimpse of the flowery design on the label as it went past him. Then it shattered against the wall behind him, spraying glass across the floor and leaving a wet blotch of dripping whiskey on the wallpaper.

"So you're going to leave me, are you?" Sierra screeched at him. "After all we've meant to each other?"

Breckinridge stretched out his hands toward her and said, "Now hold on a minute. It ain't like there was ever anything serious goin' on between us—"

Sierra exclaimed, "Oh!" and started looking around for something else to throw. Breckinridge hoped it wouldn't occur to her to grab the chamber pot.

Even though he knew it might just make things worse, he went on, "I mean, you never stopped goin' with other fellas and takin' their money to, well, you know . . ."

"That's my job, you idiot!" She glared darkly at him, her breasts heaving with emotion under the thin dress she wore. Mad or not, Breckinridge thought she was more beautiful than he had ever seen her. "None of those men meant anything to me! I never charged *you*, did I?"

"Well, not after that first time . . ."

She came at him, fingers hooking into talons, evidently intent on clawing his eyes out. Breckinridge caught hold of her wrists before she could reach his face. She started kicking at his shin, but in a soft slipper, her foot didn't do any damage through his thick, high-topped moccasins. Breck barely felt the kicks.

"Dadgum it!" he burst out. He had thought Sierra might be a little upset when he told her he was leaving for the Rockies, but he never expected such a violent reaction. She knew he had been talking right along about making such a trip, and she had known why he was going to meet Tom Lang and Colonel Baxter.

But clearly, knowing something and accepting it were two different things where Sierra was concerned.

He pulled her closer, then risked letting go of her wrists. He bent, wrapped his arms around her waist, and lifted her off the floor. That wasn't quite as easy as it looked. Sierra was lushly built and had a good amount of meat on her bones, something that Breckinridge had never complained about before. But with his great strength, he was able to pick her up, take two strides that brought him to the bed, and dump her on the mattress, where she bounced a little.

Breckinridge was ready to try to hold her down on the bed and talk some sense into her, but she surprised him again, this time by rolling onto her side and starting to cry. She put her hands over her face and wailed and sobbed, and he was left staring at her, dumbfounded as to what he should do next.

After a while he eased a hip onto the bed next to her, put a hand on her shoulder, and said, "Sierra, honey, I sure never meant to upset you like this—"

She jerked away from him and said between ragged sobs, "Just . . . just leave me alone! If you're going to . . . to abandon me . . . why don't you just go ahead and go?!"

"Well . . . the expedition's not leavin' for a couple of days yet . . ."

Sierra's wails grew louder, but then she pressed her face into the pillow and that muffled the cries somewhat.

Breckinridge wondered if there would ever come a time when he understood women. He wasn't going to count on it.

Eventually, Sierra settled down. She wasn't happy that Breckinridge was leaving St. Louis, but she seemed to accept the fact. She even went out of her way to make sure his last couple of days in town were as pleasant as possible. They seldom left her room in the boardinghouse.

Breckinridge had to get out some, though. Even though Colonel Baxter was outfitting the expedition and furnishing most of the supplies, there were some things Breck wanted to pick up for himself, such as extra powder and shot. He didn't want to take a chance on running out of ammunition at the worst possible time, like in the middle of a fight with hostile Indians.

On the night before he left, he used the rest of his

money to take Sierra out to eat in one of the nicest restaurants in St. Louis. It was nice compared to their usual haunts, anyway, and certainly Breckinridge had never seen tables donned with linen cloths or candles that burned in crystal chandeliers hanging from the ceiling. He knew that some of the other customers gave him and Sierra funny looks, as if thinking they didn't belong here.

Well, they were right about that, Breckinridge thought . . . not that he gave a damn.

"Thank you for bringing me here, Breckinridge," she said. She looked lovely in her nicest gown with its bits of lace at the throat and sleeves. "I never thought to set foot in a place such as this."

"You deserve it," he told her. "You're as fine a lady as any of the other gals in here."

"We both know that is not true . . . but thank you for saying it, anyway," she said with a smile. "You are a sweet boy. I will miss you when you're gone."

"I'll miss you, too."

"But you will come back to me."

"I'll do my best," he said. "You can't never tell what's gonna happen out there in the wilderness."

"I know. There are wild animals. Savage Indians. So many dangers of all sorts."

He grinned and said, "Yeah, but I'm pretty good at takin' care of myself."

"I know. Can I ask you to be careful?"

"Why, sure. I'll do my very best to come back with a whole hide. You can count on that."

When they got back to her room, she made sure his last night in St. Louis was one to remember for a long time. Maybe always. When Breckinridge finally went to sleep, he fell into a deep, dreamless slumber.

Sierra was gone when he woke up in the morning.

He figured at first she had just stepped out for something, until he spotted the note leaning against the cold candle on the night table. He picked it up and read the message she had written on it.

Breckinridge,

I cannot bear to say good-bye to you. I know it is foolish for a woman such as myself to feel this way, but you have brought something into my life I have never before known. I have feelings for you the likes of which I have never experienced. And so I cannot face the pain of our parting. Please do not search for me. I know St. Louis better than you. You will not find me. Just go with your friends and know that you take my heart with you. You can restore it to me when you return.

Sierra

"Well, hell," Breckinridge muttered as he lowered the paper. He would have liked a chance to say so long to her. On the other hand, it was unlikely they could have come up with a better farewell than the one they'd had the night before. So maybe it was better this way, he thought with a sigh.

He dressed, gathered his gear, and headed for the docks. The Baxter expedition would be leaving from there.

When he reached his destination, he saw a dozen canoes lined up in the river, next to one of the docks. Men were loading supplies into them as Colonel Baxter stood there supervising. The colonel wore buckskins, but they were a lot fancier than any

Breckinridge had ever seen before, covered with fringe and beaded decorations. Baxter also wore a broad-brimmed brown hat with an eagle feather sticking up from its band.

Breckinridge didn't see Morgan Baxter at first, and he hoped that meant the young man had decided not to come along. But then he spotted Morgan walking along the street from the other direction, talking to Tom Lang as the two of them approached the docks. At least Morgan was dressed in good quality working-man's clothes, not like the resplendent outfit his father sported.

Tom Lang saw Breckinridge and raised a hand in greeting. Colonel Baxter noticed him, too, and said, "Ah, there you are, Wallace. I was beginning to think perhaps you had reconsidered your decision to accompany us."

"Nope, I'm here and rarin' to go," Breckinridge said, although that was overstating the case a little. A part of him still wished he had set out for the mountains on his own.

But he had agreed to this deal, and now he was bound to make the best of it.

Tom Lang said, "How about you comin' along in my canoe, Breck? I'll be out front, so you might not want to be there. We'll be the first ones into any trouble."

"That sounds mighty fine to me," Breckinridge said, then glanced at Baxter and added, "If that's all right with the colonel. He's in charge."

Baxter waved a hand and said, "Of course, of course. That's fine. I, of course, will be in one of the middle canoes so that I'll have a good vantage point of the entire party."

And so that there would be men all around him to protect him if they were attacked, Breckinridge thought, but he kept that to himself. He supposed Baxter had earned that much, since it was his money funding the whole expedition.

Breckinridge stowed his gear in the lead canoe. The canoe at the back end of the line was packed full of supplies and attached by a rope to the craft in front of it, and more supplies were spread out through the other canoes.

The group's imminent departure had drawn some interest from the people working on the docks and also the men who frequented the nearby taverns. A crowd had gathered to watch. Breckinridge scanned the faces, thinking that maybe Sierra had changed her mind and might show up to say good-bye to him.

He saw no sign of her, though, and that came as no surprise. Once she made up her mind about something, she was too strong willed to change it.

Tom Lang was already in the canoe. He held up a hand to Breckinridge to help steady him as Breck stepped into the canoe. This was his first time in one of the lightweight craft, and balancing himself wasn't easy.

"Careful there," Tom said with a grin under his bushy white beard. "Big fella like you, step down too hard and your foot's liable to go right through the bottom."

Cautiously, Breckinridge lowered himself onto the middle of the three seats.

"Can't put you in the back or the front," Tom said. "You'd weigh down either end too much and maybe capsize us. We got to spread out that weight."

"All right, I think I'm set," Breckinridge said. He

picked up a paddle. "I've never used one of these things before. Hope it don't take me too long to get the hang of it."

"Just watch me," Tom advised. "Do what I do, and you'll be fine."

Within a short time, all thirty-three men in the group had climbed into the canoes. Men on the dock untied the lines holding the canoes. Breckinridge and the others began working the craft away from the dock and out into the river. He followed Tom Lang's suggestion and watched the old scout closely, trying to imitate all his actions with the paddle. With Breck's natural athletic ability, he soon began to feel comfortable in the canoe.

"You're gettin' it," Tom told him. "Just like I thought you would."

From behind them, Colonel Baxter called in a booming voice, "Off to the mountains, men! Let the great adventure commence!"

Tom glanced over his shoulder at Breckinridge, grinned again, and said quietly, "He's a stuffed shirt, but he ain't a bad sort for all of that."

Their canoe took the lead as Breckinridge, Tom, and the third man, a stolid gent named Akins, paddled steadily and smoothly. Breck looked over his shoulder and saw the way the canoes were arranged. Two of the craft traveled side by side about twenty yards behind the lead canoe. Next came three abreast, with Colonel Baxter in the middle one. Morgan was in the canoe flanking his father's canoe to the right. Two more pairs followed, and finally came a single canoe towing the one loaded with supplies. Breck wondered if they would follow that same pattern all the way up the river.

He knew from his time on the *Sophie* just how strong the Mississippi's current was, but the canoes were light enough to skim along the top of the water without encountering too much resistance. Paddling upstream was actually easier than he had thought it would be. He soon fell into a rhythm and knew he could keep this up tirelessly for a long time.

After a while they came to the place where the Missouri River flowed into the Mississippi. The Big Muddy joining the Father of Waters, Breckinridge thought. He had never seen anything quite so impressive. He was sure the Rocky Mountains would be even more so, once he got to them, but for now Breck was content to gawk at the junction of the two mighty streams, the biggest rivers on the entire continent.

With Tom Lang setting the pace, the lead canoe veered into the waters of the Missouri. As Breckinridge paddled, he asked, "Do we follow this river all the way to the mountains?"

"That's right, son," Tom said. "You can't hardly get lost. All you got to do is follow the river."

Breckinridge had no idea what was a good distance to cover in one day, but Tom Lang seemed pleased with their progress when they camped that night. As the men set up tents, Tom told Breckinridge that he could bunk in with him.

While two members of the party were cooking supper, Tom went to Baxter and said, "Colonel, we'll need to post sentries tonight. Since we have plenty of men, I'd suggest three at a time on two-hour shifts."

Morgan was standing nearby, as was Breckinridge. Before the colonel could answer, Morgan said, "Why in the world do we need guards? We just left St. Louis earlier today. Surely there aren't any hostile Indians this close!"

"Probably not, but I don't rightly feel like bettin' my hair on it." Tom nodded toward Breckinridge and went on, "Breck and I can tell you how the Injuns can jump you when you ain't expectin' it. That happened to us last year, didn't it?"

Breckinridge nodded solemnly, remembering how his friend Lieutenant Mallory had died during that battle.

"Not only that," Tom continued, "but you got a whole canoe full o' supplies, and that might be a temptin' target for fellas who ain't too particular how they outfit themselves for a trappin' trip."

Colonel Baxter frowned and asked, "You're saying we might be set upon by thieves?"

"It could happen. Again, we're probably too close to the settlement for that . . . but you never know."

Baxter rubbed his chin as he deliberated. Glaring, Morgan said, "Really, Father, are you going to listen to this man? *You're* in command of this expedition, not him."

"That's true, but Mr. Lang has a great deal more practical experience than I do," the colonel said. "If he thinks it's wise to post sentries, then I suppose that's what we should do. You'll see to it, Tom?"

"Sure, Colonel. Be happy to."

Breckinridge could tell that Morgan was upset with his father's decision. The matter was a minor one, piddling, really, but Morgan didn't like the way Baxter had paid no attention to his opinion.

Breckinridge saw the way Morgan looked at Tom

Lang, and he knew that rightly or wrongly, the old scout had made an enemy tonight.

That wasn't the end of the friction between Morgan Baxter and Tom Lang. Over the next few weeks, as the members of the expedition paddled steadily up the Missouri River, Morgan seized every opportunity he could find to undermine Tom's advice to the colonel.

Some of that hostility was directed toward Breckinridge as well, since he and Tom were friends. Morgan made jeering comments about Breck's size and intelligence, suggesting that the two were in inverse proportion. Breck wasn't sure what that meant, exactly, but he knew Morgan was calling him dumb.

He kept a tight rein on his temper, but he was afraid it was only a matter of time until real trouble erupted between him and Morgan. Tom Lang was old enough to let the veiled—and not so veiled—insults roll off his back, but Breckinridge had more trouble following the scout's lead. Anger and resentment festered inside Breckinridge.

Luckily the group didn't run into any other problems. The only Indians they encountered proved to be peaceful, and they didn't even see any other white men. Storms rolled in and dumped some chilly spring rain on them for a couple of days, but the trappers were able to push on through the bad weather.

They passed the Kansas River, the Platte River, the Niobrara, Tom Lang pointing out each of them in turn. One day, after the storms had all cleared up and left the air crystal clear, Tom leveled a finger toward the west and said, "Breck, you see that dark line, way over yonder on the horizon?"

Breckinridge peered over the seemingly endless plains and said, "Reckon I do. What is it?"

"Those are the Black Hills," Tom explained. "Sacred ground to the Sioux. They call 'em the *Paha Sapa* and believe that the spirits live there."

"Are we goin' there?" Breckinridge asked.

"Naw, no real reason to. Trappin' ain't bad, from what I hear, but you run too big a risk of gettin' the redskins all het up if you go in there. Trust me, there ain't nothin' in the Black Hills worth gettin' yourself killed over. Where we're goin' is a lot better."

They pushed on, each day much like all the others that had preceded it. Tom had studied a map along with Colonel Baxter, pointing out various landmarks on it and explaining where they were going, and Breckinridge had taken advantage of the opportunity to look over Tom's shoulder during the discussion. He knew they would follow the Missouri to the mouth of the Yellowstone River, then veer southwest on the Yellowstone across another stretch of plains and finally to the mountains.

Breckinridge was ready to be there.

All the men had bushy beards now except Colonel Baxter and Morgan. They shaved every day, using a looking glass they had brought along. Breckinridge thought that was sort of a waste of time. Besides, most of the mornings were still pretty chilly, and a beard felt good. But whatever the Baxters wanted to do was really none of his business, he supposed.

He tried to avoid Morgan as much as possible, since the man clearly didn't like him, but one morning not long before dawn when Breckinridge walked from camp down to the river, carrying a bucket, Morgan was there shaving, wearing his trousers and a pair of long underwear. The suspenders attached to the trousers were let down.

Morgan was trying to hold the looking glass with one hand and shave with the other, since there were no trees or any other place to hang the glass. He was having trouble since he didn't have a free hand to pull the skin of his throat tight. He looked around, saw Breckinridge, and snapped, "Here, Wallace, put down that bucket and hold this glass for me while I shave."

The imperious tone of command in Morgan's voice rubbed Breckinridge the wrong way. It reminded him too much of the way Richard Aylesworth talked to those he considered his inferiors, which was just about everybody but especially Breck.

"Akins sent me to get some water for the coffeepot," Breckinridge said, not bothering to keep the surly tone out of his own voice. "You'll have to manage your own self."

Morgan lowered the mirror and the razor and scowled at Breckinridge.

"Blast it, I'm the second-in-command of this expedition," he said. "I gave you an order, Wallace, and I expect you to obey it."

"If it was somethin' to do with the expedition, I might do what you say." *Might* was as far as Breckinridge would allow. "But I ain't your personal manservant, Baxter, and I don't have to help you shave."

"That's *Lieutenant* Baxter."

Breckinridge thought about John Francis Mallory, a good man who'd actually earned the right to use that rank. As far as he could tell, Morgan was just calling himself a lieutenant with no real basis in fact.

This whole thing was stupid and a waste of time as far as Breckinridge was concerned. He said, "I've got real work to do," and started to turn away.

"By God, I won't stand for such disrespect!"

Breckinridge heard Morgan moving and glanced back to see the young man striding toward him and swinging his right hand as if he intended to slap Breck with it.

Then the light from the cooking fire that was already burning reflected off the blade in Morgan's hand, and Breckinridge realized what was about to happen here.

Morgan was trying to slash him with that razor!

Chapter Twenty-five

Breckinridge reacted instinctively, swinging the bucket up so that it blocked Morgan's arm. The bucket cracked hard against the young man's wrist. He cried out in pain as his fingers opened and he dropped the razor.

"Have you lost your mind, Baxter?" Breckinridge demanded angrily. "You tried to cut me!"

Morgan bellowed, lowered his head, and charged. Morgan was a good-sized man, but he probably wouldn't have been able to budge Breckinridge if not for the fact that Breck was standing a little lower on the bank where it sloped down to the river, and he was slightly off balance.

Morgan rammed his head into Breckinridge's chest. Breck went over backward, but he grabbed Morgan and took the other man with him. Water flew up in a huge splash as they landed in the Missouri River.

Morgan slugged away at Breckinridge, but the blows were wild and frenzied and most of them missed their target. Breck was able to shrug off the ones that landed. He grabbed Morgan's shoulders and shoved him away, then rolled over, thrashing a little in the water, and struggled to his feet.

The commotion had drawn the other men to the riverbank, including Colonel Baxter. The colonel called, "What the devil's going on here? Morgan, is that you?"

Morgan came up out of the river smeared with mud and with water streaming off his clothes. He lunged at Breckinridge again and swung a punch. Breck didn't want to hurt him, so he leaned aside and let Morgan's fist go past him. Using Morgan's own momentum against him, Breck grabbed him under the arms and heaved him onto the bank. He landed rolling as the other men jumped back to get out of the way.

"Here now!" the colonel shouted. "Stop that! Stop that, I say!"

Breckinridge was more than willing to stop fighting, but that was going to be up to Morgan. When Morgan stopped rolling, he pushed himself up on his hands and knees and glared murderously at Breck. Snarling, he surged up and charged again, ignoring his father's shouts.

Breckinridge darted aside, but Morgan was fast and got a hand on him. Their legs tangled together and they went down in the mud again. Morgan locked his hands around Breck's throat and started squeezing, obviously intent on choking the bigger man to death. Breck heaved up from the ground and threw Morgan to the side.

Clearly, there was only one way to end this fight.

When Morgan came up off the ground this time, Breckinridge was ready for him. Breck set his feet and swung his right fist in a tight arc that ended at Morgan's jaw. The blow sounded like someone splitting wood. Morgan's head jerked around under the force of Breck's fist, and his eyes went glassy and then rolled up in their sockets. He dropped straight down to the ground and didn't move again.

Breckinridge became aware that everything was silent now except the murmur of the river and the pounding of his own heart. He looked around and saw the other members of the expedition staring at him in awe. After a moment, Tom Lang expressed what seemed to be their common sentiment when he blurted out, "Good Lord, boy, did you kill him?"

Breckinridge looked down at Morgan and saw his chest rising and falling. Breck said, "He's alive, just out cold." He turned to Baxter and went on, "I'm sorry I had to hit him like that, Colonel. I didn't want to hurt him . . ."

"But he gave you no choice," Baxter said. "I know, Wallace. I saw him. My son has a . . . problem . . . with his temper."

"Reckon you can say that again," Tom Lang muttered. Then he said, "Sorry, Colonel."

Baxter sighed and shook his head.

"It's all right, Tom. I know Morgan's shortcomings. My hope was that this journey might help him grow up a bit. Perhaps it still will." Baxter turned and gestured curtly to the others. "A couple of you men drag him away from the river and throw some water in his face to wake him up. Make sure that punch didn't break his jaw. Then we'll continue preparing to move out." The colonel gazed off to the northwest. "We still have a lot of miles to go."

* * *

The only good thing about the fight with Morgan Baxter was that afterward Morgan seemed to focus all his anger and hatred on Breckinridge. He didn't try to cause any more trouble for Tom Lang. Breck was grateful for that, anyway.

Morgan came up with every dirty job he could think of to hand to Breckinridge, and he made scathing comments about him to anyone who would listen. Breck put up with the harassment stolidly, although it wasn't easy for him to keep his temper under control. He hoped that eventually Morgan would get that anger and resentment out of his system, but he wasn't going to hold his breath waiting for that to happen.

They continued up the Missouri River, and as they did, Tom Lang got more worried. One night as they sat next to a campfire, the old scout told Breckinridge, "I could feel eyes on me today, son. They were out there, watchin' us."

"Indians, you mean?"

Tom sipped his coffee and nodded solemnly.

"But if they could see us, why couldn't we see them?" Breckinridge asked.

Tom chuckled and said, "That's just the way it is out here. You won't never see a Injun unless he *wants* you to see him. They can hide where you think there ain't a bit of cover."

"What tribe do you think it is?"

"Hard to say. Sioux, Crow, Arikara . . . Could be any of 'em, but it don't really matter. They all hate us and want to take our hair."

Breckinridge looked at the fire with some alarm and said, "Maybe we should've made a cold camp tonight."

"That don't matter, either," Tom Lang said with a shake of his head. "They'd know right where we are whether we built a fire or not. The only question is whether or not there's enough of 'em that they think they can jump us and have a good chance of killin' us. Could be it's just a small band and they figure there's too many of us, too well armed. They're savages, but they ain't stupid. They only attack when the odds are on their side."

Breckinridge frowned and said, "Seems like the farther we go . . ."

"The more the odds turn against us," Tom said. "Yep. You're right about that, boy."

The scout suggested to Colonel Baxter that they increase the guards. Baxter went along with it, and for once Morgan didn't try to talk him out of following Tom's advice. Breckinridge thought maybe the isolation was getting to Morgan. He might have realized that they were a long, long way from civilization, and everything Morgan had counted on to keep him safe in the past—the law, his father's money and influence—didn't mean a blasted thing out here.

Even though Tom hadn't spelled out his suspicions to the whole group, an air of tension gripped the expedition as it set out the next morning. The men looked nervously from side to side as they paddled up the river, as if they expected to see feathered, war-painted figures appear on the banks at any moment.

As they approached an area where the stream ran

past some high bluffs on the left, Tom waved the canoes to shore.

"Gotta have a talk with the colonel," the old scout said to Breckinridge. "I don't much like the looks of what's up ahead. That's a good spot for an ambush."

"There's no other way for us to get where we're goin', is there?" asked Breckinridge.

"No, there ain't, not without takin' the canoes out of the water and portagin' around. And that's pretty dangerous, too, not to mention a lot of danged hard work."

"What do you figure on doin', then?"

"I thought maybe if there's a surprise waitin' for us, we could spring one of our own," Tom said, but he didn't go any further into detail.

Once they were ashore, Tom and Colonel Baxter walked off a short distance by themselves and had a long, earnest conversation. Breckinridge wished he knew what they were talking about, but he hadn't been invited to the discussion.

Neither had Morgan, and that obviously rubbed him the wrong way. Whatever decisions were being made, he thought he had a right to be in on them.

Finally Tom Lang and the colonel came back over to the others, and Tom said to Breckinridge, "Get your rifle. You're comin' with me."

"Where are we goin'?"

"On a little scoutin' trip. We're gonna circle around and come up on those bluffs from behind."

"So we can see if there are any Indians lurkin' up there," Breckinridge guessed.

Tom smiled and nodded, saying, "That's right."

"We haven't seen any hostile Indians the whole time we've been out here," Morgan said. "I'm starting to think the threat they pose has been greatly overstated."

"Well, I'd rather be wrong and keep my hair than be wrong and lose it," Tom said. "It won't hurt to have a look."

Morgan looked at his father and said, "I should go with them."

Breckinridge bit back a groan. Having Morgan Baxter come along on what might be a dangerous mission was just about the last thing he wanted.

"You should have a representative there, Father," Morgan went on. "That way when these men report back, you'll know they're telling the truth."

"Now hold on just a minute," Tom said, frowning now. "Are you sayin' Breck and me might lie to your pa about what we find?"

"I'm trying to prevent that from happening," Morgan replied coldly.

"No one's casting aspersions on your veracity, Tom," the colonel said. "Perhaps it wouldn't hurt for Morgan to join you, though. I'd like for him to get some experience at scouting. He might as well learn from the best."

Scowling, Tom said, "If you're tryin' to flatter me, Colonel, it ain't gonna work. This is no job for a greenhorn."

"You're taking Wallace along, aren't you?" Morgan demanded. "He's never been this far west, either. He's as much a greenhorn as I am."

"I wouldn't go so far as to say that. He was part of that army surveyin' party I was with last year, down in Osage country."

"Please, Tom," Baxter said. "I think this would be a good experience for Morgan."

Tom sighed and said, "You're the boss, Colonel." He fixed Morgan with a hard stare and added, "Get your gear. And you'd better do everything I say out there, or else I'm liable to leave you."

"That's right, son," Baxter said. "Tom's in charge of this scouting expedition. His word goes."

"All right," Morgan said, but his agreement didn't sound all that sincere to Breckinridge's ears. He didn't trust Morgan and hoped that Tom had enough sense not to, as well.

As they gathered their weapons, Tom glanced at the sky, where the sun was past its zenith.

"Give us a couple of hours," he told Baxter. "If we ain't back by then, you'll have to make up your own mind what to do, Colonel. If you decide to run that stretch of river up ahead, take it fast and don't never slow down, no matter what happens."

"All right, Tom. Good luck to you." Baxter gripped Tom Lang's hand and added quietly, "Look after my boy. I realize he's headstrong, but he's all I have left in the world."

"I'll do what I can," Tom agreed. He turned to look at Breckinridge and Morgan and inclined his head to signal that they should follow him.

The three men set out, walking in a straight line away from the river's southern bank. After a few minutes, Breckinridge asked, "If somebody's up on those bluffs waitin' to spring an ambush, won't they see us leavin' and maybe figure out what we're up to?"

"They might," Tom allowed, "but that's why I picked the place to come ashore that I did. See that little rise yonder, between us and the bluffs? It's just high enough I think there's a chance it'll hide us."

Morgan said, "If they've been watching us, won't they realize there are three fewer men in the party than there should be?"

As much as he disliked Morgan, Breckinridge had to admit that was a pretty smart question. Morgan had some ability in a fight, although he hadn't really learned how to handle himself, and his mind was sharp enough. It was just a shame he was such an arrogant, stiff-necked bastard.

"They might," Tom said in reply to Morgan's question. "Seems like a longshot to me that they would've studied us that close, though. Now if half the bunch was gone, that they'd notice, for sure. That's why I figured on such a small scoutin' party."

"If we find that there's an ambush waiting for us, what will we do?"

"Well, we'll have to get back and tell your pa in time to keep him from goin' on through and paddlin' right into trouble."

"But you said there was no other way around except by, what was it, portaging?"

"Yeah. We take the canoes out of the water and carry 'em. Have to make a big circle and come back to the river farther west. It'll add days and miles to the trip, but we may not have any choice."

From a distance this terrain looked relatively flat, but as the three men crossed it Breckinridge discovered just how rugged it actually was. There were a lot of gullies and ridges that had to be crossed as the scouting party turned in a more westerly direction and began approaching the bluffs from behind.

"Careful now," Tom Lang said quietly. "We don't

want to get ourselves caught. If there is anybody up here, they're liable to have posted guards."

"You think it might be Indians?" Morgan breathed.

"Injuns or thievin' white men, it don't make much difference. They'd all cut your throat as soon as look at you."

Most of the country through which the expedition had passed had been grassy plains, but in recent days Breckinridge had noticed more brush and even some trees, although they were a lot smaller than the towering growth he was used to back in Tennessee. He and Tom Lang and Morgan skirted one such clump of trees now, and as they passed it something caused the skin on the back of Breck's neck to prickle. He knew better than to ignore such an instinctive warning. He whispered, "Tom . . . !" and started to turn.

The warning had come too late. Half a dozen men stepped out of the trees and leveled cocked rifles at the three scouts.

For an instant the urge to fight anyway was almost overpowering inside Breckinridge. He figured that if he flung his rifle to his shoulder and fired, he could get one of the varmints. Then, even wounded, he might be able to drag out his pistols and touch off a couple more shots . . .

Before he could do anything, something hard poked into his back. Tom Lang said, "Just hold on there, son. You try anything and I'll blow your heart out, and it would purely pain me to have to do that."

"What the hell!" Morgan blurted.

"Shut up," Tom snapped. "Drop your rifle, Baxter. I'd just as soon not kill Breck, but I don't give a damn about you, you nasty little piss-ant."

"You . . . you've betrayed us!"

"Smart as a whip, ain't you?"

Breckinridge said, "Tom, what are you doin'? Who are these fellas?"

They weren't Indians, that was for sure. The six men threatening them were white. Bearded and roughly dressed, they were hard-featured men who looked like they wouldn't hesitate to kill. Breckinridge was certain that was the case.

"These are my partners," Tom Lang said. "Fella there is the boss of the bunch. Name's Pete Hargrove."

One of the men stepped forward with a sneer on his ugly face, which looked like it had been hewn out of wood with a dull ax. He said, "You go ahead and move away from these two, Tom, and we'll get rid of 'em."

"You might better think about that some more, Pete," Tom advised. "You know how well sound carries out here. You shoot these two and the others will be liable to hear it, back yonder at the river."

"We'll kill 'em quiet-like, then," Hargrove said. "Up close with knives."

"Might not be as easy as you think. I've seen this big fella here account for several men in a fight. That's why I want to talk to him before we do anything else."

Breckinridge's head was spinning. He struggled to wrap his mind around Tom Lang's apparent betrayal. Why was it that *nothing* in his life ever seemed to go the way he thought it would? Why in blazes did fate or destiny or pure bad luck keep jerking him back and forth this way?

He knew one thing, though, and he expressed it by saying coldly, "I don't want to talk to you, Tom. I don't have a damned thing to say to you."

"You're wrong, Breck. I'm givin' you a chance here,

oy. You can throw in with us, and we won't kill you.
'ou'll be one of us."

Hargrove frowned and said, "I never told you you
ould bring somebody else into the bunch."

"Listen to me. You want Breck on your side. He's
he fightin'est fool you'll ever see."

"Not a big enough fool to throw in with a bunch
of no-good thieves," Breckinridge said.

"You can see it's a waste of time," Hargrove growled.
"Let's just go ahead and kill 'em."

"What are you gonna do, Tom?" Breckinridge
asked. "Go back to the colonel and tell him there ain't
no ambush, so he and the other fellas will paddle
right into it?"

"That's the plan," Tom Lang admitted. "And when
we're done, we'll have us the best trappin' outfit in
the Rockies. Baxter sunk a lot of money into this expedition."

Morgan said, "So you'd commit mass murder just
to steal some traps and supplies?"

Hargrove came closer and said, "That's the kind of
thing somebody who'd never been poor would say.
You never had to scramble for a crust of bread to keep
from starvin', did you, you little bastard?"

"Even if I did, I wouldn't let it turn me into a thief,"
Morgan replied. His voice was a little shaky, and
Breckinridge could tell that he was mighty scared.
Morgan was trying not to show it, though, and Breck
had to give him credit for that.

"Last chance, Breck," Tom Lang told him. "Say that
you'll join us. Otherwise we won't have no choice but
to kill you."

Breckinridge turned his head to look at the scout
and said, "Why, Tom? Just tell me that."

"Why? 'Cause I'm old, damn it! How many mor[e] years I reckon I got in me? How many more years yo[u] think I can survive out here in the wilderness? I wan[t] to find me a front porch some place where I can sit i[n] a rockin' chair and whittle and have some sippin[g] whiskey. One more year—this year—and then that'[s] how I want to spend the rest o' my days. Back yonde[r] in Saint Louis, Pete offered me enough of a cut t[o] make it happen. I feel bad about it, but I got n[o] choice."

Breckinridge drew in a deep breath and let it ou[t] in a sigh. He said, "I feel sorry for you, Tom."

Then he exploded into action, twisting away from the barrel of Tom Lang's rifle and sweeping a leg around to knock the old man's feet out from under him. As he came up again, he tried to raise his rifle[,] but Pete Hargrove sprang in, striking with the speed of a snake. He jerked a tomahawk from behind hi[s] belt and slammed the flat of its head against Breckin[-] ridge's arm. The blow knocked the rifle loose from Breck's grip.

A few feet away, several of the men swarmed Morgan Baxter. He tried to fire his rifle, but as he fumbled in an effort to cock the weapon, one of the thieves wrenched it away from him. The men knocked him down and started kicking him.

Hargrove reversed direction with the tomahawk and clipped Breckinridge on the jaw with it. Breck's beard cushioned the blow slightly, but it was enough to set his brain to spinning anyway. He felt his balance going and fought to stay upright, but one of the men slammed a rifle butt into the back of his right knee and made that leg buckle. Another kicked him be- tween the shoulder blades and drove him forward.

This wasn't a tavern brawl. These men were hardened killers, the most dangerous adversaries he had faced since those Chickasaw renegades back in the Blue Ridge foothills. Breckinridge knew they would stomp and club him to death if they were able to pin him to the ground, so he rolled over desperately and brought a foot up into the groin of one of his attackers. The man screeched in agony and doubled over. When he fell to one side, that gave Breck an opening. He surged up.

But he had barely reached his feet when something hit him in the head with stunning force. Red explosions went off behind his eyes. He fell to his knees and the men closed in around him, kicking and slugging.

Then a harsh, guttural voice he hadn't heard before ordered, "Stop! Do not kill the big one! Do not kill either of them."

That command drew angry curses from Hargrove and the other men, which was a little puzzling. Tom Lang had said that Hargrove was the boss of this band of killers and thieves, and yet he was taking orders from somebody else. Reluctantly, Hargrove withdrew a few steps, as did the others.

Breckinridge's head was spinning and he knew he was about to pass out. He hadn't given a good account of himself in this fight, which was disappointing. But at least he was still alive, as was Morgan Baxter, judging by what the newcomer had said.

"Why the hell did you stop us?" Hargrove demanded. "We don't need these two. We ought to just go ahead and kill them."

A figure stepped up and loomed over Breckinridge. With the sun behind the man, Breck couldn't make out much about him except a silhouette. Something about it was all wrong. After a moment he realized that was because the man had several feathers braided into his hair, sticking up at different angles from his head.

"I stopped you because I claim this one as mine," the Indian said. He leaned closer, and the last thing Breckinridge saw before he lost consciousness was a hideous face twisted in a savage smile, like a demon out of hell looking forward to inflicting eternal torture on some hapless sinner.

The last thing he heard was that same devil saying, "Hello, Flamehair."

Chapter Twenty-six

It took a long time for Breckinridge to come fully awake. Before that he was only vaguely aware of several different sensations.

Heat. A pounding noise that assaulted his ears. Sickness that roiled his stomach and made his head spin.

Gradually he realized that he was angry, too, and that anger was what finally energized his brain and prompted awareness to grow. He remembered Tom Lang and the way the old scout had betrayed not only him but also everyone else in the expedition. Breckinridge clung to the rage he felt at Tom Lang and drew strength from it.

Eventually he figured out that he was lying on the ground with his arms pulled behind his back and his wrists and ankles tied. He forced his eyes open and winced as the garish light from a nearby campfire appeared. He was lying close enough to the flames that the heat was uncomfortable.

Squinting against the glare, he saw a grotesque figure on the other side of the fire. The buckskin-clad man stood there, hunched slightly, as he used one hand to beat on the hide drum he cradled against his body with his other hand. A huge, ugly scar marred the left side of his face, ran down onto his neck, and disappeared under his buckskin tunic. The skin was pulled so tight by the old injury that the Indian's left eye appeared to be bugging out all the time. He stared through the flames at Breckinridge with an implacable hatred the likes of which Breck had never seen before.

This was the man who had stopped Hargrove, Tom Lang, and the other thieves from killing Breckinridge and Morgan Baxter. The Indian had called him Flamehair, Breck recalled. An apt enough name, he supposed, but to the best of his memory no one had ever called him that before.

Where in blazes did the Indian know him from? He wasn't one of the Osage warriors who had jumped the surveying party the year before. If anything, he looked more like one of the Indians from back home. . . .

A memory was teasing at Breckinridge's brain when a strained voice said, "You're awake. Thank God. I was convinced you'd gone and died, Wallace."

Breckinridge turned his head, thankful for the interruption. He had been staring at the leering, hate-filled visage of his captor like a small animal transfixed by the gaze of a deadly serpent.

A few feet away, Morgan Baxter was sprawled awkwardly on the ground, too, with his arms and legs bound in similar fashion to Breckinridge. His face was bruised and swollen, and blood had dried on a gash in his forehead. He went on, "I knew you were alive when that Indian stepped in to stop the beatings, but

I was afraid you'd died after they brought us here. After all, you were shot in the head."

"Shot . . . in the head?" Breckinridge rasped.

"Yes. I think the ball just nicked you, though." Morgan's eyes were wide with fear. No, not fear, Breckinridge thought, but rather sheer terror. Morgan went on shakily, "It doesn't really matter. They're going to kill us anyway!"

"Where are we?" Breckinridge asked. He tried to look around, but he couldn't see much because of the fire's glare.

Morgan had to swallow hard before he could answer. He said, "It's some sort of Indian village. I don't know anything about how to tell which tribe. Is it important?"

"I don't reckon it is," Breckinridge said. "Are Tom Lang and the rest of that bunch here?"

Morgan shook his head.

"No, they . . . they brought us here and then left." Morgan swallowed again. "I heard a lot of shooting not long after that."

Breckinridge nodded and said, "The ambush at the bluffs."

"Do you . . . do you think my father is still alive?"

Breckinridge answered honestly. He said, "I hope so, but I sure wouldn't count on it, Morgan. I wouldn't be surprised if they wiped out everybody else in the expedition. But they might've taken a few prisoners, so don't give up hope just yet."

Bitterly, Morgan repeated what he'd said earlier: "It doesn't matter. They either died then, or they'll die later. Just like us."

"We're still drawin' breath," Breckinridge said.

"Where I come from, that means we've still got a chance."

"I don't see how," Morgan insisted. "I don't know what that scar-faced devil is waiting for." His voice rose raggedly. "Why doesn't he just go ahead and kill us and get it over with?"

Breckinridge didn't say anything, but he thought he knew the answer to Morgan's question. The Indian wanted to draw out their torment as much as possible. He was enjoying their suffering.

A commotion nearby drew Breckinridge's attention. He craned his neck enough to see the teepees of the Indian village. A number of white men were entering the village. Breck spotted Tom Lang and Pete Hargrove among them. The thieves had returned.

They brought a handful of prisoners with them, too. Breckinridge saw Akins, who had shared the lead canoe with him and Tom Lang for weeks. Four more trappers were with Akins, all of them battered, disheveled, and sporting bloodstains on their clothing.

Morgan could see them, too, and a choked sob escaped from his throat. Colonel Baxter wasn't among the prisoners, and that could only mean one thing.

"Hold on," Breckinridge told him. "It's bad, but it ain't over."

"My father is dead," Morgan said dully.

"More than likely, but he wouldn't want you to give up. He'd want you to keep fightin'."

"How can I do that? I'm bound hand and foot!"

The Indian stopped pounding on the drum, and with a final sneer for Breckinridge, he went over to talk to Tom Lang and Hargrove. The other men herded the prisoners forward at gunpoint until they were near Breck and Morgan. The captives were forced off their feet and tied up.

Akins said, "I wondered what became of you two. Once the ambush started I figured you were dead and Lang had lied about that like he did about everything else."

"What did he say when he came back to the river?" Breckinridge asked.

"That the bluffs were clear and it was safe to paddle on past them. He said he'd left you two up there on guard and you'd signal us if anything was wrong. So we started on upriver . . . and paddled right into the worst storm of lead I've ever seen. It's a miracle some of us survived . . . for all the good it'll do us."

His attitude seemed as bleak as Morgan's. Breckinridge supposed he couldn't blame Akins for feeling that way. The odds against them were mighty high.

"How did Lang get out of bein' in the canoes with you?" Breckinridge wanted to know.

"He said he was going back up to the top of the bluffs to fetch the two of you. Pretty slick work all the way around . . . the son of a bitch."

Morgan said, "My father . . . did you see what happened to him, Akins?"

"Yeah. He was shot through and through. At least four times, I'd say. Like most of the rest of the fellas, he never had a chance." Akins paused, then added, "Sorry, Morgan."

None of the other men in the expedition had liked Morgan Baxter much, although they deferred to him since he was the colonel's son. Morgan was arrogant and disrespectful. But this tragedy had forged some bonds that hadn't been there before. The seven prisoners were all in the same trap, facing the same fate.

Whatever that might be.

Tom Lang nodded to the scar-faced Indian and then came toward Breckinridge and the others. As he came to a stop he thumbed back his broad-brimmed hat and said, "I surely am sorry about all this, boys. I don't reckon any of you did a damned thing to deserve what's gonna happen to you. Well, 'cept for you, Breck. Ol' Tall Tree's got hisself a personal grudge against you."

"You're talkin' about that scar-faced Indian?" Breckinridge asked. "What the hell did I ever do to him?"

Tom Lang looked a little surprised as he said, "Why, you're the one who put that scar on his face, son. Don't you remember?"

And just like that, Breckinridge did remember. His mind flashed back to that day in the thickly wooded foothills of the Blue Ridge Mountains, the day he had fought with those four Chickasaw renegades and used a tomahawk to lay open one warrior's face to the bone . . .

"Tall Tree," Breckinridge repeated. "That's him? I never knew his name. I didn't even know he was still alive."

"Probably didn't know he calls you Flamehair, either," Lang commented. "But that's the way he's thought of you all this time while he was nursin' his grudge against you."

Breckinridge's mind was spinning again, but whether it was from confusion or the blow to the head he had suffered, he couldn't say.

"How the hell did he wind up all the way out here, almost to the Rocky Mountains?"

"Well, *you're* here, ain't you? Life has a way of takin'

folks down some funny trails. You wind up in places you never thought you'd be, doin' things you never even considered."

"Like betrayin' the fellas who trusted you," Breckinridge snapped.

Tom Lang's face darkened.

"I tried to talk Tall Tree into killin' you fast, so you don't suffer," he said. "Keep actin' like that and you'll make me sorry I did."

"Yeah, but it didn't do any good, did it?"

Lang shrugged and said, "None to speak of. He still plans to torture all these other fellas to death and make you watch, 'fore he gets around to takin' his turn with you. Don't seem to be a thing in the world I can do to change his mind." The old scout glanced overhead at the night sky. "Come sunup, I reckon the screaming'll start."

Breckinridge kept an iron grip on his nerves during the long night. A part of him wanted to give in to his fear and whimper and sob like Morgan and some of the other prisoners, but he wouldn't allow it. For one thing, to do so would be admitting that he had given up hope, and he wasn't going to do that.

Sometime along toward morning, when the eastern sky held the faintest trace of gray, the renegade Chickasaw came over to Breckinridge. Exhaustion had finally claimed the other captives. Breck was the only one still awake. The flames had died down, reflecting only a red glow rather than the nightmarish glare. Tall Tree still looked like something out of a bad dream.

"You come to pound on that drum some more?"

Breckinridge asked. "That godawful noise is about as bad as any other torture you could come up with."

He didn't know if Tall Tree spoke English, other than the rudimentary greeting he had used earlier, but it seemed possible considering that Breckinridge had seen the Indian talking to Lang and Hargrove. Of course, the two white men might have been speaking Chickasaw, although that seemed unlikely.

Tall Tree hunkered on his heels and said, "You are full of talk, Flamehair."

"My name's Breckinridge Wallace."

Tall Tree ignored him. The renegade went on, "You must pay for what you have done. You maimed my face, you killed my friends, you made my people lose respect for me. After that, no one wanted to join me in waging war against the whites. In time I was driven from my own land, this time by my own people."

"Probably because you're a crazy son of a bitch," Breckinridge said.

Tall Tree didn't rise to the insult. Instead he said, "I was forced to wander for many moons, starving and alone, until I fell in with the one called Hargrove and his friends. They thought the tribes out here might be more likely to leave them alone if they had a redskin in their midst." Tall Tree let out a short, guttural laugh. "White men are fools. Why would Crow care whether they have a Chickasaw among them? These Indians are not my brothers. I am nothing to them. Less than nothing, because I have cast my lot with whites. The only reason they have not risen up in anger is because this band was plagued by sickness. Most of the warriors died last winter. The few who are left were no match for Hargrove and his men. They have taken over, eaten the people's food, taken the women, and none dare fight back." The renegade looked pleased with himself. "They fear me most of all. They say an evil spirit lurks under my skin." He leaned closer to Breckinridge and smiled. "They are right."

It was a long speech, and an unnerving one. Breckinridge knew that was the way Tall Tree intended it. This was just one more way for the renegade to torment him.

"I reckon there's nobody more long winded than an Indian who's learned English," Breckinridge said. He wasn't going to let Tall Tree get under *his* skin.

The Chickasaw's smile vanished. As he straightened he said, "All your talk will soon vanish. Your mouth will be too full of screams to hold any words."

With that he turned and stalked away.

In a quiet, miserable voice, Morgan Baxter said, "Why did you have to antagonize him like that, Wallace? Isn't what he's going to do to us bad enough already?"

"Thought you were asleep," Breckinridge said.

"I dozed off a little, but who can sleep facing death like this?"

"Listen to me, Morgan. I know I'm younger than you, but I've learned a few things this past year. If we don't give Tall Tree what he wants, we've kept him from winnin'. That may be the only thing we can do, but I plan to try my hardest. And if I get a chance to go out fightin' . . ."

"What chance is there of that?"

Honestly, Breckinridge didn't know. But he didn't want to give up hope, so he said, "Life's got a habit of springin' some surprises, especially when I'm around."

He didn't add that usually, those were *bad* surprises life threw his way.

A short time later, one of the Indians approached the prisoners. Breckinridge had caught glimpses of them during the night, but none had come close. This one was an old man, and he carried a water skin.

He stopped in front of Breckinridge and said in a cracked, reedy voice, "The one called Tall Tree says you should all drink."

"Doesn't want us to die of thirst, eh?" Breckinridge said wryly. "That's mighty nice of him."

The old man looked over his shoulder as if to make sure that no one else was close enough to overhear, then hunkered on his heels and said quietly, "No, he is as evil as you think he is. He knows that men who are losing blood will live longer if they have had plenty of water. He wants to prolong your agony."

"You speak pretty good English," Breckinridge commented.

"Years ago a missionary came among my people. He taught some of us the white man's tongue, so we could pray better to your God. I say what kind of Creator would not understand the words of all his creations? The black robe lost much patience with me." The Indian held the water skin to Breckinridge's mouth. "Here. Drink."

Breckinridge drank. The water had an unpleasant musty taste to it, probably from the skin, but he was thirsty enough after the long night that he didn't care.

After he'd licked his lips, he asked, "How many of the white men are there?"

The old man hesitated, then answered, "As many as the fingers of both hands, twice."

"And how many warriors are left in your village?"

The old Indian still looked wary, but he replied, "Six. But some are hurt."

"Can they fight?"

"They can," the old man said with a slow nod.

"There are seven of us. With your six warriors, that's thirteen men. Thirteen against twenty ain't too bad when it comes to odds."

"Our warriors are guarded, and they have no weapons. To fight is to die."

"To live is to die," Breckinridge said.

The old man looked at him for a long moment, then nodded again.

"I would not have thought to find such wisdom in one so young. Our women could distract the guards, but someone would need to release our warriors. I could do that."

"We're all tied up, too," Breckinridge pointed out. "We'd need to get loose somehow. They've got men watchin' us, but they don't seem to be payin' much attention. All we'd need is a knife . . ."

"Look beside your left leg," the old Indian said quietly.

In the dim gray light, Breckinridge saw the small knife lying there on the ground. He shifted his leg a little to conceal it, just in case one of Hargrove's men came strolling over.

"You old rascal," he said as a smile tugged at the corner of his mouth. "You came over here intendin' to talk me into tryin' to escape and take the fight to those varmints, and I just played right into your hands."

"You have the look of a man who will fight. I thought it would be worthwhile to make the attempt."

"Spread the word to the other prisoners while you're givin' 'em water," Breckinridge suggested. "I'll get my hands on that knife and start sawin' on my bonds." He glanced at the sky. "Tall Tree's plannin' on torturin' us, startin' at dawn, so we don't have much time. We'll have to be ready to make our break then. Your warriors, too."

"All will be ready," the old man assured him. "And those white men will learn how dangerous it is to hurt the Crow."

"What's your name, anyway, old-timer?" Breckinridge asked as the Indian struggled to his feet on bones that cracked and popped.

"They call me Antelope, because I was a very fast runner when I was young."

"You may have to move pretty fast to get out of the way when hell starts to break loose at sunup," Breckinridge said.

Chapter Twenty-seven

As the old man gave water to the other prisoners, they glanced at Breckinridge, some in alarm, some in grim determination. He knew that Antelope was passing along the details of the escape plan to them. As long as they didn't react strongly enough to draw the attention of the guards, Breck didn't care.

Every time one of them looked at him, he gave a tiny nod of encouragement. Even the men who looked frightened managed to return that nod, as if to tell him that they would do their part when the time came.

He shifted around carefully on the ground, his movements slow enough that the guards didn't notice. Finally he was able to get his hands on the knife Antelope had left for him. He turned it so that the blade rested against the rawhide thongs around his wrists, then began sawing. Now and then the knife sliced flesh instead of rawhide, but Breckinridge ignored the stinging pain. All that mattered was getting free so he could fight.

He glanced at the sky periodically and tried not

to panic when he saw the gray light was growing stronger. There wasn't going to be time for all the prisoners to free themselves, he realized. He might have to settle for getting himself loose so he could force his captors to kill him in battle rather than torturing him to death. If he was gone, Tall Tree might be content to just kill the others out of hand instead of making them suffer in order to torment Breckinridge.

The last strand of rawhide was being stubborn. Breckinridge lost his patience for a second and flexed his arms and shoulders, putting all his strength behind the effort as he strained against the thong. Suddenly, it snapped, and he almost flung his arms out to his sides as the rawhide's resistance vanished. That could have been a catastrophe. His muscles trembled as he forced his arms to remain fairly still.

He realized he was breathing a little hard. He brought that under control and bent his knees to bring his bound ankles closer to his hands. He stretched one arm down toward them, again being careful not to move too fast, and started cutting those bonds.

That went much faster. The rawhide thongs fell away from his ankles.

Morgan Baxter was the man closest to him. Morgan had been watching what Breckinridge was doing. Breck said to him in a half-whisper, "I'll toss the knife behind you. Cut yourself free and pass it on."

Morgan was still wide eyed with fear, but he nodded in understanding. Breckinridge waited until none of the guards were looking in his direction, then made a behind-the-back toss of the knife. It landed about six inches from Morgan's hands. Breck motioned with his head for the other man to scoot back a little. Morgan did so, and a moment later his fingers closed around the knife's handle.

Breckinridge couldn't really see how well Morgan was doing, but he saw the look of intense concentration and strain on the other man's face. Morgan worked at it for what seemed like a long, long time, and as he did, the sky grew maddeningly lighter. The heavens had a faint rosy tint to them now.

The sun would be up in less than an hour, Breckinridge thought. And then Tall Tree would come for them.

Breckinridge kept his arms pulled back as if his hands were still tied, but he flexed his fingers and his arm and shoulder muscles to loosen them up and keep them that way. He planned to explode into action when he got the chance, so he needed to be ready.

Morgan nodded to him. Breckinridge took that to mean he'd succeeded in cutting himself loose. Breck watched closely and could tell when Morgan flipped the knife over to the prisoner closest to him. All they could do was keep working as long as they had this opportunity.

More time dragged by, and then Breckinridge stiffened as he saw Tom Lang walking toward the prisoners. Dawn was close enough now that Breck had no trouble seeing the old scout turned traitor.

Lang stopped in front of them and said, "Breck, I just wanted to tell you again how sorry I am about all this. I was really hopin' you'd join us so that you and I could still be on the same side."

"I'm startin' to wonder if we were ever on the same

side," Breckinridge said. "I don't reckon you've got a side except lookin' out for yourself."

"Well, if that's true it just makes me the same as 'most ever'body else in the world, don't it?"

"Not really."

Tom Lang looked angry for a moment, but then he went on, "Anyway, when I made you that offer, I didn't have any idea Tall Tree even knew you, let alone had been holdin' such a grudge against you. To tell you the truth—"

Breckinridge snorted in contempt at that idea.

Lang ignored him and went on, "The rest of us are a mite leery of that crazy redskin. I've been talkin' to Pete, and I've got him convinced that we'll come out ahead on the deal if we trade you for Tall Tree."

Breckinridge frowned and asked, "What the hell do you mean by that?"

"I mean if you agree to throw in with us and give me your word you won't double-cross us, we'll kill Tall Tree."

"You'd spare these other fellas, too?"

Tom Lang hesitated, which gave Breckinridge all the answer he needed. The old scout said, "Well, no, we can't really do that. We couldn't never trust the Baxter boy, after us killin' his pa and all, and the others, well, they ain't really worth much to us. That'd just make everybody's share smaller, don't you know? No, the offer's just good for you, Breck, but I'm sure hopin' you'll take us up on it."

Morgan had a worried look on his face, as if he thought Breckinridge might agree to Tom Lang's proposal. But Breck just shook his head and said, "I can't do that, Tom, and you should've knowed better. You can either let us all go, or else I'll take what I got comin' along with the rest of these boys."

Tom Lang heaved a disappointed sigh.

"I was afraid you'd say that. It's too bad, but there ain't nothin' else I can do for you. If it's all right with you, I won't be around when Tall Tree starts gettin' up to his mischief. I've seen a heap o' bad things in my time, but I don't reckon I can stomach what that crazy redskin—"

He didn't finish, because at that moment an angry shout echoed through the pre-dawn gloom somewhere else in the village, followed by the heavy blast of a gunshot. Breckinridge knew there was only one explanation for that.

The captive Crow warriors were making their desperate bid for freedom.

He came up off the ground with all the speed and power he could muster, well aware that this would be his only chance. Tom Lang had jerked around toward the commotion, but he must have seen Breckinridge moving from the corner of his eye. He tried to turn back and swing his rifle around, but he was too late.

Breckinridge's right fist crashed into Lang's jaw with all the big man's weight and strength behind it. Lang's head slewed far to the side. Breck heard a sound like a branch snapping and knew he had just broken Tom Lang's neck.

The old scout's knees unhinged, dropping him straight down to the ground. He let go of his rifle at the same time. Breckinridge snatched it out of mid-air and snapped it to his shoulder.

About ten yards away, the guards Hargrove had posted were still confused about what was going on, but one of them spotted Breck on his feet and yelled in alarm. He started to lift his rifle, but the one Breck held roared first. The ball struck the man in the chest and drove him backward.

Breckinridge lunged toward the other two guards, reversing his grip on Lang's rifle as he did so. He swung it like a club and shattered the stock against one man's skull, which caved in under the awful impact. In a continuation of the same move, Breck raked the broken weapon across the other man's face and blinded him as jagged wood tore through his eyeballs.

Breckinridge glanced over his shoulder and saw that Morgan Baxter was on his feet and had the knife again. Morgan raced from prisoner to prisoner, cutting them loose as fast as he could. As the men struggled up, Breck called to them, "Grab any weapons you can and fight for your lives, boys!"

Two of the guards he had just disposed of had pistols stuck behind their belts. Breckinridge bent and grabbed the guns. He had a pistol in each hand as he straightened and strode forward like some avenging colossus.

Shouts, screams, and gunshots came from the other side of the Indian village. Breckinridge figured that was where the fight was going on between Hargrove's men and the wounded warriors Antelope had freed, so he headed in that direction.

Morgan Baxter ran up beside him clutching a rifle. The other men followed him, trotting to keep up with Breckinridge's long-legged strides.

"We'll catch Hargrove and those other murderin' bastards between us and those Crow warriors," Breckinridge told his companions. "They outnumber us, so we need to hit 'em hard and fast."

"Just lead the way, Wallace," Morgan said. "We've all got scores to settle."

Breckinridge liked the sound of that. Morgan might turn out to be all right after all . . . if he lived through this fight.

They charged through the scattered teepees and came in sight of the melee. Breckinridge wanted to bellow in anger, but that would just warn the thieves they were coming so he kept quiet and attacked in silence.

He slammed a pistol butt into the back of one man's head and knocked him unconscious. Another of the thieves tried to aim a rifle at him. Breckinridge shot first, thrusting a pistol out and triggering it so close to the man's chest that sparks from the muzzle landed on his buckskin vest and started it smoldering. The shot made the man fly backward, and when he landed he didn't move again.

Breckinridge turned and fired the other pistol, this time blowing away a large chunk of a man's skull just as he was about to drive a knife into the chest of a fallen Crow warrior. Breck dropped the empty pistols, stepped over to the corpse of the man he had just killed, and picked up the knife.

Some instinct warned him, and he ducked just in time to avoid a sweeping blow from a rifle swung by Pete Hargrove. Breckinridge whirled around and brought the knife up to plant it in Hargrove's belly. He heaved up on it and twisted the blade so that it opened up Hargrove's guts from belly to breastbone. Hargrove dropped his rifle and screamed thinly as his insides began to spill out over his futilely pawing hands.

Breckinridge ripped the knife free and shoved the

dying Hargrove aside. He twisted his head one way and then the other as he searched the dawn light for one particular figure.

He was looking for Tall Tree.

A ragged screech like the wail of a banshee came from behind him. Breckinridge whipped around to see Tall Tree flying Breck's way. The sun had just peeked above the horizon and the bloodred light was behind the hate-crazed Indian. If Tall Tree hadn't cried out in rage, he might have succeeded in burying the knife he held into Breck's back.

As it was, steel rang against steel as Breckinridge parried the thrust with his knife. The blades struck sparks against each other. Tall Tree's momentum carried him into Breck, and both of them went down from the crash.

Breckinridge saw the renegade Chickasaw's knife right in front of his eyes and jerked his head aside. The blade's tip drew a fiery line across his cheek as it slid off and hit the ground. Breck rammed his left forearm under Tall Tree's chin and shoved the Indian aside. He thrust with his knife but Tall Tree writhed out of the way like a snake. The Indian brought his knee up, aiming the treacherous blow at Breck's groin. At the last second, Breck blocked it with his thigh.

Fighting like a wildcat, Tall Tree got on top of Breckinridge and tried again to drive the knife down into him. Breck's left hand shot up and locked around Tall Tree's wrist, stopping the blade just short of his chest. He thrust up with his knife, but Tall Tree grabbed his wrist. They lay there like that, faces scant inches apart, as they struggled mightily against each other. Breck was considerably larger than the

Chickasaw, but Tall Tree fought with the strength of madness and that made them roughly equal.

Breckinridge's breath hissed between his clenched teeth as he tried to hold off Tall Tree's knife. The tip of the blade touched his shirt, then penetrated and drew blood. Tall Tree grinned and panted, "I will have . . . my vengeance!"

"Like . . . hell!" Breckinridge gasped back at him.

Slowly, his strength began to assert itself. Tall Tree's knife had barely pricked his skin. He forced it away from his chest. At the same time, he brought his blade closer and closer to Tall Tree's throat. Tall Tree's left arm shook as he tried to hold off the cold steel.

Neither man asked for quarter. Neither of them would have given it, and they certainly didn't expect it.

Guttural words spilled from Tall Tree's mouth. Breck might have thought the Chickasaw was cursing him, but he remembered hearing that Indian languages didn't have any curse words in them. A chill washed through him as he realized that Tall Tree was singing a death song.

Now it was only a matter of which of them would die.

Tall Tree's arm suddenly buckled. Breckinridge's knife flashed in the sunlight as he sunk its length in Tall Tree's neck with such force that the blade penetrated all the way through. Breck felt the steel grate against bone and shoved harder. Tall Tree's right eye bugged out to match the left one as Breck cut all the way through his spine. The knife slipped from the renegade's fingers. Breck grabbed Tall Tree's hair and heaved.

Not much was left to hold Tall Tree's head on his shoulders. Breckinridge ripped the head free and tossed it to the side, where it bounced grotesquely and rolled over a couple of times before coming to a stop.

Blood poured from the neck of the Indian's decapitated corpse. Breckinridge shoved it aside so the hot flood wouldn't get all over him. He rolled in the other direction and came up on his knees, looking around to see who he needed to fight next.

No one was left. All of Hargrove's men were down. So were some of the trappers and some of the Crow warriors who had battled so valiantly against superior odds.

But Morgan Baxter was still on his feet, and he hurried over to Breckinridge.

"Wallace!" he exclaimed. "You're alive!"

"Yeah," Breckinridge said. He glanced at Tall Tree's head with its sightlessly staring eyes and tried not to shudder. "It was pretty damned close, though."

Wearily, Breck climbed to his feet. He watched expressionlessly as some of the Crow women checked the bodies of the vanquished enemies. Any of Hargrove's men who were wounded but still alive didn't stay that way long, as the women casually cut their throats.

"My God, this is a savage place!" Morgan said.

Breckinridge thought about the things that had happened to him in Knoxville, Cooter's Landing, St. Louis, and just about everywhere else he had been, and he said, "I don't reckon there's any place under the sun that ain't."

Breckinridge, Morgan, Akins, and one other man named Fulbright were the only survivors from Colonel

Baxter's expedition, and they all had bumps and scrapes that needed to be patched up. Breck postponed any medical attention for himself while he went in search of Antelope.

He was shocked to find the old man lying dead with several women kneeling around him, weeping and wailing. From the looks of the numerous bloodstains on his buckskins, Antelope had been shot several times.

One of the Crow warriors who spoke English told Breckinridge, "He came to free us while the guards were not looking, but they realized what was going on and opened fire on him. He could have run away, but he stayed to cut our bonds, even after he had been shot. Swift Antelope gave his life to help us defeat these white invaders."

"Swift Antelope, eh?" Breckinridge said. "That was the old-timer's full name?"

The warrior looked at him gravely and said, "He was one of the most famous chiefs of all the Crow people."

That came as a surprise to Breckinridge. The chief of this band had lowered himself to bring water to prisoners, to act as a servant for the conquerors . . . but all the time he had been planning to strike back and free his people.

"It is an honor to have known him," Breckinridge said softly.

The warrior said, "That mad one called you Flamehair. This is your name?"

Breckinridge started to deny that, then decided it didn't really matter. Flamehair was as good a name as any for him, where these Indians were concerned.

"That's right," he said.

"From this day on, the Crow will consider themselves Flamehair's friends."

"And you and your people are my friends," Breckinridge said. "We will not make war on each other."

He held out his hand, and the warrior took it, sealing the bargain.

Morgan Baxter came over to Breckinridge a little later and asked, "What are you going to do now, Wallace? We're a long way from civilization."

"We're not all that far from where we were goin' to start with," Breck pointed out. "I figured I'd head on to the Rockies and try my hand at trappin', just like I'd planned. That is, if you'll let me take one of the canoes and some of the supplies. Reckon we've got plenty now."

Morgan rubbed his jaw and said, "I thought I might leave some of the supplies here in the village. From what I hear, they've had a tough time of it. Between sickness and what Hargrove's bunch did, they may have difficulty making it. Some supplies might help."

"That's a mighty fine idea," Breckinridge agreed with an emphatic nod.

"As for the rest . . ." Morgan took a deep breath. "Akins and Fulbright intend to go on to the mountains, too. I could start back to Saint Louis by myself, but I have a feeling my father would want me to try to make a success of the expedition regardless of everything that's happened. I was thinking . . . hoping . . . that maybe the four of us could, well, continue to be partners."

A big grin spread across Breckinridge's face. He said, "That sounds like a mighty good idea to me,

Morgan. How about you start callin' me Breckinridge, though, or Breck?"

"I suppose I can do that." Morgan shook his head. "This whole ordeal has really knocked some of the stuffing out of me, I think."

Breckinridge didn't say it, but he reckoned they might all be the better for that.

A couple of days later, they put two of the canoes back in the river and started west, towing two more canoes loaded with supplies. Breckinridge kept his eyes turned toward what was in front of them. In a few more days, they would begin to see the mountains in the distance, he thought, and that majestic sight would just give them more resolve to carry on despite all the tragedy that had befallen the group.

There was no way of knowing what waited for them in the Rockies. More danger, certainly. Death, quite possibly. But Breckinridge had sworn a vow to himself and made a promise to John Francis Mallory as well, and he intended to follow through on those pledges. He would make it to the mountains. He would become a trapper.

And then he would discover the surprises destiny had waiting for him next.

America's most popular Western novelists,
WILLIAM W. JOHNSTONE AND J. A. JOHNSTONE,

continue their bold new series
featuring Breckenridge Wallace,
a big, strong, fierce kid fighting for a home
in the towering Rocky Mountains . . .

Keep reading for an excerpt of

THE FRONTIERSMAN
River of Blood

Chapter One

Breckinridge Wallace ran for his life.

Behind him, an enormous bear lumbered after him, moving with shocking speed despite its great size.

The same could be said of Breckinridge, who stood several inches over six feet, making him close to a head taller than most men, and whose shoulders seemed to be as wide as an ax handle. Bundles of corded muscle in his arms and shoulders stretched the buckskin shirt he wore. He was a giant among men, and he sometimes joked that he was still young and hadn't gotten his full growth yet.

He wouldn't get much older if he wasn't able to outrun that damn bear, he thought as he raced across a flower-dotted mountain meadow toward a line of trees.

The scenery surrounding him was beautiful, and he would have been able to appreciate it better if he hadn't been running for his life. Snowcapped mountain peaks loomed majestically over the lush meadows on the lower slopes. Off to Breckinridge's right, a fast-flowing stream bubbled down from the heights, seeming to laugh and sing as it raced over its rock bed. Towering pines reached for the deep blue sky.

Those pines offered Breckinridge his only real hope of escape. If he had to keep running, sooner or later the bear was going to catch him.

He had to climb if he wanted to live.

Mentally, he cursed his foolishness. Even though he hadn't been in the Rocky Mountains for very long, common sense alone should have told him that it was a bad idea to have anything to do with a bear cub. Having grown up in the Smoky Mountains back in Tennessee, he knew good and well that messing with any animal offspring was dangerous.

The fuzzy little thing had been so doggoned adorable, though, as it rolled around in the wildflowers, and Breckinridge hadn't hurt it. All he'd done was pick it up . . .

Then the mama bear had exploded out of some nearby brush with an ear-shattering roar, and the race was on. Breckinridge had spied some trees in the distance, so he dropped the cub and lit out toward them.

Bears could climb trees, of course, but a man could climb higher—or at least so Breckinridge hoped. All he had to do was stay out of reach of that maternal rage until the mama bear got tired or distracted and moved on.

Assuming, of course, that he was able to make it to the trees before she overhauled him.

His long, bright red hair flew out behind him as he ran. Some Indians he'd run into in the past had dubbed him Flamehair because of it. He was running so fast now that it seemed like his hair might actually catch on fire because of his speed. Breckinridge knew that was a pretty fanciful notion, but it crossed his mind anyway.

He looked over his shoulder, saw that the bear had gained on him, and tried to move even faster. That wasn't possible, though. His long legs were already flashing back and forth as swiftly as they could. He covered ground in great leaps and bounds. His salvation, in the form of those pine trees, drew ever nearer.

But so did the bear.

Breckinridge was still carrying his long-barreled .50-caliber flintlock rifle. He tossed it aside to lighten his load. A few steps later, he pulled the pair of flintlock pistols from behind his belt and threw them aside, as well. Breck hated to discard his weapons, but they were only slowing him down. He could always pick them up later—if he survived.

For a second, when the mama bear charged him, he had thought about shooting her. He'd abandoned that idea pretty quickly for a couple of reasons.

One, he wasn't sure he could bring down the bear with a single rifle shot, and he didn't figure the pistols would do much damage to her.

And two, he didn't want to deprive that cub of its mother. The little varmint might not survive without somebody looking after it, and it wasn't the cub's fault that Breckinridge was such an impulsive galoot.

The bear was so close behind him now that the earth seemed to shake under him every time its ponderous paws slapped the ground. He thought he felt the creature's hot breath searing the back of his neck, but that was probably just his imagination. If the bear was really that close, it would have already laid him open with a swipe of the razor-tipped claws on its paw.

He was only a few yards away from the closest tree

now. He saw a likely branch about eight feet from the ground and barely slowed down as he leaped for it.

His hands slapped the rough bark and closed around it with a desperate grip. His weight and momentum swung his body forward. With the athletic grace he had been blessed with since childhood, Breckinridge kicked his legs upward, continuing the swing and twisting in midair so that he was able to hook a knee over the branch, as well.

Below him, the bear roared and reared up on her hind legs to swat at him. Breckinridge felt the claws rake through his hair. That was how close he came to having his head stove in like a dropped melon.

He reached up, grabbed a higher branch, and the powerful muscles in his arms and shoulders bunched and swelled even more as he pulled himself higher in the tree. The pine's sharp needles jabbed at his face, but he ignored the discomfort. It would be a lot more painful to fall into that bear's not-so-tender embrace. He got a booted foot on another branch and pushed himself up.

Below, the bear stopped trying to hit him and started climbing instead. The branches were close together, though, and the beast had trouble forcing herself through the dense growth. Breckinridge, even with his broad shoulders, was able to twist and writhe as he climbed, making his ascent easier.

The branches got thinner the higher he went, and so did the trunk. Breckinridge felt the tree start to sway a little from the combined weight of him and the bear. He started to worry that the tree would lean over so far the bear would be able to get at him easier.

For a second, he dropped his right hand to his

waist and closed it around the bone handle of the hunting knife with its long, heavy blade. If he had to, he would draw the knife and try to fight off the bear with it. Cold steel against fang and claw. He still didn't want to hurt the bear, but he would defend himself if it became necessary. His instincts wouldn't let him do anything else.

He climbed until he was a good thirty or forty feet off the ground. The view from up here was spectacular, he thought briefly, but he was more interested in what was directly below him by about fifteen feet.

The bear had stopped climbing, perhaps sensing that the trunk was getting too thin to support her. With her claws dug into the rough bark, she roared in anger and frustration and shook the tree. Breckinridge had moved in closer to the trunk himself, so he was able to throw his arms around it and hang on for dear life as the pine tree rocked back and forth.

That went on for several minutes, long enough that Breckinridge felt himself getting a little sick to his stomach. Finally, though, the bear stopped shaking the tree. Making grumbling, disgusted sounds almost like a human, the huge, shaggy beast began climbing back down.

Breckinridge clung to the trunk and tried to catch his breath. His pulse was pounding inside his head like a blacksmith's hammer beating out a horseshoe on a forge.

The bear dropped the last few feet to the ground, then started pacing around the tree. From time to time she looked up and bellowed at Breckinridge. He wondered just how stubborn she was going to be

Chapter Two

Trouble had a way of finding Breckinridge Wallace. It wasn't that Breck ever went out looking for it . . . well, maybe he did every now and then . . . but for the most part he was a peaceable young man.

True, he had a thirst for adventure, for new places and new experiences. That fiddlefooted nature surely would have led to him leaving his family's farm near the town of Knoxville, Tennessee, sooner or later. He knew his pa and his four older brothers could take care of the place just fine without his help.

It wasn't like he'd ever been that diligent about carrying out his chores anyway. As far back as he could remember, every chance he'd gotten he would run off to the woods to hunt and explore and just be out in the world, enjoying it.

Now and again those adventures had landed him in trouble, of course, like the time those four Chickasaw renegades had tried to kill him. That had gained him a bitter enemy in the person of the scarred, vengeful warrior called Tall Tree.

Tall Tree was dead now, but Breckinridge Wallace had other enemies in the world, through no real fault of his own.

Take Richard Aylesworth, the son of a wealthy merchant in Knoxville who had been Breckinridge's main rival for the affections of the beautiful Maureen Grantham. Of course, as it turned out, the rivalry hadn't really amounted to much. Maureen had chosen Aylesworth over Breck without really hesitating. Aylesworth was handsome and rich, after all, a polished and sophisticated gentleman, instead of a big, redheaded galoot with none of the rough edges knocked off.

To be fair, though, Maureen hadn't married Aylesworth until after Breckinridge was gone from the area, having taken off on the run from a dubious murder charge that, when you came right down to it, was Richard Aylesworth's fault.

Fleeing the law, away from home for the first time in his life, Breckinridge had fallen in with assorted shady characters, found himself in and out of danger, lost everything he had, fought river pirates and Indians, shot a man in St. Louis who had it coming, scouted for the army, and made a good friend, Lieutenant John Francis Mallory, with whom Breck had made a pact to go west to the Rockies, known by some as the Shining Mountains, and become fur trappers.

Mallory hadn't lived to see that day arrive, but to honor his friend's memory Breckinridge had followed through on the plan they had made. After a disastrous trip home, back to Tennessee, Breck had hired on with a party of trappers headed up the Missouri River.

That just led to more trouble, of course, since it

had a way of finding Breckinridge. Trust had been betrayed, lives had been lost, old scores had been settled, and four survivors from the party had continued on west.

In addition to Breckinridge, the other men were Morgan Baxter, Roscoe Akins, and Amos Fulbright. Baxter was the son of the man who'd financed the expedition, and as the sons of rich men usually were, at least in Breck's experience, he was a real jackass starting out.

The hardships and tragedies they had suffered along the way had forced Morgan to grow up a mite, though, and Breck had come to like him.

Akins and Fulbright were typical trappers, rough, stolid men without much education or imagination, but you could count on them when the chips were down, and out here that was perhaps the most valuable quality of all.

After the violence that had shrunk the group to its current level, the four men had pushed on upriver, into the heart of the Rockies, until they found this long valley with its lush meadows and numerous streams.

This was prime beaver country, Breckinridge thought, although from everything he had heard back in St. Louis the beaver weren't as plentiful anywhere as they had once been. Trappers had been coming out here for more than twenty years, and their efforts had shrunk the beaver population.

Breckinridge and his companions meant to give the business a try anyway, so they had set up camp and gone about running traplines along the creeks in the area. Every day they split up to check those traps, and

that was what Breck had been doing when he spotted
something that made him curious and wandered away
from the creek to look at the little bear cub . . .

And that was how he'd come to find himself up a
tree with a couple of thousand pounds of furry rage
pacing around below him, waiting to tear him apart.

The mama bear was nothing if not stubborn. She
stalked around and around the tree for what seemed
like hours while Breckinridge waited up in the
branches. He was starting to get hot and thirsty, but
he didn't have any water with him. He tried not to
think about it, but that didn't always work.

Morgan, Akins, and Fulbright were elsewhere in
the valley, probably within a few miles. If he'd been
able to fire a shot, they might have heard it and responded to see what was wrong, but his rifle and
pistols were lying out there in the meadow. The guns
might as well have been back in St. Louis, for all the
good they could do him right now.

He had his powder horn, though, along with steel
and flint. Maybe he could start a signal fire . . .

And burn the tree down around him. Yeah, that
was a fine idea, Breckinridge told himself caustically.
He needed to do a better job of thinking things
through. If he'd done that in the first place, he would
have stayed far away from that bear cub and wouldn't
be in this fix now.

No, he was just going to have to be patient. There
wasn't any other way around it.

Once he had come to that conclusion, he decided
that he might as well put the time to good use. He
used the rawhide strap from his powder horn to tie

his left wrist to a sturdy branch, then wrapped his legs around a lower branch, leaned against the tree trunk, and went to sleep.

Breckinridge had no idea how long he sat there dozing, but after a while he heard shouts that jolted him out of his slumber. He lifted his head and shook it to clear out the cobwebs of sleep. He heard a chuffing and growling below him and knew the bear was still maintaining her vigil.

"Breckinridge! Breck! Where in blazes are you?"

"Hey, Breck! You around here?"

Breckinridge recognized the voices of Morgan Baxter and Roscoe Akins. A moment later Amos Fulbright joined in, calling, "Hey, there! Breck Wallace!"

The three voices came from slightly different directions. Breckinridge figured they had returned to camp from checking the other traplines, then when he didn't show up, too, they had come to look for him. They knew which direction he had gone when he left that morning, so it wasn't difficult to follow his trail.

He untied his wrist from the branch and looped the powder horn strap around his neck again. Standing up carefully, he balanced on a branch and parted some of the other growth to look out across the valley.

His keen eyes spotted a man wearing a buckskin jacket and a broad-brimmed hat of brown felt about a quarter of a mile away. That was Morgan Baxter, Breckinridge thought.

He held on to the tree with one hand and cupped the other to his mouth as he shouted, "Morgan! Hey, Morgan! Over here in the trees!"

Morgan's head lifted, telling Breckinridge that he'd heard the shout. He turned and called to the other two men, then started loping toward the trees, carrying his rifle.

"Morgan, don't get too close!" Breckinridge yelled. "There's a bear!"

He kept calling the warning until Morgan slowed down and waved to the others to be careful, as well. Morgan came to a stop about a hundred yards away and cupped his hands to shout, "Breck, where are you?"

The bear's head swung toward him. Folks said that bears couldn't see very well, but that they had excellent senses of hearing and smell and relied on them to locate enemies. Breckinridge didn't know for a fact that any of that was true, but this bear heard Morgan, no doubt about that.

"Stay back!" Breckinridge called again. "Don't come any closer!"

"Good Lord!" The exclamation came from Fulbright. "That griz has run him up a tree!"

"Breck, are you all right?" Akins called.

The bear's head swung back and forth as she tried to figure out where all the humans were. The way the voices were coming from different directions seemed to have confused her. That gave Breckinridge an idea.

"Boys, keep yellin'! Whoop it up!"

The three trappers followed Breckinridge's suggestion. They whooped and hollered and created a racket that echoed back from the hills at the edge of the valley.

At the foot of the tree, the bear lurched one way and then another, growling and occasionally bellowing in frustration. She wasn't sure which way to turn because she had no way of knowing which of the humans represented the greatest threat to her cub.

Her exasperation led her to rise up on two legs, paw viciously at the air, and let loose with a tremendous roar.

Then, muttering almost like a person again, she dropped back to all fours and started toward the creek. Breckinridge figured she had decided her best course of action would be to return to her cub and forget all about these crazy two-legged critters.

Morgan, Akins, and Fulbright waited until the bear was several hundred yards away before they approached the tree Breckinridge had climbed. Breck was still up there in the branches, gazing off into the distance.

"You can come down now," Morgan called to him. "The bear's gone."

"Or are you stuck?" Fulbright asked with a grin on his whiskery face.

"No, I ain't stuck," Breckinridge replied with a little annoyance of his own. "I just noticed somethin'. Looks like somebody else heard all the hollerin' that was goin' on."

He lifted a long, muscular arm and pointed at a thin, broken column of smoke rising in the distance.

Smoke signals. Indians were talking to each other over yonder . . . and Breckinridge had a pretty good idea what they were talking about.

Keep reading for a special preview of
the next epic from National Bestselling Authors,
WILLIAM W. JOHNSTONE AND J. A. JOHNSTONE.

THE TRAIL WEST: MONAHAN'S MASSACRE
The accidental gunslinger Dooley Monahan
has quit wandering and settled down to a
farmer's life. But when the itch for adventure
gets too strong, he packs up and rides west.
Along with his horse, General Grant, and Blue,
a dog who's too smart for his own good,
Dooley rides for the Black Hills to strike it rich in
the gold fields. But fate has other ideas.

When the trigger-happy Dobbs-Handley gang
holds up the Omaha bank, Dooley is mistaken
for one of the robbers and a price is plastered
on his head. With every lawman in the territory
hot on his trail, Dooley has no choice but to join up
with the murderous outlaws. If the hangman
doesn't get him, his new friends will, but Dooley
won't turn back. With Blue and General Grant at his
side, Dooley will make his fortune—come hell,
high water, and everything in between.

Coming this March.

Prologue

Naturally, Dooley Monahan had never cared a whit for Nebraska. After all, when a man is born in Iowa, he frowns upon that great state due west that lay just across the Missouri River. Come to think on it, Dooley never liked Illinois much, either, over to the east. And especially not Missouri, what with its bushwhackers and outlaws such as the James boys and the Younger brothers and that crazy governor named Boggs the state south of Dooley's home state had once had elected. Had he ever really given Wisconsin or Minnesota much thought, Dooley might have decided that he didn't care much for those places, either.

But Nebraska had always been something of a rival of Iowa, at least from what Dooley had been reading in the *Council Bluffs Journal* that he had found accidentally put in with his mail at the general store in Des Moines. Well, actually, it wasn't so much all of Nebraska that the editor, one Jonas Houston, waxed most violently against with his poisoned pen. Just Omaha, which lay just across the wide Missouri River from Council Bluffs, Iowa.

When Dooley crossed the ferry and landed in Omaha, he didn't see what all the ballyhoo was about. Nebraska, and Omaha, looked fine—maybe even, Dooley had to reluctantly admit—a sight better than rickety, ramshackle, and rank-smelling Council Bluffs. But not Iowa, overall, with its rolling hills and verdant pastures and corn and mud and everything that Dooley had grudgingly grown to like over the past two years back on his farm.

Omaha, Nebraska, was all right, Dooley had decided as he loaded up his supplies into the saddlebags, gave his blue dog a bite of biscuit, and swung into the saddle on his bay gelding.

A minute or two later, Omaha and Nebraska—and Dooley Monahan's life in general—went straight to hell.

Chapter One

As he rode west down the wide, muddy street, Dooley Monahan felt content. He had a belly full of coffee and biscuits and gravy, a newspaper article—torn out from page three of the *Council Bluffs Journal*—and enough supplies, or so the merchant at the general store had told him, that would get him to the Black Hills of Dakota Territory, where Dooley had decided he would make his fortune at that gold strike up yonder. And a fellow he had met at the Riverfront Saloon had sold him a map that would take him to the Black Hills and avoid any Sioux warrior who might be after a scalp or two. Two blocks back, he had even tipped his hat to a plump blonde who had not only smiled at him, but also even offered him a "Good morning, sir."

"Yes, sir, ol' Blue," Dooley told the blue-eyed dog walking alongside his good horse, "it sure is shaping up to be a mighty good day."

That's when a bullet tore through the crown of his brown hat.

A couple of years had passed since, as best as

Dooley could remember, somebody had taken a shot at him—but Dooley had not been farming for so long that he forgot how to survive in the West. Ducking low in the saddle, he craned his head back down Front Street where the shot had come from while his right hand reached for and gripped the Colt .45 Peacemaker he wore in a well-used holster slickened with bacon grease.

On one side of the street, that plump blonde girl dived behind a water trough. On the south boardwalk, a man in a silk top hat pitched his broom onto the warped planks, slammed one shutter closed, and dived back inside the open door of his tonsorial parlor.

What looked to be a whole danged regiment of cavalry charged toward him, the hooves of wild-eyed horses churning up mud like a farmer breaking sod— but only if that farmer had Thoroughbreds instead of mules, and a multidisced plow that could rip through the ground at breakneck speed.

"The James boys!" came a shout.

"It's the danged Youngers!" roared another.

"The Reno Gang!" yelled someone.

"We're the Dobbs and Handley boys, you stupid square-heads!" shouted a man with a walrus mustache. He rode one of those wild-eyed horses that were coming straight for Dooley Monahan; his dog, Blue; and his gelding, General Grant.

"Bank robbery!"

"Murder!"

"St. Albans!"

Dooley had read about St. Albans—not in the *Council Bluffs Journal*, but some other newspaper, maybe one in Des Moines back when he was living with his mother and father and long before he got the urge to ride west and find gold and had made a name for himself as a gunman who had killed a few outlaws. St. Albans was a town in Vermont or New Hampshire or Maine or maybe even Minnesota—but not Iowa or Nebraska—where Confederates had pulled a daytime robbery of a bank during the Civil War. So whenever the James-Younger boys or the Dobbs-Handley Gang or some other bunch of cutthroats or guerillas robbed a bank in daylight hours, folks still cried out . . .

"St. Albans! St. Albans! Foul murder! Robbery!"

Or:

"Get your guns, men, and let's kill these thievin' scum."

The men of Omaha, Nebraska, had taken up arms by now. Bullets whined, roared, and ricocheted from barbershops and rooftops, from behind trash bins or water troughs. Panes of glass shattered. The riders thundering their mounts right at Dooley Monahan answered in kind.

General Grant did two quick jumps and a stutter step, which caused Dooley to release the grip on his walnut-handled Colt. His left hand held the reins. His right hand gripped the horn. And seeing his dog bolt down the street, leap onto the north-side boardwalk, and move faster than that dog had ever run gave Dooley an idea.

He raked General Grant's sides with his spurs and felt that great horse of his start churning up the mud of Front Street himself.

Later, when Dooley Monahan had time to think everything through, when he came to realize every-thing that he might have done—*should* have done—Dooley would realize that perhaps his best move

would have been to dive out of the saddle and over
the hitching rail and fall onto his hands and knees on
the boardwalk. Then, he imagined, he would have
crawled rapidly east—toward Iowa—until he reached
the water trough, where he gallantly would have dived
and covered the body of the plump blonde, shielding
her with his own body, earning much praise for his
heroics and chivalry from the editor of the Council
Bluffs Journal and maybe even Omaha's *Weekly, World,
Herald, Register, Call,* and *Mormon Prophet.* General
Grant, most likely, would have galloped off after Blue,
found shelter down an alley, and Dooley Monahan
would have avoided confusion and near death. A
parson would have found his horse and dog and
led them back to the saloon on Front Street where
Dooley would have been talking to the plump blonde.
She would have kissed Dooley full on the lips for
saving her life, Dooley would have been given a
couple of cigars and a bottle of whiskey, and he would
have continued on to the gold mines of the Black
Hills—if there were mines, or maybe he would just
have filed a claim on some creek. Either way, he would
have been well on his way to a fortune, and not running for his life.

Yes, that is what Dooley should have done.

But when a man is mounted on a fast-running
horse and facing a charging horde of rough-looking
men, with bullets slicing dangerously close, even an
experienced farmer turned cowboy turned gunman
turned gold seeker turned amnesiac turned recovered amnesiac turned farmer turned fortune hunter
does not always elect to do the smart or proper thing.

Instead, Dooley did what came to him first. He
spurred his horse, and General Grant led him westward

down Front Street. He leaned low in the saddle, and almost not low enough, for one bullet grazed the skin tight across his left shoulder blade.

The frame, sod, and bricked buildings of busy Omaha seemed blurry as Dooley glanced north and south. He saw the flashes of guns from a few windows or doorways, but none of the bullets came that close. Still, he managed to yell, "Don't shoot at me, you fool Nebraskans! I'm just trying to save my own hide!"

They couldn't hear him, of course. Not with all the musketry and the pounding of hooves and, perhaps, even Dooley's own heartbeat.

General Grant had always been a reliable horse, and as fast as many racehorses. But Omaha's streets had become a thick bog after a bunch of spring rains, and the fine bay horse had spent the past couple of years on an old farm a few miles outside of Des Moines—so he wasn't quite up to his old form. Before he knew it, Dooley felt riders on both sides of him. He wanted to slow down, but even as he eased off his spurs, General Grant kept running as hard as his four legs could carry him. And Dooley understood that the bay gelding really had no choice. Too many horses were right behind him. Even if the horse or Dooley could have stopped, they would have been trampled by outlaws and bank robbers trying to get out of Omaha as fast as they could. Dooley could not go to the left, because a bearded man on a buckskin mare blocked that way. Dooley could not veer off to the north side, either, because a tobacco-chewing man wearing a deerskin shirt and riding a black stallion held Dooley and General Grant in check. There wasn't much Dooley could do except ride along with the flow of the outlaws and pray that he didn't get killed.

Of course, later, Dooley thought that maybe, had he drawn his pistol and shot one of the bad men riding along either side of him, he might have been able to leap General Grant over the dead man and save his own hide.

Which never would have worked in a million years.

On the other hand, had Dooley possessed the sense of mind to draw his hogleg and put a bullet through his own brain, that might have been the easy, if a coward's, way out.

The man with the deerskin shirt pulled ahead of Dooley, but a rider in striped britches on a pinto mustang quickly filled the opening. The man in the deerskin put his black mount right in front of Dooley and General Grant.

That, Dooley decided, wasn't such a bad thing to happen. No fool Nebraskan would now be able to shoot Dooley dead, mistaking him for one of the bank robbers. At least these men of the Dobbs-Handley Gang were protecting Dooley's life.

By now, Dooley was sweating. His lungs burned from breathing so hard. His butt and thighs ached from bouncing around in the saddle. Mud plastered his face from the black stallion galloping ahead of him. Mud splattered against his denim trousers and stovepipe boots. He glanced to the south and saw the bearded man riding the buckskin mare stare at him. Dooley tried to smile. The man turned away, raised the Remington .44 in his right hand, and snapped another shot toward some citizen and defender of Omaha, Nebraska.

Then the outlaws, with Dooley right among them, turned north.

More gunfire. More curses. More mud and shouts.

Dooley glanced up at a three-story hotel. A man on the rooftop stood up, did a macabre dance as bullets peppered his body. The Winchester rifle—or maybe it was a Henry—pitched over the hotel's façade, and the protector of Omaha—for Dooley glimpsed sunlight reflecting off a tin badge on the lapel of the man's striped vest—followed the repeating rifle and crashed through the awning and onto the boardwalk in front of the hotel.

That caused Dooley's stomach to rumble. He thought he might turn to his side and lose the whiskey he had downed at the Riverfront Saloon and the biscuits and gravy and coffee from Nancy's Diner. But he did not vomit, and he thought that power might have saved his life. For surely had he sprayed the man on his right, the man in the deerskin shirt on the black stallion would have shot him dead.

And that man was a mighty fine shot, for he was the one who had killed the lawman on the rooftop of the hotel.

The horses kept running, though by now the gunfire was dying down. And the buildings weren't so close together anymore. Before long, the Dobbs-Handley Gang had put Omaha, Nebraska, behind them.

They kept their horses at a gallop.

And Dooley Monahan had no choice but to keep galloping with them.

Chapter Two

Eventually, the lead rider's horse began to tire—as did the mounts ridden by the other outlaws—and the pace slackened, but did not stop. Dooley wanted to say something, but, on the other hand, he really didn't want to get killed. He swallowed any words he thought of, especially when the men to his side began shucking the empty shells from their revolvers and reloading. They filled every cylinder with a fresh load—most men, including Dooley, usually kept the chamber empty under the hammer to make it less likely to blow off a toe, foot, or kneecap. When they had their six-shooters loaded, they began filling their rifles or shotguns, too.

They did this while their horses kept at a hard trot.

Which took some doing.

Dooley kept both hands on his reins. He didn't even look at the Colt in its holster. At least, Dooley thought he still carried the revolver. For all he knew, it might have been joggled loose during that hard run and was buried in Omaha's mud or the tall grass they now pushed through.

They turned south, swung a wide loop to avoid any trails, farms, travelers, or lawmen, and kept their horses at that bone-jarring, spine-pounding trot. Dooley felt, more than heard or saw, a couple of the riders in the rear pull back. Most likely, he expected, to watch their back trail and let them know if any posse took off after them. From Dooley's experience, posses could be slow in forming—especially when that posse of well-meaning but not well-shooting citizens knew it would be going up against the likes of Hubert Dobbs and Frank Handley and the murdering terrors who rode with them.

South they traveled without talking. General Grant, though, kept tossing his head back, hard eyes trying to lock on Dooley, and probably cursing him in horse-talk for running him this hard for no apparent purpose. Dooley wondered what had happened to that blue-eyed dog of his. Well, Blue wasn't actually Dooley's. The dog didn't belong to anyone, as far as Dooley knew, but he had more or less adopted the dog some years back. Fed him. Befriended him. He sure hoped he hadn't lost him again. Good dogs—any dogs—were hard to come by.

Of course, when the outlaws finally stopped running, Dooley would be able to go back to Omaha and maybe find old Blue and—

When they stop, most likely, they'll kill me.

The thought almost caused Dooley Monahan to pull back on the reins, but he quickly stopped an action that would have caused quite the horse wreck. And if spilling members of the Dobbs-Handley Gang, maybe laming a mount or two, and busting collar-bones and wrists and arms of outlaws, didn't incite murder among those owlhoots . . .

Ahead, he saw the river, and now all of the horses slowed down. Oh, no one stopped. The leader jumped off what passed for a bank, and Dooley and the men riding on either side followed.

The water felt good as it splashed over Dooley's wind-burned, mud-blasted, sweaty face. General Grant's hooves found solid bottom, and the gelding pushed through the water toward the shore.

This, if Dooley had his bearings straight, would be the Platte River. Wide, but not that deep, even after all those thunderstorms and being fairly close to where the river flowed into the Missouri. It was wet, though, and Dooley took a moment to scoop up some with his right hand. He splashed it across his face, repeated that process, then found another handful and brought it to his mouth. There wasn't that much to swallow, but what did go down his throat felt good, replenishing, but most of the wetness just soothed his dried, chapped lips.

The two riders on his left and right pulled ahead of him, but Dooley knew better than to try to escape now. He tried to think up various options, but no matter what idea came to him, the end result most likely would lead to Dooley Monahan's quick and merciful death. Unless Handley or Dobbs decided to stake him out on an ant bed, cut off his eyelids so the sun would burn his eyeballs out before the ants started eating him alive. Then that death wouldn't be anything close to quick or merciful, but it would most certainly be eternal death.

Those three riders had reached the banks about twenty yards ahead of Dooley now. He heard horses snorting, and men grunting behind him.

Water cascaded off the horses as they climbed up the bank. The riders—that bearded man on the buckskin mare, the man in the deerskin shirt, with a cheekful of chewing tobacco, on the powerful black stallion, and the puny gent in the striped britches, who rode a brown and white pinto mustang—turned around, drew their revolvers, cocked them, and waited.

The Platte began to get even shallower, and soon General Grant was carrying Dooley out of the wide patch of wetness. Behind him came the other riders, who grunted or cursed or farted. Dooley let his bay horse pick its own path up the bank until he reined in in front of the three men. He stared down the barrels of a Smith & Wesson, a Colt, and a Remington. Behind him he heard another noise.

You never forget what a rattlesnake sounds like. Maybe you think you know how it sounds—or how it makes you feel—but once you hear that rattle, you know exactly what it sounds like and you know it will practically make you wet your britches.

Quite similar to the whirl of a rattler is the cocking of a single-action revolver . . . the thumbing back of two hammers on a double-barreled shotgun, and the levering of a fresh cartridge into a Winchester or Henry rifle or carbine. Those were the sounds coming from behind Dooley Monahan.

Not the rattlesnake, of course. Not that sound. Though right then, Dooley would have preferred it to those metallic clicks.

Dooley eased the reins down, letting them drop in front of the horn. The horn he gripped with both hands, and leaning forward, he nodded his head at the men in front of him.

"Who the hell be you?"

That came from the man in the deerskin shirt. He wore a wide-brimmed dirty hat that might once have been white but had been dirtied up and sweated through over some years. Or it could have been gray, but had been faded from so much alkali dust and the blistering sun of the Great Plains. Dooley didn't think the hat had ever been black.

Brown juice came out of the man's mouth like he had opened a spigot, and he wiped the tobacco juice off his lips with a gloved left hand. The right held a large Smith & Wesson pistol that looked just a tad smaller than a cannon. He was the biggest of the men, which explained why he rode that giant black stallion. Dooley couldn't quite guess, but he had to figure the man stood six-foot-four in his boot heels, and had to weigh around two hundred and forty pounds. Maybe more.

"Name's Dooley," Dooley said. "Dooley Monahan."

The bearded man on the buckskin mare pursed his lips as if in deep thought. Thinking did not mean the man took the .45 caliber Colt away from Dooley's chest. He just thought.

He appeared to be more medium size, maybe not even as tall as Dooley, but tougher than a railroad tie and maybe twice as solid. Muscles strained through his muslin shirt, and Dooley couldn't quite remember when he had ever seen a beard that long on any man. There had been that woman back at that circus in Davenport that time, but you expected that when you paid two bits to see the bearded lady at a circus in Davenport. Her beard didn't seem real, though. This gent's certainly wasn't glued on.

"We ain't got no one goin' by Dooley in this gang, does we?" the man on the massive black mount finally asked.

"Ain't got nobody usin' the handle Monahans, neither."

That sentence came from the third cuss, the one with the striped britches. He was puny. A spring wind might have carried him off like the furs on whatever those weeds with the furlike tops were called. Puny, and pale, with the coldest blue eyes Dooley had ever seen, sunk way back in his head. His blond hair, soaked by sweat and some Platte River water, hung like greasy rawhide strings. He was even uglier than that bearded lady back at that circus eighteen months back in Davenport, Iowa.

The man seemed so sickly, the big Smith & Wesson never steadied in his pasty white hand, but neither did it ever exactly not aim at one of Dooley's vital organs.

"Monahan," Dooley corrected. "No s. Just Monahan. Dooley Monahan."

He thought if he kept talking, they might not kill him.

"Shut up," barked the man on the black horse.

"Kill him, and let's ride," said the one on the buckskin mare. "Posse'll be chasin' us directly."

"How did you come to be ridin' with us?" asked the sickly one on the pinto. "Dooley *Monahans.*" He stressed the last name and especially the *s* on the end of it, even though it wasn't Dooley's name.

Dooley shrugged, but kept gripping that saddle horn. If he let go, those men would think he was going for his Colt, and he'd be plugged before he could explain by a .45, .38, and .44 bullet—and no telling what calibers or gauges from the men behind him.

"Came to Omaha to stock up," Dooley said honestly. "Was riding out down that main street when you boys started whooping and hollering and riding."

"And shooting," said someone behind him.

"And shooting," Dooley added.

The men behind Dooley chuckled. The ones in front of him did not even blink or crack a smile.

"Y'all kind of swept me up," Dooley went on. "Wasn't anything I could do but keep riding. If I stopped, you would have run over me. That would've caused quite the spill. Probably got one of you boys caught, if not killed."

"We're obliged to you for that," said another voice behind him.

"Do you know who we are?" asked the tobacco-chewing man on the big black.

Dooley's mouth went dry. He could only shake is head.

"Hubert," came the first voice behind him. "My horse's gone lame."

"Now do you know who we are?" The man spit out more tobacco juice and shifted the quid to the opposite cheek.

Dooley just swallowed, but what he swallowed was mostly air. His mouth felt dried out like his skin did when he was farming. And his muscles did not respond when he tried to shake his head.

"C'mon, boy," said the man with the long beard. "How many bank robbers you ever heard called Hubert?"

"Shut the hell up, Frank," barked the tobacco chewer. "Hubert ain't no name to be ashamed of.

Belonged to my grandpappy on my ma's side, and his grandpappy's long before that."

The bearded man grinned. "And now you know my name, Dooley Monahan." At least he pronounced Dooley's name correctly. "Frank Handley."

"Which," said the big man on the big black, "makes me Hubert Dobbs."

"Which makes us," said the thin man on the pinto mustang, "the Dobbs-Handley Gang."

"A pleasure," Dooley managed to say.

"Step down off that horse," said the man who had not introduced himself.

"But first," added Frank Handley, "pull that hogleg from your holster . . ."

"Real careful," warned Hubert Dobbs.

"Real careful," coached the second voice behind Dooley.

"And," said Handley, "drop it to the ground."

Dooley Monahan obeyed.

"Let go of the reins and step away from the horse. Kinda in my direction." The tobacco chewer spit again. "That way. That's good. Two more steps. Now one more. Now don't move. Good. You take directions real good."

"Thank you," Dooley said.

The puny man leaned over in his saddle, and now managed to steady the .38 caliber Smith & Wesson. "Do I kill him now, Hubert?"

"No, Doc," Hubert Dobbs said. "Gunshot would draw a posse."

Which meant the sickly-looking man on the rangy pinto would be Doc Watson, the coldest and most vicious killer to ride with the Dobbs-Handley Gang.

"I can slit his throat," came a new voice behind Dooley Monahan.

"You could," Frank Handley said, "but Dooley Monahan rode with us. Maybe by accident. And maybe for just a few miles. But he rode with us. And we don't murder men who rode with us. It ain't in the code of the outlaw."

Dooley's heart skipped a beat. His mouth started to open to thank, to praise, Frank Handley.

Then everything went black.